G
WITH
THE
FLO

M.D. RANDALL

SLOW HOUND
MEDIA

1

I'm Flo.

And I've been here before.

Not this womb, of course. A different one.

Not this hospital. A different one.

One that boasted a slightly less depressing shade of green.

Not this life, in fact.

I say I've been here before. That's not strictly accurate. *I* haven't. Not like this. I don't want that. That was a right fuck up. Last time. And it'd be weird. And confusing as hell not just for me but for those I met, loved, raged at, sent inappropriate pictures to. Weird for those who remain.

It doesn't work that way.

Which generally is a good thing.

It really isn't too confusing. I get it and I'm a baby.

But then I know how it works. You would too if you'd been subjected to the process. Most of us have been, some just don't realise it. The man with the red spectacles explained it to me. You know him? Ken. Works in Halfords. He's a bit odd. Obsessed with lubricants. Thoughtful though. The sort who does a random act of kindness but doesn't feel the need to subsequently pebbledash it over four different social media platforms.

If I'm honest I think I knew without Ken telling me. He told me the day he was awarded employee of the month so he had a lot on his plate. Still found time for me though, which was nice of him. By way of thanks, I bought him a chocolate muffin (and didn't post the handover on Instagram).

I remember the day well since it was my sixteenth birthday.

Death clicked and collected me two days later.

But all that doesn't matter. Not really. Because you're either aware of a situation like mine, or you aren't. If you are, you can strike a different pose, lay down in a meadow that *isn't* ant infested. You can look again, learn from the mistakes you made (not *you*—we've covered that—pay attention) in order to manipulate situations, circumstances, people. You'll have an ability to make better choices; ones you might not ordinarily have made. If you aren't aware of this special situation then that's all OK too because your default state will be blissful unawareness. If that's you, feel free to merely sigh, put your hands behind your head and enjoy the ride.

But... blissful unawareness comes with a warning because unless you're the lucky kind, the ride will be bumpy as hell, and you're going to make mistakes. Big ones. The sort of fuck ups you never live down. The kind your friends mention to strangers at a party.

But I'm aware.

I'm determined not to mess things up. Again.

I'm going places.

Looking adorable? Check.

Debatable moral compass? Check.

Eyes open? Check.

Which is ironic since my last memory is of them being shut. Shut against the blinding, gravitational light. I'm battling *towards* the light now. But in a good way. I will bend life like a prism bends light. Just watch me. I'm unstoppable. I'm a blimp, rising above the mediocrity, giving myself a blast when I need to break free. Down there the ants hurry about. They fret. You fret. People get bitten. But only because they don't know how to escape, or how to change direction. In short, it's easier to carve out a path for yourself if you can see where you went wrong last time. Much easier.

You've heard of life after death, right? Well this is nothing like that. Everyone knows that the whole life after death hypothesis dictates you return with no memories and as a rabbit or a tree, or if there's been a monumental DNA screw up, an Aled Jones/Rod Stewart hybrid.

This is very, very different.

Because this is life before birth. And a life lived before, if you can retain the details, is one you can learn from, draw upon—the minutiae of your life before birth.

And with that comes 20-20 vision, or at the very least, hindsight.

And from now on there are going to be some changes around here.

I'm Flo.

I'm a kicking screaming 7lbs of possibilities.

Watch me fly.

2

At some point I'll explain life before birth properly. You'll need the basics if you're to travel with me.

But right now, the light is drawing closer. There's a lot of movement; so much so my internal gyroscope is all out of kilter and I long for my sea sickness bracelet. Pushed from behind and pulled from in front, it's taking an age. As a vessel it's comfy enough I suppose, but if I'm entirely honest, it's too hot, too unstable and there's been some sort of chemical leak.

Someone once likened this malarkey to a cork springing forth from a bottle, but as an analogy it's shite. For starters the pop of a cork is a wondrous thing. It promises so much and always delivers. Also as an act, it's hellishly quick. Granted, there can be a degree of initial mess but that's easily resolved by the running of a tongue along the sodden work surface. Granite, preferably. Wood's too absorbent.

In the end, after much drumming of fingers on pelvic floor, there'll be a champagne delivery here too, but no one in their right mind will be running their tongue over the spillage after this cork pops.

Right, here goes.

I'm giving 10/10 for concerned faces, but I'll be deducting one star from my Trip Advisor review for the cleanliness of the male midwife. If I didn't know better, I'd suggest he has a piece of tinned spaghetti in his beard.

3

I read a book once. I think it was called *This Is Your Life (Before Birth)*. Ken lent it to me. He'd inserted a tree-shaped air freshener at page five. As a bookmark it was functional but a tad piney for my liking. Page five was so interesting that I also read pages one to four. And six to two-hundred-and-sixty-one.

Page five gave an example of life before birth. It works on the principle that up to the age of thirteen or fourteen, children hold memories from previous existences, though these recollections weaken as they grow older. Various theories exist as to why these memories are short-lived. Some say it's because the mind becomes increasingly full, and to file new stuff, older clutter must first be jettisoned. Others suggest that as a child's innocence evaporates, so too do its memories. Memories that are seen by the child as increasingly irrelevant to living in the moment—childish fantasies that should be usurped in favour of the immediacy of adolescent thrills.

Page five sent a charge arcing across my brain. I recognised the type of scenario. It could have been me.

Page five describes a family unit travelling by car for a holiday. They travel a long way, over four hundred miles from home. Having left the motorway behind, a rural carriageway serves up some spectacular views.

'I spy with my little eye, something beginning with *N*,' father says.

Mother looks straight ahead. 'Nissan,' she says with a measure of faux excitement. 'Too easy!'

Father shakes his head. She tries again. 'Numpty,' she offers as an Audi overtakes and cuts across them.

Father's fingers tighten around the steering wheel, he eases back on the throttle, and smiles.

'Nope.' He looks over his shoulder. 'Tommy, your turn to guess.'

Tommy thinks. Screws up his eyes. He looks to his left across a small meadow. He sees sheep, grass, and a fence. There's a building beyond. None of the things he initially sees begin with the letter N, though. He smiles and turns front, delivers his guess to the back of his parents' heads.

'Nana,' he announces, before returning his attention to a set of dinosaur Top Trumps.

For a while the only sound is the thrum of rubber on tarmac. It's followed by the unmistakable drumming noise of two wheels riding first one cat's eye, then another, before father recovers concentration and repositions the car. Mother and father exchange glances.

'Why did you say Nana, darling?' Julie asks as she peers around the headrest. She's aware she's trying too hard to be breezy.

'Daddy said, "*I spy with my little eye, something beginning with N*",' Tommy replies, matter-of-factly. 'Nana.'

More silence. Julie and Mike aren't sure whether to point out the obvious.

Tommy gives a drum roll with his feet on the back of his dad's seat, neatly packs his cards away in their plastic container, then presses an index finger to the glass. 'Nana's buried there. By the church,' Tommy adds before either parent can settle on a suitable retort.

The problem Tommy's parents have isn't that Julie's mother *isn't* buried in the churchyard Tommy's pointing at. She is. The fact that Nana died fifteen years before Tommy was born shouldn't be troubling either. Lots of people die before their kids have given them grandchildren. What's making Julie and Mike feel decidedly uneasy is the simple truth that their five-year-old hasn't visited the grave before. Neither has he been within two hundred miles of their current location. They haven't even visited Scotland since he was born. In addition, they're as sure as they can be that their son won't have been party to any documentation listing his grandmother's resting place. Julie takes a deep breath. It must be a coincidence.

A hush settles. A welcome one, yet still stifling in its presence.

A minute goes by. Two. Time and distance become Julie and Mike's friends. Mike eases his shoulders back into his seat's lush upholstery. Julie shoots her husband a reassuring look, places a hand on his knee, then switches her attention to a bird of prey perched on top of a broken, lifeless tree.

'Mummy. I hope the broken heel of Nana's nice shoe is still there. Do you think it is Mummy? Grandad put it there. It was broken at a dance they went to, remember?'

4

I'm cleaned up, wrapped in a towel and passed first to the midwife, then to a concerned-looking gentleman in a white coat. The process seems a little rougher than is strictly necessary, like a game of pass the parcel amongst Category-A inmates. The figure sporting the white coat will be a doctor. Experienced looking. He nods to the midwife who wastes no time in taking me from him and placing me in a Perspex box. The doctor is handed a clear tube which, despite me wriggling in protest, he seems hell-bent on inserting into my face. Various other bits and pieces are stuck to my naked body.

A machine growls, wheezes and beeps, and there's a great deal of movement around me. Calm but firm voices ping instructions back and forth, and after some time, the doctor peers into my temporary plastic house, offers a nod first to his right, then his left, before retreating from my terrarium.

I follow his head as he nods. To my left is a striking woman on a hospital bed. As she leans towards me, one of the birthing team dives forward with additional pillows, presumably to give the exhausted woman some support. She's alongside me now. Moisture filled eyes sit at the centre of a beautiful, oval, unblemished face framed by long dark curls. If I inherit this woman's genes I'll be more than happy.

She looks to the doctor for permission to reach in and touch me. Permission is granted and she runs a moist finger along my cheek before stroking the top of my head. Moist eyes become wet as she passes a look over the top of the incubator, presumably in the direction of my father. I wonder if he will be equally as handsome.

I turn my head and the tube in my nose snags. Can we have more slack on this twatting tube, I think. The midwife, almost certainly a mind-reader in *his* life before birth, springs into action, fiddles with the apparatus attached to my face and steps back satisfied with his work. About time, I think. These moments are important; first impressions stay with you and I don't want the first image of my father to be partially obscured by a bit of clear, cheap tubing.

A new-born's eyesight isn't the best, that's common knowledge, but I'm staring at an equally handsome face. Strong features. Piercing blue eyes—mercifully dry. Blonde hair cropped short. My parents exchange a warm smile over the top of my oversized Tupperware box, and hands are stretched across until they intertwine with each other. I look back to study my father once more. Tube or no tube, my first impressions were correct. My father is very definitely *not* my father. I know this because he most likely isn't *anyone's* father—on account of him being a woman. A beautiful one. Do I have two beautiful women as my parents?

The blonde woman makes her way around the trolley my box perches on and squeezes in by my mother's side before the pair embrace lovingly. This is followed by a cupping of hands around each other's faces, and finally a kiss. One bursting with happiness and love. And long.

Not really the time or place to be copping off, I think— *Er... hello?... baby here... with tubes sticking out of it... child clinging to life.* In order to redirect their attention, I manage a cry. One that's noisy as fuck. After all, this moment should be all about me.

After the all-clear from the doctor, some weighing, hosing down and a great deal of faffing about later, I'm handed to the female couple. Their eyes widen, lips part, and some sort of ridiculous noise springs forth from the dark haired one's mouth—a noise that even the earliest homo sapiens would have been embarrassed to call a language.

And then it comes, proving that these people do indeed have the power of speech.

Three words. Short ones at that.

'Our little girl!'

5

Against all the odds, given my age, I know three words of my own.

For.

Fuck's.

Sake.

I've used them before. Ken wasn't a fan. He argued the use of such a phrase betrayed my innocence, and more importantly demonstrated a limited vocabulary. I pointed out to Ken that the man who tried to return the bike lock because he'd lost the key probably wasn't going to be too familiar with the more classical alternatives on offer from our wonderful language. I did concede that when I addressed the individual concerned, a better approach would have been to incorporate the word bellend.

Seriously, I'm to be parented by a same sex couple?

This isn't good. In my previous life, Barry Todd's parents were divorced because his father decided he preferred men. Ricky Henshaw's father to be precise. Those two kids endured years of insufferable torment, the pair of them always on the horns of a nervous breakdown.

But wait, that was years ago. Times will have changed, surely? People will be more tolerant. Live and let live, right? Children will undoubtedly still be cruel but I can handle them. In fact, I can use this situation to my advantage. Hindsight, see. Things are shaping up nicely. No one's ever going to believe either of these two women is my birth mother anyway. Not unless I grow up looking like Billie Piper. I mean, they're blindingly beautiful but check out the overbite on the pair of them.

I wonder what kind of a house they live in. Fingers crossed it's in a decent area. It's so much easier to carve out a satisfactory life for yourself if you have a head start. Y'know... nice house, nice clothes, nice school, Mindful Chef. I need to be mixing in the right circles from day one. With any luck, my parents will boast a wine cellar and be patrons of the local theatre. At the very least I expect them to own a TV that's superior to the one in this room. How can anyone watch a box set on this piddling thing? It's tiny, and the odds of it having Netflix are considerably slimmer than the guy with spaghetti in his beard.

Right, I don't know about the rest of you but I'm ready to go. I've got things to do. I intend being an arsehole of a baby, before turning into an arsehole of a teenager, and at the end of all that, probably marrying an arsehole.

Quick look to the midwife, a nod of my purple head by way of saying thanks for a job well done, then I direct my gaze to my new mothers and weigh up which one I'll have most luck playing off against the other.

If I could wink to the camera, I would.

6

Two days on from my delivery into the same world that I remember from my life before *this* birth, I leave with my parents. They've bought all the gear, I'll give them that, although I silently question whether an SUV the size of a shipping container is strictly necessary. There's only three of us and I'm tiny.

'Just you wait 'til we get you home, kitten. We have a lovely surprise for you,' says the one with short blonde hair called Bridgette. Either they've left the hospital with the wrong species or they're the sort to have annoying nicknames for everything. It's too soon to tell.

'Ooh yes,' says the other woman. 'Bridgette's right. Shall we ask Bridgey what we've got waiting at home for our little kitten?' On hearing the name *Bridgey*, Bridgette casts a sharp glance to her left and offers an unambiguous look to her partner—the sort which sees both eyebrows raised and thin lips retreating as they fold under one another. This is clearly a source of contention between them. A bit rich when they aren't calling me by *my* name. Wait, what *is* my name? A feeling of dread washes over me as I consider that my name might actually be Kitten. It's the kind of name given by a rock star to their first-born, safe in the knowledge the child will never be bullied for it. Rich, famous kids don't get teased.

'Penny's right, kitten. We've bought you a puppy!'

Considering I seem to be called Kitten, it's a toss-up whether the creature waiting for me at home is a dog or a brother. I'm hoping it's the former. Being an only child is what I have my heart set on. I'll need all possible attention and money directed my way if I'm to achieve my life goals this time around.

7

I take notice of the approach to the place I'll be calling home in my new life. My vision's somewhat restricted because I'm seated low and the car's glass starts too high above my head. I can see trees though, and they seem a fair distance from the road edge. The illusion is one of a wide boulevard and chances are this is a respectable, leafy, neighbourhood with a low crime rate and a small Waitrose.

The car slows and my new mothers (becoming comfortable calling them that may take some time) get disproportionately excited as they announce our arrival in a sing-songy way even a *CBeebies* presenter would flinch at.

Once out of the car, when Penny turns to Bridgette to ask if she has a front door key, I get the benefit of a three-hundred-and-sixty-degree panorama. It's a decent road, comprising mainly older houses but with a few new soulless red-brick infill plots. An elderly couple tend to the garden on my right. They offer up half-hearted waves; ones which are undoubtedly well-meaning and neighbourly yet manage to portray an awkwardness at finding themselves living next door to a same sex couple. They look kind people though, and merely part of a world that's overtaken them faster than they can adapt.

'Good luck,' the elderly woman says with a smile and in the loudest voice she can muster, before turning her attention back to the rambling rose that, along with the world she inhabits, also seems to have got too much for her.

Bridgette looks first at me, then to the couple. 'Thanks Mary. We'll need it!'

I try not to be offended at being projected as some sort of difficult, hard to manage basket case before we've even stepped over the threshold but snap out of my self-pity upon hearing a noise that, to be frank with you, is an assault on my delicate ears.

Penny lowers my basket to stripped pine floorboard level. There's a scuff mark that I'm guessing no-one has owned up to yet. And there it is, bounding towards me at pace. I'm praying it's the all-bark-no-bite type, but it's small and they're usually the ones who'll gnaw your arm off given half a chance.

The primitive language delivered in an unfeasibly high-pitched voice makes a return. Bridgette, this time. 'Kitten. This is Martha. Oh, yes it is. And aren't you lovely? Yes. You. Are. And are you going to be a good dog for our new baby? Ooooh what's that you say, Martha? I love babies. *Do* you Martha? Did you hear that kitten? Martha loves babies!'

What I heard was a series of questions. Presumably rhetorical ones given that my parents must surely be aware that neither the hound from hell in front of me nor I have yet acquired the gift of speech. Martha is kind of cute though and looks eager to please. I decide to give her the benefit of the doubt, though the barking will need to stop if we're to get along. At the appropriate juncture I'll point out to her that historically, serial killers learn their craft on family pets before progressing to more worthy prey. That should do the trick.

16

Luckily for Martha, I have no intention of becoming a serial killer, or criminal of any sort. There won't be time for that nonsense.

8

Five years on and I have things to report. My mothers Penny and Bridgette are doing an acceptable job of parenting me. The initial drive for the accolade of favourite parent has slowed somewhat but I can tell that each of my mothers believe themselves to be my favourite. That's all my doing. Occasionally I'll give one or other a cute giggle or hold eye contact for longer than is strictly necessarily. The real clincher though, rests with a widening of my eyes, suggesting that as a child, the world around me—selflessly provided for me by my wonderful parents—holds endless wonder. It doesn't, because I've seen it before, though things are slightly different now, of course. Cars seem to be plugged in when not in use and televisions are even thinner than I remember. Indeed, most things have got smaller, but surprisingly, mobile phones are larger. I'll make sure I own one of those as soon as I can. I'll play the "safety card" when the time's right.

There's something else I need to tell you. Penny and Bridgette's friend Laura Pollard spends quite a lot of time with us. She's really cool. Her and Penny grew up together, skipped school PE lessons together, found boys together (albeit one with more enthusiasm than the other), and shambled their way through music festivals together. The friendship went through a hiatus when Laura married Scott and moved to the Lake

District. But she's back in her (and our) home village of Loxby.

Minus Scott.

Oh, did I mention Martha died?

9

Before you ask, Martha's death had nothing to do with me. I actually loved that dog, and even learned to tolerate her high-pitched bark. Old age claimed her. Despite being introduced to me as a puppy, she was in fact eight years old when she came to live with us. She was re-homed with us after her previous owner was sadly no longer able to take care of her.

On many occasions I'd talk to Martha, confide in her, and she would listen, her head cocked to one side, ears standing to attention. I was comfortable telling Martha about my life before birth. In truth, there wasn't much to tell, but nowadays I find I'm remembering scraps. They arrive as flashes; sheet lightning that disappears in a fraction of a second but leaves behind a residual light—a scar on the sky, and on my brain. When the bolt retreats, you only have moments before the brilliant, focused light and the memories that hitchhike in on it disappear. I'm left with a jigsaw puzzle of fragments that seem impossible to piece together. Right now, I can't even complete an edge.

I remember Ken's warning about memories fading, and accordingly I'm keeping a notebook. My handwriting is quite refined, presumably because I've learned before, but I choose to write in a clumsy fashion, with bubble-shaped letters so as not to arouse suspicion in my mothers. The last thing I need is for them to think they have a child protégé on their hands.

You know the sort: the boy able to paint the Houses of Parliament from memory and in perfect detail; or the girl who works for GCHQ as a code-cracker at the age of twelve. I need to shape my own life; one that doesn't include a paintbrush or a logarithm.

My class at school has twenty-four pupils. I count them when Miss Finch is reading to us from some book about donkeys. When she asks us to repeat words, I can't be the only one who's aware she's silently performing a phonics screening test on each of us. Given Alfie Musgrove's difficulty in blending graphemes, I'm not convinced he's going to be one of life's high-flyers. Mollie Sawyer on the other hand carries the air of a child who's perplexed at the painfully slow rate of learning. Her parents will have already filled out her application for King's College and affixed a second-class stamp.

Of course, every classroom in every school up and down the country contains a mix of abilities. Did you ever wonder why? Ken knew, and he told me when we stepped outside for a cigarette on an unusually hot day in April. The perceived wisdom, he explained, after nudging his red specs back to the bridge of his nose, is that children's brains develop at various rates, each having an intellectual ceiling distinct from each other. This made little sense, according to Ken. The range of abilities witnessed in a classroom is too great, and the proportion of pupils demonstrating capacity for true genius, too low.

Consider the child who has had a life before birth—like me (and Ken). I've been taught how to speak and write before. Details are sketchy, but I'm guessing I was hopeless at it to begin with. Technically, I'm learning from scratch now in my new life, but my comprehension is accelerated. Muscle memory if you will. But I won't outperform my fellow pupils in *all* subjects, likely only the ones I was interested in or encouraged in before. The girl who cracks codes at GCHQ may have had multiple lives before birth so it's no wonder she's a child genius. But ask her to catch a ball and her lack of developed hand-eye co-ordination may see her rank bottom of her class because she's never been encouraged in that direction. Why would she be?

Of course, not everyone has the capacity to call on learned skills from their life before birth. Remember I said some people are blissfully unaware of the process? Well, that's those guys. It has nothing to do with intelligence, rather the parts of the brain given over to imagination and memory. Ken reckoned the group with no recall make up 'a good 99.5% of the population', but to me that sounded like a statistic he plucked out of thin air. I liked Ken, but at times he could be a bit of a bullshitter.

10

Laura picks me up from school on Mondays, Wednesdays, and Fridays. Between them, Penny and Bridgette contrive to collect me—usually a few minutes late—on the remaining two days. I'm told Laura's working hours are flexible which enables her to help out with me. She works part-time at the florist in the village, and her house is even nicer than ours. It's huge, and clearly far too big for one person. It's the sort of home I'll strive to own when I'm older.

Today is Friday, and Laura drives me to her house to kill the couple of hours before Penny and Bridgette are released from their respective workplaces. Bridgette isn't having a great time of it at work, and yesterday I overheard her bemoaning her boss.

'I'm not sure how much longer I can put up with that goose-stepping Nazi,' she said to Penny. 'I'm that close to telling him where he can stick his job.'

Penny, while unloading the dishwasher, was keen to encourage Bridgette in that direction.

'You should… Tell him to stick his job, I mean. You could start out on your own. Or with me. We've talked about it enough.'

The last word on the subject was, 'Hmm,' muttered by Bridgette as she cleared the dinner plates away.

Laura's house is what experts would label as child unfriendly. It's all furniture with square edges, bleach-filled cupboards without safety catches, fireplaces devoid of guards, and power sockets minus those silly blanking plates. Those aren't the most dangerous items in Laura's home though. That accolade goes to a ginger, teeth-bared, claws-extended predator who goes by the name of Duncan. Miss Finch would call him a Kh. Ah. T.

Duncan doesn't like me and the feeling is mutual. Laura tells me that Duncan only likes being stroked in a certain way. Well, I've tried nigh on two hundred different petting techniques and he's hissed at every single one of them. There must be something wrong with him; I'm guessing he was dropped as a kitten. Why can't he be more like Martha. Martha used to roll over for me to tickle her tummy. Get within twelve centimetres of this hellcat's belly and you'll likely be taking your own severed hand in a bucket of ice to A&E.

I miss Martha. I miss her cuddles and her big soulful eyes. The licking could get a tad wearisome, but I compartmentalised that along with the relentless barking, and loved that animal to bits.

Duncan has commandeered the chair by the fire; the one I like to sit on. It's a deliberate, antagonistic move on his part, of course. Before I rocked up for the first time at this house, his perch of choice was the round velvety thing Laura calls a pouffe.

'Good boy Duncan, you sit there. I don't want fur all over my pouffe,' Laura says now, before disappearing into the bowels of the house where the kitchen can be found. Later in life, I come to find that line amusing.

I set my schoolbag down and for no good reason swing my arms left and right, like an athlete might do as part of a warm-up routine. My gaze falls on the staircase in front of me, and I cock my head towards a shoulder, let my arms flop to my sides, and steer my focus upwards, inch by inch, tread by tread until it settles on the dark landing at the top. It dawns on me that I've never been upstairs in Laura's house. When I've needed the toilet, I've used the one downstairs, the one with black and white movie posters on all four of its walls. *The Seven Year Itch* is one. I asked Penny about it in the car when she collected me last Tuesday. She told me it's a funny story with a pretty girl in it. I accepted her brief synopsis but I'm struggling to comprehend how such a long-lasting affliction can ever fit neatly into the genre of comedy. I wouldn't find it remotely funny.

Duncan yawns and his gums smack together as his mouth slams shut. It's enough to rouse me from my fug. Laura will be in the process of making me a snack. That's the routine, but I'm curious to see what lies beyond the dark landing. Can I just wander upstairs without asking first? That's precisely the sort of thing grown-ups get spikey about, and I don't want to upset Laura, she's nice. After a quick glance towards the kitchen and a rough calculation of time available to me, I develop a rudimentary plan and make my move.

I approach Duncan all smiles and he fixes me with a look a hammer head shark would be proud of. In a move borne principally out of self-preservation, I change tack and approach him from the rear. Duncan, in his quest not to appear intimidated doesn't turn around, but merely tilts his head a few degrees by way of making the point he knows I'm behind him. I pause. Duncan swivels an ear at the silence. A stand-off. I eat up the last few yards in a flash, scoop up Duncan and with the thrashing cat in my arms, hightail it up the pine staircase. I deposit him into the first room I see, and in return receive a scratch that extends from elbow to index finger.

Free to explore, I waste no time opening doors and peering inside rooms previously unknown to me, all the while careful to keep an ear out for Laura freeing herself from her kitchen duties.

There's not a lot to report. Each bedroom is tastefully decorated and expensively assembled, and if there's any furniture carrying veneer in this house, I'm yet to find it. The bathroom looks to be bigger than my classroom at school. It has floor to ceiling white porcelain tiles and taking pride of place in the centre of the room sits a freestanding bathtub which would swallow me up many times over.

My own reflection in the bathroom cabinet gives me a start but I recover my composure, reach up and pull open its double mirrored doors to find a large number of medicine bottles, most of which, judging by their labels, appear to be prescribed. I sincerely hope Laura isn't poorly, or if she is, that the pills are doing a good job of keeping her well.

I complete the remainder of the first-floor tour in record time, mainly owing to there being only one door left to open, which as it turns out merely houses a hot water cylinder and a large dead moth. I shrug my shoulders and out of respect for the recently deceased lepidopteran, quietly close the door.

But something niggles me; something I know I must double-check, so I pop my head into each room one last time.

Satisfied with my findings, and aware that I've been snooping for longer than intended, I resolve to head downstairs whereupon I hear an anxious shout from Laura.

'Flo. Where are you?'

There's a scurrying of slippers on floorboards, and an irregular panting. From my vantage point I see the front door being flung open and Laura's panicked expression when she realises I'm nowhere to be found. I feel terribly guilty for causing her to worry, though if I'm entirely honest I'm more worried for myself and the potential bollocking that could be heading my way, so I decide to bring this particular game of hide and seek to an end.

I retrieve the somewhat bewildered Duncan, and shout as I descend the stairs, 'I'm here, Laura. Duncan ran upstairs with one of my gym socks. I've got it back from him though.'

'Oh Lord,' Laura says, leaning against the door frame for support, while patting her free hand against her chest by way of some amateurish CPR.

'Sorry,' I say sheepishly as I reach the bottom step. 'Am I in trouble?'

Duncan wriggles free, a claw snagging on the scratch he gifted me a few minutes earlier, causing me to stifle a yelp. He skulks off, keen to put distance between us.

Laura rushes to me, crouches down so our eyes are level, and with an expression that screams relief at not having lost her friends' daughter to an opportunistic child snatcher, gives me a playful wink and whispers, 'No, of course not darling Flo. Duncan was being silly taking your sock. He's only playing though.'

Laura looks across to her cat who carries the look of a creature who realises he's been taken advantage of. He makes to spring onto the chair, thinks better of it given the unwelcome escapade that ensued the last time he settled there, warily eyes up the pouffe and opts instead to trudge towards the utility and his cat flap.

'Silly Duncan,' Laura repeats, chuckling and turning back to face me with an impossibly wide smile. 'Right Flo, I've got some humus and crackers with your name on them. Follow me.'

'Will there be carrots for dipping?' I ask, still feeling guilty for making Laura anxious. 'I like carrots better than the cucumber sticks.'

'I know you do, love,' Laura says, easing herself to her feet. 'No cucumber, I promise.' Laura winks again, then in a hushed, conspiratorial tone adds, 'It'll be our secret!'

We start for the kitchen, Laura leads the way, her backless slippers skating along the pine with me in her slipstream. I glance around the living room and the study beyond, and the images bouncing back at me confirm the findings from my tour of the house's first floor. *Findings* is the wrong word though. It's rather what I *didn't* find that strikes me as odd.

An absence of any photographs.

Not one single record of family or friends.

Not even a snap of gorgeous me!

11

'Miss Finch. What's a goose-stepping Nazi?'

We've all been tasked with colouring in a picture of a duck, so my waterfowl themed question seems wholly relevant.

There's a shift in Miss Finch's demeanour. Gone is the self-assured, all-seeing-all-knowing façade. Her eyes flit nervously around the classroom searching for tell-tale signs of other pupils' interest being piqued. It's nearly twenty-past-three and she's been promised an after-school glass of wine with Mr Ball who, amongst other subjects, teaches us PE. We're only a group of five-year-olds but the irony of his name isn't lost on us.

Miss Finch valiantly regains her composure and in a gentle voice says, 'Flo. That's not a question for now. I'll speak to you after class.' She rounds her speech off with a half-arsed effort at a smile, no doubt intended to gloss over the awkward hush that still hangs over the classroom.

***

Miss Finch pulls up a chair and leans forward, placing her elbows on a desk that would never make the cut as a piece of furniture in Laura's home.

'It's not a question I expect to hear from any of my year one pupils, let alone Flo,' Miss Finch says, looking to each of my mothers in turn as she speaks. 'I have to say I'm more than a little concerned she's repeating this sort of thing in my classroom. There are very good reasons why Nazism is a subject matter covered much later in a child's school life.'

Penny shoots a glance to Bridgette that's loaded with reprehension.

Miss Finch sets down her pen, leans backwards, raises both hands in a gesture of surrender, and affords the pair a smile. 'Look, I'm hoping it's just a misunderstanding. Perhaps Flo has stumbled across some reading matter at home?'

'It's my fault,' Bridgette says sheepishly. 'I was talking about my boss. Flo must have overheard. We'll try and be more careful.'

Penny's head snaps around, and she casts an accusing look directly at her partner, her eyes blazing over the use of the word '*We'll*'. She clearly resents the implication they were somehow jointly responsible.

Miss Finch assures my mothers there's no harm done and the conversation between all three is wrapped up following a brief *all-friends-again* superficial chat about the school's upcoming sports day.

We drive for ten minutes in silence other than Bridgette pointing out a porch extension and a pigeon. It's done in an attempt to convince everyone that it's business as usual again. I look at the small row of shops to our right. A woman exits the hairdresser's while self-consciously touching her lacquer-sprayed bob. Penny breaks the lull in conversation.

'We're sorry you overheard Bridgette saying bad things about her boss,' she says with a smile, her face peering around the headrest. 'Can I ask you to do something for me, Flo?' I nod and look to my left as we overtake a middle-aged man attempting to commit suicide by jogging. 'Next time you'd like to ask a question, we'd like you to ask *us*, Flo darling. Is that OK?' I nod again. 'I mean it's great that you want to know the answers to things, it really is. We don't want you to stop asking about stuff that interests you. Maybe ask *us* about things you hear at home and ask Miss Finch about things you hear at school. Is that OK kitten?'

Page eight of the bloody school prospectus states that *"... children's thirst for knowledge is actively encouraged in all aspects of their learning."* I know this because Penny read virtually the whole booklet aloud one night, despite Bridgette only having asked what the fees were.

I contemplate quoting page eight. In fact, I nearly piped up with it in our "chat" with Miss Finch after school. I decide against it.

'Did you hear what Penny said to you?' Bridgette asks softly while negotiating the filter lane to turn right into our road.

'Yes Mummy,' I say.

'So you know you can ask us anything, Flo?'

I nod my agreement but neither of my parents are looking my way so aren't aware of my acknowledgement.

'Flo?' Penny says. 'So you can ask us anything, right?'

I realise they need to hear it from my lips. 'Yes,' I reply and gaze to my right.

'Good girl,' Penny says in a voice that indicates she considers the matter dealt with.

We're nearly home and I have a question; because I'm in their company, it qualifies as one to be addressed to my parents. I'm not sure if I ask it to satisfy my parents' desire for me to communicate directly with them, or whether I ask in order to fulfil my own curiosity.

'Penny?' I pause while I search for the right words. 'Why are you called Penny when you used to be Zoe?'

12

If I could have words with Ken right now, I would. Stern ones. I'm seven years old and flashbacks to my life before birth have been scant at best. Ken was insistent that most people remember snippets from their previous existences by finding themselves in close proximity to where they grew up, around familiar people, or stumbling upon memory-jogging landmarks. It can be something as simple as a shop front that triggers a memory of a childish prank or first kiss. If I've lived in this village before, it's not bloody-well making itself apparent to me. More to the point, I don't recognise any of the *people* living here. It also troubles me greatly that I don't know when I died, and without my old name, I have little chance of finding out.

I pause to do some simple maths. Technology can move very quickly, but that said, I don't see wholesale changes around me; we aren't all flying planes to work or having sex with robots. After some counting on fingers, I estimate I last saw Ken between eight and nineteen years ago. That was two days before I died. I haven't seen a Halfords on our travels so I'm guessing I've been born into some place new.

I'm allowed the use of a laptop at home now, so I'll make it a priority to try and locate Ken. I'd like to know how he's doing. Might he have found some less ridiculous-looking glasses? Might he have been promoted? Might he have finally found himself a girlfriend? Unlikely, I think, given that his name is Ken. I shudder slightly as it occurs to me that my friend might now be dead.

I don't know my name from my life before birth, which frustrates me greatly. It would be so much easier to recall details from my previous existence if I had my name as a starting point. I sometimes lie in my small bed willing the memory of it to come forward. And just as I think I'm within reach of it, something trivial pops into my head and displaces it—like yesterday when David Anderson admitted in class he'd 'had an accident'. Anyone with even the most rudimentary sense of smell realised a major incident would soon be declared long before David made his announcement. Martin Stewart, from the back of the classroom shouted, 'No shit!' As a retort I remember thinking it was quick witted and well in advance of his tender years. The delivery was slick too, much like the eruption that emanated from poor David's backside.

**

We as a family visited a boating lake the week before last. It was to celebrate Laura's birthday. She's forty-five, the same age as Penny. Bridgette is two years younger.

Penny, Bridgette, Laura and me all shoe-horned ourselves into a rowing boat that, judging by its paintwork, offered little guarantee of seaworthiness. Despite the worry of capsizing hanging over us, we had a great time. The sun shone, and we splashed water of dubious purity on each other's faces to a chorus of shrieks and giggles.

During our impromptu water-fight, an oar slipped from Laura's grasp and floated off toward a flock of swans who didn't see the funny side. Fortunately, a boat carrying a more skilful oarsman than us headed off in the direction of the stricken paddle. After the man had retrieved it, he rowed back to us and gently handed it back to Laura who blushed and said thank you at least eight times too many. He was handsome though. The sort of guy who, when I'm older, I'd be more than happy to engage in flirty banter with about rudders and rollocks. He'll invite me back to his huge pad and we'll set about having children (by which I mean the process—the fun bit minus the actual responsibility of kids at the end of it).

When our two hours were up, we stepped from the boat in turn, all of us making undignified exits onto the pontoon. It wasn't until we'd secured ice creams from the park café, and when our giggling had started to subside, that Laura touched one of her ears and rather mournfully announced she'd lost an earring. Ice creams were hastily finished, giving rise to bouts of brain freeze in Bridgette and Penny, and we all undertook the task of hunting for Laura's lost earring.

Twenty minutes of searching on hands and knees later, and Laura called a halt to the search. Secretly I was pleased since my knees were starting to feel raw. At the same time, I remember thinking that should *I* have gone missing instead of a piece of jewellery, I'd have hoped the search would go on considerably longer, and with more volunteers recruited.

Laura clambered to her feet, sighed, and with her best brave face declared the earring likely lost to the murky depths of the boating lake. For my benefit, she likened it to treasure lying on a seabed, left there by pirates as they swam from their sinking treasure-laden galleon.

It was a trigger; I knew that instantly. Treasure on the seabed was my sheet lightning. It meant something to me but try as I might, I couldn't lock on to its significance. Had I lost something in my life before birth? Something precious to me? Was it taken from me by bad people? One thing is for sure, I know it meant something, and in all probability it had nothing to do with pirates.

Later that day when we returned home, I scribbled the day's revelation in my notebook. I study it now. I'm careful to enter the few flashbacks I've had thus far as part of a wider recap of the day in which it occurred. This way, if Penny or Bridgette become inquisitive and reach for my book, they will merely see something resembling a diary. I write:

"Today was a lot of fun but Laura lost an earring which made her sad. She thinks she dropped it in the water. One day someone might find it like treasure left on a seabed by a pirate."

I flick back to my previous entries. There aren't many. The last was more than a year ago, but every so often I reacquaint myself with each written event in the hope that as I add more, the scribblings won't seem so disparate from each other.

"We went to the countryside today and had a picnic. Penny made egg sandwiches and humus. I left the cucumber sticks. I don't like cucumber. We got too hot and sat under a big tree. Bridgette said it was an oak tree and that we should look out for squirrels in case

they steal our food. Oh we also ate cake. Oh and we didn't see any squirrels."

I thumb back another page and read quietly:
"Brigetts car broke today a man had to come and mend it he had lots of tools and we stood at the side of the rode and play I spy. the man was nice and he made us all laff and when we got home we told Laura all abowt it."

Page one of my notebook contains one line:
"Brigit showd me some photos today they were lots of Penny and Laura when they were litel gurls like me"

13

8. That's what it says on the badge I'm wearing. It's in large print and surrounded by stars and unicorns. To be honest it's a bit bloody embarrassing. I'm eight years old, not three. Next, they'll be asking me to blow candles out on a cake and make a wish. I'll wish my badge gets stolen. I think I've worked out who's responsible for buying it: Bridgette. Strikes me she's struggling to come to terms with her baby growing older. She still talks to me in a lullaby voice and makes jokes about me having a boyfriend.

By the way, the boy Bridgette thinks is my boyfriend is Marcus Fraser. He's a complete bellend. He still wears t-shirts with dinosaurs on them and his mum calls him a scamp. If *he's* had a life before birth, he hasn't managed to recall any experiences of human development to allow him to bypass this lame phase.

I'm torn. In some ways it suits me to have my parents see me as intellectually on-par for my age. This way I can go under the radar in my quest to achieve the high life. I can lurk in shadows where they won't be looking for me. On the other hand, it's humiliating and an insult to my intelligence. For a brief second, I think about telling my parents that Marcus isn't my boyfriend because he has a tiny penis. I consider how much fun it might be to watch my parents squirm; squirm like I'm doing now in front of my friends with my oversized badge and butterfly hair clip. But I decide to keep the status quo and refrain from telling them. Apart from anything else, there'd be an excruciating conversation that followed; the pair of them viewing the moment as a trigger to be responsible parents, revving themselves up to deliver some wise words on sex education. They'd be keen to be all liberal about it, but still fuck the whole thing up by talking about kittens and puppies. He hasn't by the way—Marcus—a tiny penis. Well, he may have, I wouldn't know because I haven't seen it.

There's some encouraging news, though. Tomorrow, we set off for somewhere called the Lake District. Laura has a house there which, somehow, everyone has omitted to tell me about during my (current) eight years on this planet. It's to be our base for a holiday for the next two weeks. Just the four of us. Laura has described the house to me, and it sounds like a fabulous place. She says we'll be paying a visit to her old school, and the cinema if it's still there. When I ask why Laura doesn't know if the cinema is still there, the three adults exchange the briefest of glances before Bridgette breaks the silence saying, 'Laura hasn't been back to her old house in a long time, Flo.'

I look to each of them in turn, blink a couple of times and force my eyes to open a little wider. 'Why not?' I ask, genuinely curious by now.

Penny dives in, 'Because Laura's home is *here* now. In Loxby, darling.'

While I'm in the swing of posing questions, I plump for another and ask, 'What happened to *Mister* Laura? Where's he?'

It's Penny's change of expression that grabs my attention. There's a panic behind her hazel eyes and a flush of red makes its way from her collarbone to her neck, like a lava flow in reverse. The heat has reached Penny's cheeks now and she distractedly fiddles with her left earlobe. Laura takes the opportunity to leave the room, making excuses about gathering up washing to take with her to put out on the line. Bridgette touches her partner's hand but Penny withdraws it immediately. Bridgette visibly bristles at the rejection.

All is not well, I think. I want to know more but I fear this particular interrogation is over. At this juncture, a well-heeled lawyer would lead their client out of the interview room, look over their shoulder and tell the detective that that specific line of questioning was over. The detective would respond with, '*For now.*'

For now, the music is lowered, lights are dimmed, and a cake complete with eight yellow candles makes the journey from kitchen to living room. The room collectively destroys a couple of verses of "Happy Birthday" and I'm asked to blow out the candles and make a wish.

So I do. And as is traditional with making a wish, it remains secret and is made with eyes firmly shut.

And that's when the sheet lightning strikes. And even through my eyelids I can tell it's more forked than sheet. With greater intensity than those that have struck me before. And what's more, this time the residual light isn't fading. It's blinding, and powerful, and vaguely terrifying.

14

Every kid has a favourite parent. Fact. Any child who claims otherwise is lying, deluded, or, in a handful of cases too kind to risk offending the least likeable parent. The also-ran.

My favourite mum is Penny. She parents me with a light touch; she's the fluffy candyfloss to Bridgette's toffee apple. As years go by though, I reserve the right to switch allegiance, since middle-aged adults often talk fondly of their strictest teachers, the ones who cut no slack and who, at the time, seemed like the biggest, scariest killjoys in the world.

While it'd be going too far to label Bridgette a killjoy, she brings an increasing tension to the household, often manifesting itself as late-night arguments with Penny. Conscious to keep their voices down, it's not often I'm able to overhear from my small bedroom upstairs. Unless wine has been drunk. Wine lends a volume to a person's voice. There must be some science behind it. Most likely it will be covered in lesson one at secondary school. When we start back at primary school after the summer break, I'll suggest to Miss Finch she join a wine club, since her voice is feeble and falls well short of the back wall of the classroom where I like to sit.

Tonight will be a two-bottles of wine affair. An inch or two will be left undrunk in the second bottle to allow my mums to congratulate each other on their restraint. A routine doctor's appointment would unquestionably see Bridgette lying about the number of alcohol units consumed per week. Penny, on the other hand, would trumpet an excess of forty units and leave the doctor in no doubt that it would be unwise to offer negative feedback on the matter.

**

This morning, I'm up, dressed and make it downstairs before the others, most likely because I haven't shovelled half a case of thirteen-and-a-half percent Merlot down my throat the night before. The dregs of the second bottle wink at me from the coffee table. Both hands are needed to raise the bottle to my lips, whereupon I take a small sip, wince, splutter and screw up my face like a footballer who's received the lightest of glancing blows to their shin. The glass of water I pour cleanses me of the worst of it.

There's virtually no chance the conversation I overheard last night will be continued in my presence over breakfast. The bone of contention lay with Penny having failed to tell Bridgette of her old identity. It does seem odd. On a wet Autumn night last year when we raced in from a downpour and huddled around the fire, the pair were poking fun at me for giving Penny such a difficult birth with labour lasting almost eighteen hours. I had asked my mums how long they'd been together before they had me.

'Two years,' Bridgette said, while poking me in the ribs. 'Two glorious Flo-free years.'

'Those were the days!' Penny chuckled, before selecting another log to add to the grate.

'Hey!' I squealed. 'I'm a good girl. You're lucky to have me.' I planted on my best mock-wounded look which prompted both my mums to exchange a warm look; one of those fuzzy ones usually reserved for the point in a movie where the leading protagonists realise they're in love.

The reason I'm telling you this—other than to give you a snapshot into my day-to-day happy life—is to press home how odd it seems to me that in ten years, Penny never thought to tell Bridgette she used to go by a different name. A few weeks later when I ask why, I hear it from the horse's mouth and am told that Penny is my mum's middle name and simply prefers it to Zoe, a fact Bridgette confirms by way of a smile and a shrug.

What a monumental anti-climax.

15

You're probably curious as to how I knew Penny used to be called Zoe. Well, truth is I didn't, at least not until I saw the stranger stepping from Hair by Zoe on the day we journeyed home from our collective bollocking from Miss Finch. As soon as my eyes went to the shop signage, I knew. Don't ask me how, I just did. If you were to ask the boy from page five how he knew his grandmother was buried in that particular churchyard, he most likely wouldn't be able to offer a satisfactory explanation either. He would simply shrug his shoulders and say, 'I just do.'

That's the thing with flashbacks from your life before birth. Ken was adamant that when you've collected enough of them, (on the proviso you've amassed sufficient quantity before you get too old) your brain will make sense of them, rearrange them into chronological order and make connections where none were previously apparent. The more pieces you can decipher early on in your life, the more fluidly the remaining pieces will float into place and complete your picture.

The trouble is, I'm already eight years old and I've scraped together such a meagre stockpile of flashbacks that I think if Ken were here sharing a cigarette with me now, he'd tell me my chances of featuring in *This Is Your Life (Before Birth)* were virtually nil.

A short-circuit. Could that be what I had when I thought Penny used to be called Zoe? Am I seeing memories when there are none? I wish I could assemble better information, like the boy on page five.

It's frustrating because I have a feeling my life was full of incident. There should be more advice on how to go about recovering your previous life experiences. Should a person refrain from actively looking, and wait for revelations to strike in their own time? I ask because sometimes I think I crave past secrets too much. The process has overtaken my quest for a thoroughly enjoyable life this time around. In truth, I'm less bothered about being an arsehole of a child in my present, and more interested in whether I was an arsehole before.

Old age is often accompanied by a desire to explore one's position in the world order. It's why genealogy companies target publications with a particular demographic, specifically those people who are nearly dead. In an attempt to hook new customers in, such organisations will sandwich their advertisement between a new denture fixative and a charity whose sole objective is to fleece an elderly person's dependants out of a much-needed inheritance.

But look at me, I'm all arse-about-face. By the time I reach old age, I'll be so thoroughly clapped out from my research into a life which no longer exists, that if Heritage Trace stick a leaflet through my letterbox, I'm likely to tell them in no uncertain terms to piss off.

Obsession. That's what this is becoming. I silently curse Ken and wish I could stick his air freshener bookmark up his skinny arse.

I have a holiday coming up. I'm banishing thoughts of old Flo to landfill.

From now on, I live in the moment.

16

'Twenty minutes, Flo,' Bridgette says. It's in response to me asking if we're nearly there yet—that line all kids trot out full in the knowledge it's guaranteed to grate on parents who are tired, hungover, and desperate to pee. Or poo, if like Penny you've made the schoolgirl error of having cauliflower soup for lunch.

We pass a hospital. An enormous monolith of a building, clad with roughcast concrete panels and boasting a line-up of information signage around its grounds that, were you to take the time to read it all, your parking charges would run into hundreds of pounds.

But it's somehow familiar to me, if not this particular hospital, then a generic sibling punctuating the horizon elsewhere in the country.

A trolley is eased from the rear doors of an ambulance. There's a person lying on it but I see no movement. Unconscious, perhaps. Or worse. A teenage girl wearing a hospital gown wanders into view alongside the ambulance.

What takes place next is unsettling. The girl slowly turns to face the car park between us and the ambulance and she stares. Despite the distance between us, I know she's looking straight at me. Not Penny. Not Bridgette. Not Laura. Me. The stare is held until our car takes us beyond our line of sight. I turn around and look through the car's rear window to find the girl still fixed on me, only now she's wearing a smile that's cartoonish in its size and grotesquely at odds with the scene unfolding around her. Then in an instant her smile drops and her eyes narrow. She nods her head once, before disappearing behind the ambulance. I know that girl. I'm sure of it.

I shudder and switch my gaze to the opposite side of the road. A bus shelter intent on baking its occupants beneath its curved plastic roof carries a poster on one end.

"Party on the Pitch."

'Can we go?' I ask.

I've done that thing everyone does where they assume others around them are seeing or thinking the same as they are. I'm met with a quizzical stare from Penny.

'There was a poster back there for a party on a pitch. Can we go? Pleeeeease? There are to be stalls and a fairground ride and people playing guitars.'

'I don't know,' Penny says with a smile. 'It might be too far away and Bridgette has already done so much driving to get us here.'

I sulk, and in case there's any doubt that's what I'm doing, I paste on a face that reflects my mood.

'I don't mind,' Bridgette says cheerfully. She aims a wink at the rear-view mirror and I smile back before she switches her concentration back to the road. 'It'll be fun,' she says. 'We'll find out where it is. Presumably it's a football pitch, or cricket, or maybe a rugby pitch. It can't be too hard to seek it out. Did you see what day it's on, Flo?'

'Sunday', Penny says flatly.

I baulk at this, wondering why I was on the receiving end of a quizzical stare not thirty seconds ago. At the time I mentioned the poster, Penny looked my way as if she didn't know what I was talking about. She obviously saw the poster, so why pretend otherwise? For some reason, it's an event she doesn't want us to be a part of.

'*Tomorrow* is Sunday. Is it tomorrow?' Bridgette asks, looking increasingly keen to make sure we attend. If she keeps this up I'll need to give serious consideration to promoting her to favourite parent.

'Not sure,' Laura chips in. 'I didn't see the poster.' She's seated next to me and has been unusually muted for the last half an hour of our journey. 'We have plenty of other lovely, fun things to do anyway.'

Penny turns around and fixes me with a reassuring smile that implies Laura's right, that there's plenty of enjoyment to be had elsewhere.

I see Penny's smile and raise it with, 'I think it said it was in a place called Denholm Water.'

Penny turns back to face the road but not before dropping her smile and exchanging glances with Laura. Distractedly, Laura reaches for her handbag, rummages around inside but retrieves nothing from it. Penny mentions something about the radio station we're tuned to being dreary.

It's my turn to speak. Time to pass on information that wasn't to be found on the poster.

'It's on the first Sunday in August. Just like it's always been,' I say, gazing absent mindfully out of the car window.

We finish our journey in silence.

17

"Lakeside". As a house name it's unimaginative and one that round these parts must thoroughly piss of the postie. We're barely two minutes into the tour of Laura's house, but a look through the floor to ceiling glass at the rear of the property and I spy water. Lots of it. The sun's rays play on the lake's slack surface like a glitter ball on a dance floor, the water beneath carrying a turquoise hue. And as spectacular as this house is, I desperately feel the urge to be outside at the water's edge.

I'm given permission and hurtle out of the huge double-height living space to freedom, across the large expanse of cedar decking until I hit lawn. I'm smiling and laughing as I run, even though the promised water seems to get no closer, so I pump my legs harder, travel over a crest in the immaculate lawn until I'm no more than thirty yards from the lake which, for the next two weeks, will become my own personal paddling pool. I wrench my shoes from my feet as I run, causing me to hop and stagger, which in turn makes me laugh and shriek.

There's a shout from behind for me to be careful. The garden is long, a couple of hundred yards perhaps, so I can't tell whose voice it is, probably Bridgette's. I slow up like a sprinter would after crossing the finish line as I arrive at a narrow, decked strip which spans the full width of the back garden. It's sandwiched between the lawn and the water and I gingerly step onto it, more aware than an eight-year-old would normally be of the risk of splinters to bare feet. It must be an unconscious, inbuilt self-preservation learned from my life before birth.

The boards are hot on the soles of my feet so I sit down and allow my feet to dangle over the deck's edge. Leaning forwards, I peer down to see water lapping all the way under the structure I'm seated on. The lake's water is clear but shallow, barely covering the rocks that line the shore, and occasionally there's a popping sound as water caresses the deck's uprights, trapping and squeezing air in the process.

I'm soon on my feet though because projecting from the deck is a jetty which extends out over the lake by thirty feet or so. There's a small but swish-looking motorboat moored-up, and I step onto the jetty to take a closer look. The motorboat is covered with a tarpaulin to keep out the worst of the weather, but I can see a black hull with alternating orange and red stripes. Its motor hangs from the rear of the boat, lifted clear of the water, no doubt well maintained and primed ready for action.

Towards the rear of the hull, near the motor, what seems to be lettering peeks out from below the bottom edge of the tarpaulin—the boat's name, I think. I kneel on the jetty's edge with the aim of peeling back the tarpaulin to reveal the lettering, but the canvas is stretched tight and just out of reach. I lean a little further and almost overbalance, so rock back on my haunches to reassess. There are two ropes securing the boat. The one nearest the rear has some slack to it, and I'm convinced if I pull on it, it will draw the boat close enough for me to grab the tarp and tease it upwards to reveal the writing underneath.

There's a shout from the garden and I instinctively look to my left to see Laura waving her arms in a way that resembles some kind of demented semaphore. She shouts again and I cup a hand to my ear to signal for her to shout louder in order for me to hear.

'Come inside now Flo, darling,' Laura hollers. 'We're going to have a bite to eat.'

'OK,' I shout back, and turn back to give the motorboat one final look.

'Now please, Flo!' Penny joins in, leaving me in no doubt the matter isn't up for negotiation.

I clamber to my feet and resolve to revisit the jetty at the earliest opportunity. After popping my shoes back on, I set off in the direction of the house but walk this time, rather than run, so I can take in the rear façade of the property.

It really is a stunning piece of architecture, being fifty-percent glass, the remaining walls a combination of vertical timber boarding and white painted render. The framing to the windows and large expanses of glass are dark grey in colour and seem to blend seamlessly with the exterior's materials they punctuate. There's a balcony projecting from an upstairs room, the view from which over the lake must be stunning. Some kind of covered pergola spans the balcony's footprint, presumably to enable its users to sit and drink in the views no matter what the weather.

I reach the house to find the promised 'bite to eat' hasn't materialised, and since the guided tour of the property has already played out, I explore on my own. The living room we walked through earlier is immense. If you were to stand in its centre and perform a twirl like a three-year-old girl might, you could take it all in with one jaw-dropping rotation. It's a stunning room; a vast Tardis of a space made to appear even larger due to an absence of clutter, the only items punctuating the space being three luxurious sofas, a coffee table, a dining table with seating for ten and a wall-mounted television that has to be at least a hundred times the size of the one in the hospital room. There's also a log-burning stove with a stainless-steel flue that kinks itself under the stone mantelpiece behind.

I skip over to the coffee table, taking a circuitous route to make the most of the room's volume. On closer inspection, the coffee table appears to be constructed from a car's boot lid; the red coloured glass of the vehicle's rear lights at one end giving it away. Well, that and the FIAT badge near its centre. The remaining edges have been finished using tan leather upholstery with cream-coloured stitching. By way of support, each of the boot lid's four corners sit on top of a moulded plastic headrest—the hard plastic type with a cut-out in its centre. I stand back to give myself a better look. No one could dispute the amount of love and hard work that's been invested in creating this piece of furniture. From my point of view, I only have one criticism of it—it looks completely shite.

Three magazines are neatly stacked on the incongruous piece of furniture. I have to lift the *National Geographic* on the top of the pile to see the others' titles. Both, as it happens, are from the same series of publications: *Classic Cars*. Laura has many interests, but to my knowledge, cars of any age is not one of them. I reason they must have belonged to Scott before he decided to leave to be with his new woman. At least that's why I assume he left. The looks Laura and Penny exchange at mention of the man lend weight to this theory, like his name is a dirty word. Well, if he wronged Laura, I'm glad he isn't around. If he were, I might even give him a piece of my own brilliant eight-year-old mind. I'll bet my butterfly hair clip that he was the one responsible for creating this atrocity masquerading as a piece of furniture. I curl up a lip at the sight of it and pretend there's a bad smell under my nose. Junk, that's what it is. Something even a scrapyard would think twice about taking off your hands.

I decide not to linger at its side any longer and walk in the direction of the mantelpiece. The blanket ban on trinkets applies here too; the clean lines of the narrow slab of granite deemed ornamental enough in its own right. It's a smart move on Laura's part, I think, to create a living environment that's simple to keep clean, one which has nothing to lift in order to dust around.

I cock my head slightly towards a shoulder and purse my lips, weighing up whether it wouldn't be nice to display at least one object. It needn't be flashy, just something modest to soften the edges. I don't know, maybe an elegant piece of glassware, or an objet d'art keepsake from a grandmother, or a family photograph.

Photographs! That's what are missing from this room, just as they are from Laura's home in Loxby. Frankly, it doesn't take a genius to work out why, and I doubt you'd have to dig too deeply to uncover the truth. It all comes back to Scott. What did he do to Laura that would cause her to obliterate his very existence from her life?

'Flo, darling? Oh, there you are,' Laura says as she bustles from the kitchen with Penny and Bridgette in tow. Each adult carries a plate laden with food, and Laura casts a wide smile in my direction. I study the face of the woman whose airy demeanour is at odds with a past that is surely an unhappy one, and I feel resentment towards the person who prompted this woman into cleansing her life of its past. In my short life, Laura has passed me nothing but love.

Hold up... that's not quite true, she's also passed me some meals of dubious quality over the years. I've noticed that in the same way some people refuse to ask for directions, Laura obstinately refuses to follow a recipe. Ingredients are never weighed or measured, simply chucked into a pot with a degree of blind optimism present only in the sort of person who watches *The Wicker Man* thinking there'll be a happy ending.

Laura nods her head at the bi-folding doors. 'It's too nice to be inside. We'll eat on the terrace.'

How posh is Laura, I think? *Terrace?* I'm sure my school friends' parents bar none would call it a patio. I was invited to Lexi Montrose's house once. Terrace would be too kind to describe the designated seating area in her garden. Patio would be a stretch too. Scrub, wasteland, or nuclear wilderness would however all make the cut.

Upon reaching Laura's decked terrace, we circle a large dining set—the sort that looks like it's made from rattan but isn't because it can't be unpicked by fidgety-fingered children like me. Plates are deposited on the table, and immediately I can discern which offerings were concocted by each respective adult. Penny's dish is well-presented and crucially carries edible, healthy-looking fare. The food heaped on the plate

Bridgette has cobbled together is devoid of anything green but contains a selection of favourite nibbles of mine. By way of a reward, Bridgette receives a grin from me and a reproachful look from Penny.

That just leaves Laura's platter. I glance from the plate to Laura to find her looking pretty pleased with herself. She exudes the confidence of a woman who's sure she's nailed her task. And she has, if her task was to stockpile the scrapings from a crematorium's burn chamber.

Penny and Bridgette sneak a look at each other, and the corners of their mouths twitch upwards. Both women try to straighten their faces to iron out the beginnings of smiles that are in danger of getting away from them, but Laura seems oblivious to it all, trained on me as she is. I plant a warm smile on my sweaty face, and tentatively reach over to stab a cocktail stick into something that is either an incinerated, carcinogenic chipolata sausage or something that used to be attached to Marcus Fraser. With my free hand I take a swig from a glass of water in a futile attempt to facilitate smoother passage for what I'm about to put in my mouth.

At the last second, I hesitate. I'm the bungee jumper whose bravado has held its hands up, muttered an insincere apology, and skulked off to the bar (via the toilet). I scold myself for my cowardice, raise myself up to my full height, pin my shoulders back, and remind myself that I'm feeling especially protective towards Laura given what she's been through.

Laura practically explodes with pride when she sees me prioritising her plate of carbon over my mums' offerings. As I force down the food, stifling the urge to gag, I hide my distorted face from Laura by looking in the direction of the jetty, and see a large crow perched on one of the two huge oak posts that serve as mooring points. It reminds me of page five of Ken's book—the foreboding image of the bird on the sterile tree. The crow's presence here lends a comparable sinister vibe; the opening sequence to a horror film, perhaps.

Farther out into deeper water, a family in a rowing boat make their way slowly past. I can hear their laughter and I'm reminded of our day at the boating lake and Laura's lost earring. The man in charge of the oars looks our way and signals for his family to wave. I wave both hands back in the direction of their smiling faces. The crow takes this moment to fly off, its squawking becoming the dominant soundtrack, the family's laughter reduced to a barely audible musical underscore.

'I don't fucking believe this!'

We all turn to face Bridgette. Her hand is shaking as she holds her mobile phone out in front of her, though there's no possibility of any of us seeing the screen's content from where we're standing.

Penny makes eye content with Bridgette and subtly nods her head in my direction. It's done as a reminder to Bridgette to keep her language in check. That done, Penny gently says, 'Hey. What's up babe?'

'Sorry,' Bridgette starts, 'It's my… I can't… Why should I…' She's unable to finish her sentence so instead shakes her head in frustration, returns her stare to the phone, starts to cry, and runs off in the direction of the house. She pauses at the bi-folds, leans on the door frame, turns to face us and mouths a 'sorry', before turning again and disappearing into the house.

18

It's a relief to be out of the house after the emotions of last night. We've been holed-up in it together for less than twenty-four hours, but today's trip offers us all a change of scene.

There is a sadness to the bones of this house, yet I can't pinpoint why. Maybe it's the yawning space within it. My room, for instance, must be eighteen feet square, the king-sized bed in its centre cut adrift from the remaining scant furnishings. When I first laid eyes on the room, I debated whether an alarm clock might need to be pressed into action, set to sound a good five minutes before I usually need to pee, just to allow enough time to reach the en-suite. Large rooms are more difficult to fill with the soundtracks of everyday life, I reason. The noise of laughter, joy and voices might never reach the walls and ceilings in this house, especially if happiness is in short supply as I suspect it is here. I catch myself and wonder if I'm not merely projecting a perceived unhappiness where there might be none at all. I mean, for God's sake, all I've seen is a crow and a lack of photographs. With that as the sum total of evidence, Hercule Poirot would hardly be herding his suspects into the ballroom ready for the big reveal.

We bundle ourselves into Bridgette's SUV. Like the house we drive away from, this oversized tin can is far too big for four people.

'Make the most of the car,' Bridgette says, failing to disguise the bitterness in her voice.

Penny looks across to her partner, smiles sympathetically, then turns front again, directing her words at the windscreen.

'Well, it's only a car. It's not like we don't have another.'

'You can borrow mine whenever you like, Bridgette,' Laura adds, leaning forward as she speaks to ensure she's heard above the engine and road noise.

'Bridgette turns her head to her left and looking at no one in particular says, 'Thanks guys. I really appreciate it.'

'Anyway, before long you'll be able to buy your own car. Better than this heap of…' Penny pauses, and checks herself, '… crap,' she finishes, looking across to Bridgette to ensure she's taken on board the reassuring words.

Bridgette has lost her job, you see. Sacked via email yesterday. It's what prompted the swearing and sobbing that started outside at teatime, and which carried on well into the evening. Fortunately, emotions flattened out when Laura discovered a bottle of French Sauvignon in her wine fridge, and tears turned to laughter as Bridgette recounted stories of tricks colleagues had played on their unlikeable boss, Steve.

Without doubt, the best prank—and co-incidentally most cruel—was when Sandra Houseman from accounts gift-wrapped a dildo which she sent anonymously to Steve on his fortieth birthday. Steve gathered everyone into his office for a lunchtime glass of Prosecco, gave some lame speech in which he likened his milestone birthday to targets met by his team since the time he had become their boss, and set about opening the few gifts lined up on his desk.

There was a book about golf, a sign which read *"Forty-year-old golfers are crazy"*, and a box whose contents were unclear but carried the slogan (presumably invented by someone who thought it to be a humorous play on words): "IT'S PAR-THREE TIME". As an aside, Bridgette broke from the story to tell us that at the time she suggested to Steve that if he wasn't such an old git, *"PAR-THREE LIKE IT'S 1999"* would have been better. In hindsight she acknowledged it's probably the reason she's now unemployed.

Steve turned to the fourth gift—the pièce de résistance—and while he teased the paper from one corner of the parcel said, 'You're naughty. You really shouldn't have!' He finished unwrapping his gift and tossed the paper to one side to reveal a shoe box. Having lifted its lid clear and taken a peek inside, he took a step backwards. And there it was, Bridgette explained, in all its glory, the bright pink member. Large. Shiny. Nestled on a bed of shredded tissue paper and accompanied by a card which simply read, *"From your secret admirer x."*

I'm only aware of this story because I overheard Bridgette—the storyteller—when I paid a visit to the downstairs toilet. Like I said before, wine equals raised voices, and in all likelihood, I would have been able to hear the tale from the next county. The three adults were roaring when Bridgette described Steve's reaction upon seeing his gift, Laura swallowing a mouthful of wine the wrong way when the story moved on to reveal what Jim from the company's copyright department had said.

'You're naughty. You really shouldn't have!' Jim had said, repeating Steve's earlier words.

Turns out Jim doesn't work at the company any longer, either.

When Bridgette asked her boss if he had any ideas where he was going to put it, Steve called a swift halt to the impromptu meeting and told everyone to get back to work. Bridgette didn't need to explain to us that Steve was a man who wouldn't tolerate jollity in the workplace, especially if it resulted in an undermining of his authority.

We continue our journey to the pitch; a rugby one as it transpires, so I'm expecting it to be dominated by short men with large bellies and all of them minus a neck.

'I hope there's a bar,' Bridgette says. 'I could do with a drink.'

To my left on the back seat, Laura delves into a tote bag and withdraws a bottle beaded with condensation. 'Who needs a bar?' Laura grins.

'Ooh, naughty!' Penny gasps.

'Hmm… Yes. Very naughty!' Laura adds.

'You shouldn't have!' Bridgette says, completing last night's joke.

The three adults snigger and I wonder if they might still be pissed. I'll let them have their secret joke, though. For now. At least it's making Bridgette smile.

It's a story that will become profoundly fucking tedious extremely quickly though, so if one of them attempts to resurrect it a second time, I'll stop it in its tracks by asking what a dildo is.

19

Orange and red. There are those colours again, just as the motorboat's livery but more vibrant and plentiful here, as corporate colours adorning the fairground rides. And just like the boat's tarpaulin, there's a splash of white which is identified unnervingly quickly by Bridgette as a gin tent.

It's not two o'clock yet but there are plenty of bodies swirling around the place. The routes they take around the pitch seem random, as if the presence of so many attractions has confused their brains, preventing them from plotting a properly sequenced route. Hearts belonging to children skip beats as they gaze in wonder at the colourful waltzers and helter-skelter. To our left there are stalls, some selling hand-made crafts, others offering teddy bears as prizes for hooking a plastic duck or chucking a ping pong ball into a glass jar.

I'm drawn to the helter-skelter and turn to tell my trio of adults that I'm going to wander over to it. Make that a *duo* of adults; Bridgette is halfway to the gin tent and gathering pace like her life depends on it.

Life. It's not lost on me that since I've been in this part of the country, recollections—that I have to assume emanate from my life before birth—have increased exponentially. No mean feat considering this is just my second day here. This place: the pitch; the stream by the car park; the woods that rise at the far end well beyond the point where the pitch's turf blurs into long grass—they all look familiar to me. All of this after spending eight barren years scratting about trying to make sense of meagre scraps of video-bytes, some of which I'm not convinced are even relevant. And it dawns on me that my sensitivity to experiences thus far aren't recollections of *specific* events, but rather generic day-to-day occurrences which, while not as dramatic individually, will be important as a collective in helping to point me towards understanding better who I was in my life before birth, and equally crucial in helping me to chart a course through this one.

Take my caution yesterday over not wanting to splinter my feet. This wariness has somehow travelled with me and is hard-wired into my brain. The next child wouldn't have hesitated at the interface between the soft, safe lawn and the rough, weathered, timber boards and, as a result, they may have injured their feet.

I think back to the incident at school where Penny and Bridgette were invited to speak with Miss Finch. I knew for a fact that, at worst, asking a question about Nazis would land me with a metaphorical rap on the knuckles, and more likely reflect badly on my parents rather than me. I know this because it's knowledge gained from living through a process twice. At least twice. It's not a specific incident I decided to repeat from before. These episodes are simply an in-built instinctive knowledge of what I can and can't get away with, what will and won't hurt me, and what I will and won't enjoy.

The anomaly thus far in my life up until yesterday is knowing that Penny used to go by the name Zoe. It's a specific piece of knowledge, one that I can't explain how I came to be in possession of. In my defence, Penny was christened Zoe when she lived in this part of the world and it lends credence to my inkling that I know this place.

Which brings me on to the helter-skelter. As I look at the faces of the fearless children spiralling downwards, my in-built *generic* recall tells me that as a fairground ride, it offers you three things that the poor bastards waiting at the top won't have clocked. Firstly, it provides you with a mat made from coir that even at the point of manufacture was no thicker than a drinks coaster. Thousands of journeys later having been sandwiched between kids' arses and splintered wood, what you're asked to plant your butt cheeks on is now the thickness of the cardboard tray from a Bounty Bar. Which is exactly why, when you ride the timber ridges where the structure has been bolted together, you're stacking up a whole raft of medical problems for later in life; anything from a hernia, to piles, to the need for complete spinal reconstruction. Secondly, the helter-skelter offers you (as near as makes no difference) zero cushioning when you're spat out at the bottom onto an oversized doormat. To make matters worse, just before being jettisoned, your coccyx will smash against another of those pesky timber ridges placed there with the sole intention of making you bite through your own tongue. Thirdly, and most dangerously, the sides that flank the helter-skelter's spiralling ramp are nowhere near high enough. You don't need to be Isaac Newton to see that. Yet parents blithely pack their kids onto these things without a care in the world, as if parental instinct was given permission to bin itself at the car park, or more probably the gin tent.

While these are generic in-built defence mechanisms that I've no doubt learned from bitter experiences, this particular helter-skelter burns a specific image onto the surface of my eyes; that of a boy toppling over the side of its ramp, barely five metres from the launch pad at the top. He was tall for his age which almost certainly contributed to the accident. That year, the summer was hot, with rainfall low, and the grass—that might ordinarily have cushioned his fall a little—was baked to the consistency of concrete. A perfect storm.

Memories flood my brain of parents screaming, shouts for help, a man rushing to the clubhouse to call for an ambulance. I remember being led away by a man whose face I can't see, the sun behind rendering him a silhouette. He holds my hand, done to reassure me that everything will be alright, as he strides quickly but calmly, putting distance between the horrific sights and sounds of the accident.

And the boy *was* alright. In the end, that is. He spent many weeks in hospital and, while he never walked in quite the same way his school chums did, he went on to regain his strength and fitness, and complete his schooling.

And the man who led me away from the boy's accident? The man who held my hand?

He was my dad.

20

'Not going on the rides?'

I spin around to find Bridgette eating up the last few yards between us, gin and tonic complete with candy-striped straw in hand.

'We'd prefer you didn't, darling.' A different voice. Laura's. I shield my eyes as the sun bounces off a silver trophy, placed there not just to blind me, but as an award for someone excelling at something trivial later in the day. Laura and Penny emerge from the brilliant light and I blink furiously to wash the black dots from my eyes.

'It's dangerous, Flo. Best not to—'

'Bollocks is it,' Bridgette cuts in, trampling all over Penny's words of warning, then immediately placing a hand over her mouth as if it's not too late to prod the swear word back inside. I snigger and temporarily place Bridgette at the top of my favourite adults list.

'There was an accident here once. And it looks like the same ride to me,' Penny says, undeterred, looking across to Laura for confirmation. Laura nods her agreement.

'I know there was,' I say. My words, like Bridgette's have tumbled out before I can stop them. Laura and Penny cease their nodding, and in an instant, all eyes lock on to my own. During the weighty hush that follows, Laura and Penny scan the pitch in an effort to locate the person or persons responsible for passing news of the horrific accident to an eight-year-old.

'Come on Flo,' Bridgette announces. She's finished her gin and tonic and uses the moment to step in and defuse the growing tension. 'You can help me buy another of these and then we'll go and explore. How does that sound?'

It sounds like a good idea. It's a tad patronising of course since I'm sure Bridgette can buy a drink without my help. She bought the first on her own, after all. But Penny and Laura look like they're preparing an interrogation and I'm not ready for a Q&A session just yet.

Heading for the tented stalls with my hand nestled in Bridgette's, a look over my shoulder reveals Laura and Penny deep in conversation and in a moment of immaculate timing, Penny looks my way and shoots me a no-teeth weak smile.

They're all smart women, make no mistake, but they all succumb to the same blind spot. To a woman they all underestimate my powers of comprehension. If you were to ask an average eight-year-old to replay the key points of the conversation that just took place between the four of us, they might touch on the ride being dangerous, the previous accident, and their parents being concerned because of it. They might also, through blushing cheeks, throw in a reference to Bridgette's swearing.

But I don't believe I'm an average eight-year-old. I'm not being boastful, and I don't have an ego, I simply have a better understanding than most of my peers of what it takes to navigate my current life on a day-to-day basis. And in the case of our recent conversation, I'm also able to recall specific episodes. Set all that to one side though, and I have something else other children my age don't, and that's an ability to pick up on nuance. I mean, sure, it's obvious from Laura's request that in order to make her happy, I shouldn't ride the helter-skelter. But what I locked onto no sooner than the words left her mouth was the word '*We'd*'. '*We'd* prefer you didn't, darling.' Why not *I'd* prefer you didn't? It struck me as phrasing a *couple* might use.

Bridgette places a ping pong ball in my hand and I'm aware I haven't been listening to the instructions provided by the heavily lined woman prowling the space behind the glass jars. I shake thoughts of the conversation from my head, after all didn't Laura and Penny grow up here as friends. Did they witness the accident together, I wonder?

'Come on Flo, we haven't got all day,' Bridgette says, slurping the remainder of her gin and tonic, a pink one this time with half a fruit salad in it.

Some glass jars are smaller than others, and the ones towards the back nearest the stall holder are spaced further apart making it less likely to land the ball in them. But hell, I'm not paying. If I were, I'd play the odds and stick to the jars that sit so close that, at a stretch, I could lean over and just drop the bloody ball in. But where's the fun in that?

I launch the ball, misjudge its weight completely and manage to bounce it off the forehead of the woman who's just relieved Bridgette of one pound. Upon impact, the woman screws up her face and impossibly adds more lines to the relief map that is her forehead. If that woman has ever been introduced to sun cream or Botox, I'll come back here when I'm eighteen-years-old and ride that helter-skelter naked.

'Not so hard, Flo, darling,' Bridgette says for the benefit of Mother Theresa. She's stifling a giggle though and it's threatening to go rogue. 'Have another go,' she says, handing another coin over.

Pretty reckless spending for someone who's just lost their job, I think.

'I don't need another go. I won,' I say triumphantly, beaming at each woman in turn. The two women exchange a glance which screams *oh bless her,* so I wait until they're looking my way again, before offering a barely perceptible nod in the direction of a jar that's sitting second row from the back. It's not hard to spot since it's the one with a ping pong ball nestling within it.

'I think I'll have the giraffe,' I say, pointing to the faded polyester creature directly behind the woman's head.

'Wait!' the woman yells, all square shoulders, hackles up, jaw set to the consistency of boron, her demeanour firmly in defence mode. 'You need to throw the ball straight into the jar.' Gone is the sickly-sweet smile she deployed to draw us to her stall in the first place. She's now a lioness protecting her cubs (and a small giraffe).

As if reading my mind, Bridgette becomes defensive herself and rises another half an inch from the turf. 'Where's it say that?'

'Eh?'

Doubt writes its name all over Bridgette's face but there's no going back now, and she knows it. We all do.

'Where's it say the ball has to go directly into a jar?'

'Well it's bleedin' obvious innit,' the woman squawks, eyes blazing.

'Don't you swear in front of my daughter!' Bridgette yells, meeting fire with fire.

I sneak a look at Bridgette just to check she's conscious of the hypocrisy that has just taken place. The briefest of looks returned my way confirms that she is.

'Connie. Belt up.' The voice is calm and soapy, and washes over us from behind. Yet there's also a firmness to it, a tone that makes it perfectly clear to those on the receiving end that non-compliance isn't an option. 'I can see a table tennis ball in a jar, Connie. Did you put it there?'

'Of course I didn't. Why would—'

'—and did you place it there, Miss?' The man directs his question at Bridgette.

We get a better look at him. His features are classical, a strong jaw framing a lean face punctured by cobalt eyes. I'm drawn to his dimpled chin and pronounced cheekbones that the sun has targeted in deference to rest of his face. He still keeps a full head of dark hair, greying a touch at the temples. Mid-forties at a guess. Maybe younger. It's hard to tell because he's in good shape, an attribute not lost on Connie, who despite her protestations can't disguise her attraction towards him.

'Me? Oh goodness no,' Bridgette says in an unfeasibly high voice, sufficiently flustered to place her palm to her chest. She'd have been better placing it on her face, at least then she could have hidden the blushing. Weird behaviour for a woman whose sexual leanings don't extend to men.

The man drops to his knees so his eyes are level with mine. I wait for a proposal of marriage that doesn't arrive.

'Well, that just leaves you, doesn't it?' He smiles using both his mouth and eyes, shaping his face into a warm canvas to reassure me he'll make everything right.

'I'm Tom. What's your name?'

At this question, other eight-year-olds might throw a glance towards their parents, seeking the required permission to talk to a stranger. But this man doesn't feel like a stranger. I know... I know... this is what the bad strangers are good at, putting you at ease, being super-friendly in order to gain your trust. I'm aware of this. Quite why I seem to know this level of detail is easily explainable too. It's like my splinters knowledge but less innocent and more graphic. I'm unsure if it's part of my sub-conscious, or knowledge directly received from my parents or Miss Finch. Either way, I'm right to be wary, and if I were alone, I reassure myself that I'd have the confidence to tell a stranger to back the fuck off.

'It's Flo,' I say, deciding that, on balance, this man is unlikely to throw me into the back of his van and cut me up into small pieces. I swing my arms from side to side like I used to when I was three. I urge myself to get a grip and pin hands to hips.

'Well, Flo. It's lovely to meet you and your... Mother?' Tom looks inquisitively at Bridgette who nods her scarlet head. 'I hope you have a lovely day.' He winks, but not in a creepy way like the caretaker at my school does. Tom then rises to his feet. He's almost upright, but a faint noise grabs his attention and he looks back to the stall to find Connie covertly retrieving the ball from the jar. 'Giraffe wasn't it, Flo?' Tom says, eyes fixed squarely on Connie's.

'You've gotta be bloody joking. It's a ricochet!'

'Ricochet?' Tom starts. 'Nope. It's not a ricochet. It's definitely a giraffe.'

Bridgette sniggers, Connie scowls. Tom leans over the stall's edge, and clicks his fingers once, whereupon the giraffe is reluctantly placed in his hand. He passes it to me and claps his hands together.

'Well, that's me,' he says. 'See you all later.'

All three of us watch him disappear into the crowd, Connie lustful, Bridgette conflicted and me stuck with a toy that I'm at least five years too old for and which, let's face it, won't carry a kite mark or whatever they use these days to prove a commitment to safety. I make a mental note to keep the thing away from a naked flame.

21

The afternoon wears on, faces become more sunburned, livers become smaller. Penny and Laura are chatting to a woman of similar age. She wears a floral print dress and canvas sandals and nods intently while Laura talks. Bridgette wanders over to join them and introductions are made.

I've been handed some coins and told I can play on a dance machine, a contraption I have no intention of setting foot on. Not after seeing a woman—who'd visited the gin tent more times than Bridgette—lose her footing, then lose her tits as they spilled over the neckline of her dress, all to the amusement of her friends (and gratification of the teenage lad in charge of taking the cash).

I've been told not to stray beyond the try-line of the pitch, or the H-shaped white posts as it was re-described by Penny when she registered my blank face. I'm starting to think I wasn't good at sports last time around. I would have been the child who couldn't catch.

I reach the posts. There are no stalls beyond this point, no organised games you can stick your name down for. I risk a glance over my shoulder to see my two mums, Laura, and the mystery woman deep in conversation. Five minutes of exploring. Just five minutes I say to myself.

The fine turf gradually gives way to knee-height grass which I wade through until I reach the woodland's edge. It's the point at which the unchecked grasses pass nature's baton on to lush ferns reclining happily in the low levels of light.

Picking my way along the woodland floor, tripping on roots occasionally, scratching a calf here and there on nomadic brambles, I happen upon a small clearing. A single shaft of sunlight hits the ground in the centre, a spot where ferns have retreated to find denser tree canopies. I position myself under nature's spotlight and imagine myself on a theatre stage being cheered on by an adoring audience. Picking three foxglove spikes, I toss them into the air and imagine them to be roses flung to the leading lady at the ballet. I curtsey, scoop up the flowers and am stopped in my tracks by a noise to my right.

Except now it's to my left. Behind me now. I spin around, dropping my bouquet, feeling panic rising. I can see nothing. Silence settles, hangs there reassuringly. There's no one there. No strangers. No predators. No ghosts. A giggle. There, definitely a noise. I didn't imagine that. Female. A girl. I step from the spotlight and gingerly creep to my right, the source of the original sound. I stoop to pick up the giraffe I'd set down earlier, pressing it to my chest now for protection, feeling momentarily guilty for mocking it before.

I'm about to retrace my steps and head back to the safety of the pitch when a face peers around the trunk of a beech tree. The face belongs to a girl, perhaps fourteen or fifteen years old, a teenager who you'd be more likely to refer to as a young woman. She giggles once more and detaches herself slowly from the tree until she stands there grinning, her hands plunged into the front pockets of her dress. I scan for adults or similar aged girls but this female appears to be unsupervised like me.

'What you got there?' she asks, nodding at my cuddly toy.

Long blonde curly hair frames an elfin unblemished face but for a few faint freckles across the bridge of her nose. Innocence personified. Pretty. Especially pretty considering she's largely un-groomed, unpainted, her good looks seemingly irrelevant to her.

'Oh, this?' I say, giving the toy creature a shake in order to impress on the girl in front of me that it isn't my answer to some sort of pathetic comfort blanket.

The girl stares at me, still smiling, and gives another small nod in the direction of my prize to suggest that I'm still to answer her question. I look first to the limp, stuffed animal in my grasp and then back to the girl. I really don't want to state the obvious. I mean, even from the distance she's standing from me, it's blatantly obvious it's a giraffe. I change tack.

'I won it on one of the stalls,' I say with the sort of shoulder-shrug championed by stroppy teenagers up and down the country.

'What's his name? If it's a *he*. Could be a *she*.'

I think hard, unsure where this conversation is going, other than nowhere.

'I haven't named it. I'll probably give it away as a present. I mean, would *you* like it?'

'Yes please. I'll name him Joyce,' the girl says, stepping forward to claim her prize.

When she's within a metre or so of me I can see she's older than I first thought. I've been deceived by her carriage and manner which suggested someone considerably younger.

'Thank you,' she says, leaning forward and planting a soft kiss on my cheek.

75

'I see the two of you have met.' I recognise the voice as belonging to Tom, the man who secured "Joyce" for me at Connie's stall. He turns his back to us and shouts in the direction of the rugby pitch, 'Penny. In here. The woods. I've found her.'

I'm led away from the tree canopy by Penny who, after thanking Tom profusely, insists on holding my hand as she strides through the long grass until we reach the pitch once more. Bridgette and Laura scurry over to join us, relief etched on their flushed faces.

'We were worried, Flo. You mustn't do that again, do you hear?' Penny urges, just about managing to keep the quiver out of her voice.

I nod.

'Seriously Flo, we were really worried,' Bridgette presses, still clutching a gin goblet.

I start to cry. I'm not sure why. I'm genuinely sad for upsetting Penny and Bridgette but there's more to my tears. Perhaps the flashback to the helter-skelter accident is to blame, perhaps it's seeing Tom—another face and voice that seems familiar to me. Bumping into that freaky fairy in the woods won't have helped either. Deep down though, I know what it is that's upset me. It's because for the first time in my life, I've remembered my old dad.

22

I silently curse myself for crying today. It hastened our departure from the party thus robbing me of a precious opportunity to look for my father. Ken wouldn't have been impressed with me for saying that. On one of our many chats on the subject, he made it clear that people who are able to remember should never attempt to revisit their past lives. I asked him why, of course. I mean, wouldn't the sight of a lost loved one bring comfort to a family, ease their grief?

Ken was having none of it. 'Firstly, you're assuming you'll look the same as before. You won't.' By way of demonstration, Ken grabbed my ponytail that was fed through the hole in the back of my cap. 'You might wear your hair short next time around,' he said, inviting a playful punch from me to his chest. 'You might be ugly,' he grinned.

'With these genes?' I said with mock offence before relaxing into a smile.

'Seriously…' Ken, it seemed wasn't finished, '… a person who recalls a past life can really screw up the lives of those still living from that time. Consider this; even though they may not *recognise* you, they'll almost certainly still pick up on simple things: mannerisms; a unique gait; a laugh that extends beyond that of other people.'

'You saying I walk funny?'

'Also, do you really think you'll be able to resist reminding them of who you are… *were*.' Ken corrected himself. I noted that he hadn't expanded on my gait.

'Well, I wouldn't blurt out, "Hi Mum! Remember me?" would I?' I said, rolling my eyes.

I remember Ken folding his arms and raising his chin slightly.

'What *would* you say, then?'

'Well, I dunno do I?' I tapped my foot in a quest for inspiration. 'I mean, I'd be more fucking subtle than that, wouldn't I?' Ken raised a reproachful eyebrow at the bad language, lifting it well clear of the red frame of his glasses. 'I probably wouldn't *say* anything. I'd maybe move a photograph slightly on my parents' coffee table, or leave a flower on my own grave, or turn the toilet roll around so the flap rests against the wall. My mum hates it when I do that.'

Ken shoved his hands into the pockets of his dungarees. 'So, what you're saying is you'd break into their house and find all sorts of different ways to be a creepy so-and-so. My God, that's the stuff of slasher horror films. Your family might be getting on with their lives, then all of a sudden there's a poltergeist with a bog roll fetish roaming the joint. After a few months when they're total gibbering wrecks, they'll call in Father Michael who'll have to turn down the gig owing to the Vatican having "retired" him five years previously after some negative publicity.'

Creepy *so-and-so*? A great example of a phrase that can be successfully superseded by one word: *fuck*. 'What the fuck are you on about? Who's Father Michael?'

'What?' Ken muttered, fiddling with his watch while nervously looking around for the presence of a supervisor.

'Father Michael,' I said, a little too loudly. Out of the corner of my eye I saw Keith, our supervisor, duck into the car battery aisle carrying a clipboard, but Ken and me both knew he was monitoring our productivity. I made a note to buy him a stopwatch for his secret Santa. I'd have got him a life but you were only allowed to spend ten quid. 'Was he a kiddie fiddler?'

'Who… what… no… I dunno… who?'

'The disgraced Father Michael, who by the way I've never heard of,' I said. He'll have been hushed-up by higher echelons, I thought.

'Well he's an exorcist isn't he?' Ken said, a sheen of sweat forming on his forehead.

'I dunno, is he? He's never been round our house,' I said, becomingly increasingly confused.

'Well, he wouldn't, you're not Catholic,' Ken said before performing a slightly comical double take. 'Are you?'

'No, but I'm thinking of becoming one. You can get away with all sorts of shit by just saying you're sorry afterwards.'

Ken shook his head in exasperation. Keith had moved closer, and now lurked in the car valeting goods aisle.

'My point is, you've *had* your previous life before birth. A subsequent life needs to be viewed… no… it needs to be *lived* as a separate, detached entity. I mean, draw upon your experiences by all means, that's not going to hurt anyone, and in all likelihood will guarantee you a smoother passage this time around.'

I nodded while smothering a smirk at hearing Ken use the word 'passage'.

'Apart from anything else,' Ken continued, 'Who's to say your previous life was better than your current one will be? It's up to you to make sure you enjoy your second, or third chance and make a better life for yourself. Be a better person. Be nicer to your current loved ones. Be happy.'

'Do you know who your old family are, and where they live?' I asked.

'I do,' Ken said, the words catching in his throat. 'I leave them be.'

I leave them be? Ken had started to talk like he was the central character in a ropey Western so I decided to wind up our chat.

'OK partner, I guess we'd best get on. Lots to do before sundown. Besides, Lurch is on the prowl.' I gave my last sentence enough volume to ensure the words reached Keith's flapping ears and made off in the direction of some car radios waiting to be security-tagged.

'Baboon.' I swung around at the sound of Ken's voice to find he hadn't moved. He stood stoically, then refolded his arms. 'Your gait. It's like a baboon's.'

'Fuck off, Ken.'

23

As I lie in my capacious room, I think back to Ken's words. Back then I was an attitude-riddled teenager who must have been annoying in the extreme. That said, Ken liked me. Ken liked Michelle in the cycle shop though, so he wasn't what you'd call discerning.

I realise I'm talking of Ken in the past tense even though there's no reason to suggest he's dead. Maybe I do it because I'm talking about *my* life. Terminated too soon, they'll have said at my funeral. Cruelly taken from the world at a mere sixteen years old, the chaplain would have addressed to the lines of disbelieving mourners.

I wonder what the eulogy will have been like. I bet it'll have missed the decent bits out, sanitised for the benefit of my parents. I'm willing to bet the story of the customer who refused my help when selecting a new car battery didn't feature. I told the man he only need tell me the make, model, and age of his car, and I in turn would advise him which of our batteries would fit. He rather pompously told me that if he needed my help he'd ask for it. Which after ten minutes or so, he did. He asked for a tape measure so he could measure the distance between various batteries' terminals. I obliged and made sure I passed him a metal one.

I like to think the deafening bang which rocked that particular part of the store when positive and negative were brought together is still talked of today, along with the ensuing commotion when three colleagues tried to prise the furious, disorientated gentleman from the windscreen wiper display he'd been catapulted into on the opposite side of the aisle. There were mutterings of a lawsuit at the time, but Keith smoothed things over by gifting the man his car battery, a foot pump and some upholstery cleaner.

If Ken was the person selected to give my eulogy, it will have been tender, heartfelt but ultimately wearisome and way too long. It would also be bereft of any swearing.

It maddens me that Ken's is the only face I remember.

Until today, that is. I sit up straight in my bed and replay the image of my dad that presented itself to me as… what… a mirage? An apparition? A ghost? It could be all or none of these things but in the instant his hand took mine, I knew I loved my dad dearly. And as soon as he was allowed into my thoughts, I could see additional pieces for my jigsaw; the piece which shows my dad schooling me on the best way to catch crabs on the seafront, another piece where he demonstrates how to set a table properly with knives and forks in all the correct places. And us standing in a large aquarium tunnel with fish of all shapes and colours swimming above our heads. Us laughing. Him holding my hand and me feeling protected because of it. Ironic since he wasn't able to save me when my time came. What I never see is his face. But I know it's him. I just know.

Laughter drifts up from downstairs. The three women—or *The Witches of Eastwick* as I've started calling them (their fault entirely since I was barred from watching it with them the other night and banished to my room)—are talking in alternate hushed and raucous tones. A loudly delivered sentence by one of them being followed by uncontrollable laughter, with a dose of pantomime shushing not far behind, presumably so I can sleep undisturbed.

Who do they think they're kidding? The shushing is akin to a wind tunnel and if I'm to drop off anytime soon I'll need to watch reruns of Keith's "Health and Safety in the Workplace" seminars.

I'm forever being told that we shouldn't keep secrets from each other, and right now that feels very much like a one-way agreement. Why can't I be involved in whatever is so funny? I console myself with the reasoning that in reality their conversation won't be that funny. Well, not unless you've put away two bottles of wine, at any rate.

A much better idea is to creep halfway down the stairs, peer around the bulkhead and watch for myself.

'Why the fuck not?' Penny says sweeping the room with her eyes to gain support from onlookers who aren't there.

'All sorts of reasons. Too many,' Bridgette responds, flopping back into her armchair, arms folded, with an expression that suggests if pressed, she might struggle to come up with any at all.

'One. Name one,' Laura says, entering the fray.

'Alright,' Bridgette says, looking around the living room for inspiration, and nearly spotting me before I retreat behind the bulkhead, out of sight.

'Flo!'

I freeze. She *has* seen me. Shit. Shit. Shit. I quickly take the decision to remain hidden and sit tight. After all, she's been drinking and may have only *thought* she saw movement when she looked my way.

'Flo?'

Bollocks, it's Penny this time. I've been rumbled and prepare to give myself up.

'Well of course we need to consider Flo,' Penny continues. 'We can co-ordinate around her schooling. Whenever we think is best.'

Whatever the three of them are banging on about, I realise their conversation is being conducted unaware of my presence.

'I don't know, she seems happy at Loxby, happy in this school,' a concerned looking Bridgette says.

No I'm fucking not. Every day I'm seated by Amy Cooper who has deplorable body odour. Yesterday a bluebottle landed on her desk before flopping onto its back, all six of its lifeless legs pointing at the culprit. Even an apocalypse-proof cockroach would be struggling within fall-out range of that girl's armpits.

It takes some willpower not to vocalise my thoughts, but I need to hear this out.

'There's no reason why she shouldn't be happy here too,' Penny argues, keeping her voice gentle and her tone low.

'Yeah I know. But what about you? I'm surprised you're even considering it.' Bridgette addresses her concerns directly to Laura. 'Are you really ready to come back here permanently, after everything that happened to you?'

Laura, who's been quiet to this point, leans forwards on the sofa and clasps her hands in front of her. She looks earnestly at my mums in turn and, with some measure of control, delivers one of the most compelling speeches I've ever heard, and that includes *Eastenders*.

'Five years ago. Wait no, a year ago, I wouldn't have even considered it. You both know how nervous I've been the last few weeks, and I've lost count of the number of times I nearly called this trip off. Even last night, cocooned in this bloody house, I felt terrified. But this is my home and… ' Laura breaks off, clearly struggling to compete with the emotions that threaten to overwhelm her. Her voice cracks as she speaks. Penny reaches over and places a hand on her arm and receives a nod by way of thanks, the action of which encourages a single tear to break free and roll down Laura's cheek. With train of thought well and truly lost, she wipes the tear away and gives her head a brief shake, clearing it of anxiety, ready to continue once more. Bridgette sits separate from the other two, looking somewhat uncomfortable around such elevated levels of raw emotion.

'Today was what I needed. It would have been easy for me to bury myself away in this house for a fortnight, away from the villagers' gaze, the sympathetic looks, the finger-pointing, the ones trying too hard to be kind… the ones finding it easy to be *unkind*. I nearly stopped you from going to the gin tent, Bridgette. I felt safer in a three. Less vulnerable. As a pair, stood in the centre of the pitch, I wondered if we weren't simply there for target practice.' Laura raises a trembling finger and points to her heart, the words she's about to utter for the benefit of partygoers from earlier who might have wished her ill-will. 'Go on, all of you. Aim here. Take your best shot. You can't miss. Oh, but I'm forgetting… you can't pierce a heart that isn't there, can you?' The trembling finger joins the others in her lap and Laura risks a glance at her two friends. 'I wanted to shout you know… today. Shout at everyone whose lives are duller for me not being around. YES I'M BACK! Missed me? Yeah, I bet you fucking did. What the hell did you find to gossip about for all these years I've been missing, eh?'

'They'll have found something,' Penny says softly. 'It's what people do. Grasp at others' misfortune in order to give their own lives a shot in the arm.'

'No, it's OK, really. Tom made me realise that. He was always understanding, quick to ring-fence me if people got too close. Today was no different. I could tell he was looking out for me, you know. And today made me realise that this is my home, and I have every right to be here, to enjoy it with my two best friends.'

Bridgette takes a sip of wine, and frowns, 'Is he single?' she asks, utterly sincerely.

'Two *best* friends? Your two *only* friends more like,' Penny quips.

Laura laughs, a quiet chuckle at first, but one which morphs into a throaty sixty-a-day bellow; and the release is visible, the muscles across her shoulders un-tangle themselves, her eyes regain signs of life, and laughter lines overshadow the worry kind.

The sight of Laura laughing is permission for the others to follow suit. Frankly, I'm so relieved Laura's speech is over that I feel the urge to join in too. I've read books, and in every single one of them, summer holidays are all about sandcastles, ice creams, water fights and dancing. Heart-to-hearts, unrelenting tears, and crippling anxiety have not, to my memory, appeared in any of them. I remain quiet.

'Ssshhh!'

The wind tunnel is back. It's more uncontrolled this time, though. There's a slackness to it. It'll be the wine. There's some unintentional spitting to accompany it, too. We've progressed from wind tunnel to a cobra on crack.

When a third bottle of wine is called for, I take it as my cue to retreat. After all, I have the day's images to convert into words for my notebook. Not to mention the time I'll need to take while I'm in bed trying to make sense of what the hell I just witnessed.

24

It's calmer today; the atmosphere, not the lake, the lake remains as flat as my chest, something I sincerely hope will rectify itself in the coming years.

Laura, spurred on by her newly acquired confidence in her surroundings, has opted to make breakfast. She's whipped up some pancakes with maple syrup and crispy bacon. Looking at the colour of the bacon, I'd say it's giving yesterday's sausages a good run for their money. On the face of it, it's considerably more dangerous than the inflammable giraffe; biting down on bacon this brittle could take someone's eye out if a shard of it flies loose. In contrast, the pancakes have barely progressed from the batter they started life as. Bridgette has been chewing her first mouthful for well over two minutes. You'd think she'd have learned to take smaller bites by now. The first jug of orange juice is devoured in record time and Penny races off to replenish it. Ken's lubricants spring to mind; I have a pressing need for something viscous to line the scar tissue that is my throat.

'You lot were loud last night,' I say, shifting focus from the food while secretly scheming in how to dispose of it.

'Oh no, were we?' Laura adopts a look of surprise, as glances and suppressed smiles are swapped between the three.

'Didn't sleep a wink,' I shoot back, careful to keep my face neutral.

'Well how about we give you some news that will hopefully make you happier?' Penny says, seeking affirmation from Laura and Bridgette who nod their consent.

'You like this house right, Flo?' I nod in a non-committal sort of way. 'And the village? The hills, the lake?'

'It's nice.' I direct this at Laura, a woman who, in my book could do with some love pinged her way. I wait for the bombshell that won't be far away now. Laura opens her mouth; she's to be the one to drop it, I think.

'How would you like to live here… all four of us… permanently, I mean. Is that something you'd like, Flo?'

This needs consideration. Not the decision to move here, that's an easy one, a slam-dunk. My *response* is what needs consideration. I know from previous life experience that the wrong approach here is to appear madly in love with the idea. Do that and I'll surrender any bargaining chips further down the line. Whereas, if I appear slightly reticent to the idea, I'm likely to receive a better gift on my next birthday, be more likely to have the final say in places we visit, be allowed to sleep over at friends' places, and blag myself a mobile phone. Things that, were I to shout from the rooftops how happy I am at the prospect of moving here, I might not be permitted to indulge in. Hindsight, see. Ken would be proud.

'I'm not sure,' I mumble. 'I have my studies to think of and friends I'd be leaving behind.'

Bridgette wriggles forward on her kitchen chair. 'We've thought about that, darling. How about we move here in a couple of years from now? That way you can start secondary school here. A clean break.'

Oh, bollocks. I've overdone it.

'Well... I mean... if it's important to you we can move here sooner...'

'No, honestly it's fine. Let's stick with the plan of moving in a couple of years' time. If... you *want* to move here permanently, that is?' Penny asks.

The air becomes heavy. Three faces trained on me, hanging on my next words.

'Yeah, I guess,' I say. 'It'll take some adjusting, but if it makes you guys happy then I'm happy to move too.'

'That's settled then,' Laura says. She instigates a group hug across the table and Bridgette comes away with maple syrup on her t-shirt.

'Wait!' I blurt out, 'Where will you work? Will you get jobs here?' I ask because employment opportunities around here must be scant unless you let a holiday home or own an ice cream van.

'We've talked about that too,' Bridgette says excitedly. Strikes me there's a lot they've talked about without sharing. *No secrets huh?* 'You know how Mummy lost her job?' I'm guessing I'm not being asked *how* Bridgette lost her job. That'll be a combination of incompetence and a pink dildo.

I settle on, 'Yes?'

'Well, Mummy is going to work for herself, from home, which means I can work remotely, from any home. Like this one,' Bridgette explains.

Makes sense, I think. Lucy Kennedy's mum works from home too. The bedroom, according to Matthew Toon.

I switch focus to Penny. 'What will you do? Where will you work?'

'I'm going to work with Mummy. That's the plan anyway. We'll see how Bridgette gets on, and if there's enough work for both of us, I'll join her. If not, I'll try and persuade my company I can work from here with just a few visits to head office each month. How's that all sound, Flo?'

Laura hasn't offered any explanation as to where she'll work, though it's unlikely she'll need to judging by the wealth in property she's accumulated.

'It sounds OK to me,' I announce.

The three women beam wide grins at each other. Plates are stacked, the table cleared of everything except me. I'm not finished.

'What's the boat called?'

25

Laura starts to arrange her mouth and tongue into shapes that will allow a word to be formed. Looks like it might be a *P*. Doesn't narrow it down much unless it's 'Peckerhead'. Unlikely to be that. There'll be rules governing the naming of vessels in the same way there are restrictions on what you're able to call your child. "Twatwaffle", for instance, wouldn't be permitted on a birth certificate. Pity, I think, Darren Tandy coming to mind as a fellow pupil who deserves to have been saddled with that name. You'd pay good money to hear a teacher demand to see Twatwaffle Tandy after class. Short of leafing through all the P's in a dictionary, my best bet remains to try and reach the boat for myself to reveal its name. I'll make it my first job this afternoon.

This morning, Penny, Bridgette, and I are heading out to a local town to buy clothes. Secretly I'm dreading it. If Bridgette has any significant input, I'll leave the store looking like one of the kids in *Little House on the Prairie*.

Ironically, when it comes to adult clothing, Bridgette has better fashion sense than Penny who, despite no longer being pregnant, persists in wearing dungarees irrespective of the occasion. She even sets older ones aside for decorating and gardening. Where Penny trumps Bridgette, though, is in her capacity to better understand what an eight-year-old needs to be seen wearing. Hopefully, I won't need to prompt her and she'll be clued-up enough to lean towards a festival vibe. I want to step through that front door later, sporting a bucket hat not a fucking bonnet.

Rapping. The knuckles-on-door kind, that is. Specifically Laura's front door. It's why the name of the boat wasn't forthcoming. It interrupted her.

Laura unties her pinafore, hands trembling, the tied bow in danger of becoming a knot. She's been out of sorts all morning, behaving oddly, though surely as a result of the previous night's soul searching. It started with a stint of weeding at seven a.m. and continued with an hour of frenzied beetroot-pickling, an activity which has left the whole house reeking of vinegar. To top it all off, a frying pan was left on a hot ring despite its contents having made their way into mouths (and bin) twenty minutes earlier. Something has rattled her for sure, and I'll bet that *something* is the owner of the fist that right now is knocking on our door for a second time.

For reasons I doubt any of us can explain, we gather as a unit in the living room and stare at the front door. Whoever turns out to be on the other side will be met with a freakish tableau of *Addams Family* proportions. Four smiling faces lined up like the Von Trapps in a doctor's waiting room. I'll lodge my disapproval of this simpering show of deference later, and only make an exception if our visitor is Neil Armstrong, Lady Gaga or Terry Nutkins.

It turns out to be two people, neither of whom feature on my list. What are the odds?

'Come in!' Laura shakes a man's hand; he baulks at the formality.

It's Tom, he of velvety voice and dimpled chin, he who fearlessly strode into the woods yesterday to rescue his princess (moi). He who—

'Candy, how lovely to see you,' Penny announces from my side.

Candy? A name—if ever I heard one—that should be added to the banned Christian name list. If I hate my child that's what I'll call it. That, or Cindy. Even if it's a boy.

Candy, the girl from the woods yesterday, is out of the starting blocks, bounding over toward me in a manner reminiscent of Martha. She flings both arms around my neck and affords me another kiss. There's something slightly erotic about it, and I daren't glance at my mums for fear they'll be standing there bursting with pride. A chip off the old block, so to speak. I notch it up as my most successful sexual liaison to date. Not hard given my pitiful track record which up until today sees Oliver Tetworth's brush of his elbow against my left breast, ranked top. Out of one.

Candy peels herself from me and races back to be at Tom's side. I'm still having difficulty zeroing in on Candy's age, but help is at hand and it arrives via an envelope passed from Laura to Candy. No time is wasted ripping open the envelope and freeing the card. It's gleefully held above head height for all to see, Candy spinning en pointe for the benefit of the royal box, upper circle, and the spider camped next to the small feature window by the stairs.

26. It reads 26. Surely an error; a card for a sixteen-year-old bought in a hurry at the end of a long day. Penny notices my slack jaw, scoops up Bridgette, me, and her handbag, and

choreographs us towards the front door as a single entity; a moving vortex kissing the pine floorboards.

In truth I'd rather stay here with Laura, Tom, and Candy. I'm curious to know how they're acquainted with each other. The sorrow I've detected in the bricks and mortar of this house is connected with Tom, I'm certain of it.

Before the door slams shut behind us, I glance over my shoulder to see Candy and Laura embrace. There's no kiss though, and somewhat unexpectedly, for a moment I feel special.

26

A friend from Laura and Penny's past. That's the sum total of information I've gleaned from Penny and Bridgette regarding Tom. I have the distinct impression there was more they could have told me, but my lines of questioning were cut off at source as the women made repeated trips from changing room to shop floor, bringing back all manner of garments, none of them suitable for an eight-year-old, all of them however befitting a stick insect on a catwalk.

Information was more forthcoming regarding Candy, though. Candy, Tom's daughter, has a condition, the name of which Penny spelled for me but which I've forgotten. The condition restricts a person's mental growth meaning that by adulthood, physicality can be drastically at odds with intellectual development. Candy sees herself not as an adult but as a much younger female. Over the years she's visited countless specialists, undergone rigorous tests, and switched schools more times than Kim Hansen's older brother (for very different reasons, I should add).

There were no solutions or quick fixes, and Tom bombarded from all quarters with advice on how he and his daughter should approach the challenges they faced.

'Back in the day, Tom being Tom took it pretty much in his stride,' Penny explains. 'He gave his daughter all the love, resources and protection she needed without smothering her,' she adds. 'He even gave up work for a while. If she was content, he was too, even if it meant a slightly unconventional life for him. Even today, you can see that her happiness means everything to him.'

It explains Candy's dress-code, outfits from H&M's early teenage range, though it's not lost on me that her youthful traits display the odd anomaly: four piercings in one ear; a small tattoo of a face on the underside of her wrist; the face of a boy, perhaps. Additions that mark out Candy as an adult and not the fourteen-year-old girl that on first inspection she appears to be.

I've met the girl… I correct myself… *woman* just twice but I feel a closeness to her, a similar affection to the one that washed over me when my dad led me away from the rugby pitch. A degree of closeness that can't be explained by a single chance meeting and daytime visit. I know this woman well; I feel her energy course through me until pictures form, indistinct ones, fuzzy, distorted, bleached around the edges. They flash behind my eyes like playing cards being scattered around a blackjack table. No image settles for long enough to be processed, though. They come in and out like stills displayed on a static-riddled portable television, and no matter how much I tweak its ariel, the pictures won't settle or sharpen. There is a sufficient quantity of flickering images for me to glimpse the sense of a theme, though.

Water.

27

By the time we return to Lakeside, Tom and Candy are long gone. Three weary people stumble from car to house with far too many shopping bags, mentally exhausted after a morning spent making all the right noises about each other's purchases. Bridgette, resembling a packhorse, having bought more outfits than Penny and I put together, doesn't have a free hand so skilfully opens the front door with her bum, drawing a sarcastic comment regarding its size, from Penny.

'At least I don't hide mine under dungarees,' Bridgette fires back.

Fearing I'll be asked to arbitrate on who has the bigger arse, I dump my shopping bags and dart for the bifold doors. With the sun on my back, I career down the garden, my big toe snagging on something halfway down the lawn. A quick glance over my shoulder as I stagger reveals no obvious trip hazard, so I feel justified in arranging my face into an accusatory look, the one deployed by everyone, everywhere, immediately after tripping.

The remainder of the garden's terrain is negotiated without incident and I stand breathless on the jetty. I take a moment to massage my toe and allow my lungs to rally, before striding the short distance to the rear mooring point of the boat.

For a minute I make no move to reach the tarpaulin cover. It's shifted. Lower. Before, I could see the very bottom extremities of what I took to be lower-case letters; specifically the ones with a 'below the line' curl. The kind that might belong to a "g" or "y", for instance. Now, even those fragments that had been visible are covered by the canvas and I muse over whether the gentle rocking of the boat could have caused the cover to slip. Surely it would be more likely to shift upwards?

A look in the direction of the house reveals Laura standing at the kitchen window, but the moment she registers my gaze, she turns her back to the garden, moves away from the glass and retreats into the room.

Kneeling, I pull on the weathered rope that tethers the rear of the boat, and the fibreglass hull edges closer. I take up all of the remaining slack but there isn't enough to form a second loop around the oak post, so I'll need to hold onto the rope while reaching forward to grab the tarpaulin.

The whole exercise seems far more exhausting than it should be, but after a change of tack that sees me grab one of the orange fenders slung over the hull's side, I manage to pull the boat the last few inches necessary for me to reach the canvas cover. Tucking four fingers under the bottom seam, and with my thumb on top acting as a clamp, I begin to prise the material away, stooping lower so I'm able to read the inscription underneath.

The sunlight bounces off the fibreglass making it hard to see, and I curse myself for becoming obsessed. Why can't I just leave it be. God, I sound like Ken, I think, letting go of the rope now that I have a firm grip on the tarp. Christ's sake, how far do I need to peel this bloody thing back?

And then it hits me square in the face.

The reason I'm struggling to read the boat's name is because it isn't there.

It was. As recently as yesterday. It's not something I imagined. What's more, the area of hull in question is cleaner than the rest. Too clean. Like a solvent solution has been applied, pressed into action after removing the vinyl lettering. It's a hurried job though, wafer thin remnants of adhesive clinging-on, leaving evidence of letters peeled away. In the main, these slithers of glue remain at what I presume to be the edges of the letters. A crime scene analyst would have a field day.

I squint against the reflecting light and estimate the removed name to be eleven or twelve letters long.

If I'm not completely mistaken, two of the letters were "y" before they were removed, though either could just as easily have been a "g"

Why remove the name? Why now? Why at all? Ever since we arrived there's been a concerted effort to conceal things from me; Tom's background, a simple motorboat's name, not to mention a reluctance to attend yesterday's party. Who's going to these lengths and why? Is it for my protection? Someone else's?

There's movement out of the corner of my eye and I release my grip on the tarpaulin. The boat floats away for a couple of feet or so until the slack in the rope is gone. It's like the boat is trying to be free of me. Keeping me at a safe distance. Or maybe me a safe distance from *it* and its secrets.

Movement again. The same as before. Closer now, though. I freeze, a shiver slashing through me, chilling my skin despite the cloudless sky. Darkness replaces light; it's subtle but it happens all the same—a shift.

Cold, black eyes stare at me, intent on giving nothing away. Secretive, like the boat not two yards from it. Silent, too.

The crow studies me from the mooring post, its head tilted to one side.

In what I take to be a warning, the creature shuffles and extends its huge wings; a dark, gothic monster unfurling its cape in readiness to enshroud the unsuspecting. A prophet tasked with delivering fear and choosing this precise moment to magnify it with a terrifying squawk that bounces from lake to mountain top and back again, scything down everything in between.

Except me. Because I run. Hard. And the splinters that spear the soles of my feet don't even register.

28

There were no more parties on pitches, or anywhere else for that matter. No further shopping trips. Not even the hike we'd planned to do as a family came to fruition.

The soreness in my feet that wasn't apparent at the time of running from the jetty, reared its head not long afterwards. A sometimes sharp, sometimes dull bastard of a pain depending on the angle I held my foot. All three adults made ham-fisted attempts to remove the timber shards, all of them on the receiving end of screams from me as the wound became angrier and the pain more intense. Bridgette's attempt was by far the worst, but then she's clumsy as fuck at the best of times. Penny's words, not mine.

This is the woman who, back in Loxby, didn't apply the handbrake to her car properly. A cheery ring on our doorbell at 6 a.m. heralding the first signs of trouble; the alarm raised by a dog-walker who didn't know whether to be angry or relieved at almost been wiped out by Bridgette's monster truck as it sailed backwards off our driveway. He simply stood at our threshold, utterly speechless, and pointed toward the scene behind him. After the car had narrowly avoided the gentleman whose expression had decided to settle on one of perplexion, it had seemingly rolled at speed across both carriageways, bounced off the kerb between two parked cars on the opposite side of the road, and eventually parked itself in the middle of the road spanning both lanes so precisely so as to prevent traffic from passing it in either direction. To add insult to injury, it was a bleary-eyed Penny who'd answered the door that day. Penny, who'd had to raise a search party to find Bridgette's car keys. And while Bridgette continued to sleep through the commotion, it was a scarlet-faced Penny who'd moved Bridgette's car while being subjected to a symphony of car horns and an unsavoury hand gesture from a delivery driver.

To this day, the incident still leaves Penny utterly bewildered as to how a person could be so simultaneously careless and lucky. You'd have got very long odds on the car hitting neither a pedestrian, a parked car, nor a passing vehicle. But that's Bridgette. Lucky.

A few years ago, during a party hosted at our house, Penny described Bridgette to a mutual friend as, 'Clumsy as fuck, and lucky as fuck.' Bridgette overhead, sashayed over, planted a tipsy peck on Penny's cheek and with a grin, added, 'and adorable as fuck!' Word has it, Bridgette—feeling pleased with herself for her coquettishly delivered witticism—backed into a table carrying a champagne glass pyramid, arranged as a centrepiece to celebrate the pair's fifth anniversary of cohabitation. Not only did the majority of the glass flutes not smash, but, owing to two guests shifting cars on the driveway, the pouring of champagne into the pyramid of glasses had been delayed by the couple of minutes it took for the guests to return, and by sheer coincidence the time during which Bridgette decided to play drinking glass Jenga.

Clumsy as fuck. Lucky as fuck.

Right now, my foot looks pretty angry. That doesn't do it justice; 'pretty angry' gives the impression of it being slightly peeved. Well, it isn't. It's positively raging. Livid. Furious. Beside itself. It's thoroughly pissed off, that's what it is. If my right foot was a light, it'd be one of those red ones in a nuclear facility; the kind which alternates between a gentle low-luminosity throb, and full-on molten hell bunny on a spike.

The doctor at A&E said the same. Well, similar. I bet I was in more pain than the bloke the doctor attended to before me. The one who'd had a heart attack. I was quick to point out to the nice doctor that my foot started out merely as mildly painful until Bridgette took up arms in the form of tweezers.

Right now, if anyone even stands within a yard of the sole of my right foot, I get fucking twitchy. Get any closer than that and I turn into a bellowing, spewing, head-spinning Regan from *The Exorcist*.

'She's OK,' Bridgette had announced to the doctor. 'Probably just the shock,' she added.

Shock?! Fucking shock?! Shock is having a day where you're finally surprised by Kinder. Shock is Neil Massey during class 'news time' revealing he doesn't wear underwear in order to combat aggressive chafing. Shock is Lily Bullimore not falling asleep in assembly (I swear that girl's a narcoleptic).

What shock *isn't*, is a level of pain that right now would register as a Richter scale 10 or a *Spinal Tap* 11. Shock my arse.

Holiday. Ruined.

29

School's out for summer, which means I'm only a couple of months shy of starting at my new secondary school in the Lake District.

The Dreyfuss Richards Embury Grammar School I'm to attend is ten miles from Laura's house. It's the closest school to Lakeside that's permitted to use the word *outstanding* when touting for business. They're not shy about using it either. The school's prospectus contains the word no fewer than eleven times, though that pales into insignificance when compared to the seventeen times the word has been machine-gunned at its website; one instance of which appears on the site's homepage in a vanity-massaging 36-point-font.

My new secondary school is an academy, placed in the hands of a trust responsible for five other schools all within a ninety-mile radius. Makes you wonder how the school has achieved outstanding status when its multi-academy trust didn't think to place the names of its founders in a different order. My mothers, in wilful neglect of their duty as parents, have literally given me the D.R.E.G.S.

I'm no less than two years late for school, which must qualify as some sort of record. Luckily for my mothers, they hadn't handed over the wad of cash required to pay for my first two years of secondary schooling at the point when Penny's job dictated we couldn't make the move so far up

North. It caused a bit of aggro at the time. Laura, it seemed, had psyched herself up for the move, and Bridgette had purchased a new mouse mat which she said would complement the décor in Lakeside's office. The day I match an office accessory to a wall colour is the day I kill myself. I wait for a flash of sheet lightning on the off chance that's how I met my death last time around, and I'm somewhat relieved when I'm not presented with the image of a me slumped against a blood-spattered wall with a mouse pad resting on my chest. Bridgette still has it by the way—the mouse mat—still in its cellophane wrapping. A frog on a red bicycle. The office is painted blue.

It's my birthday in just under a week's time, and I've been gifted an early birthday present in the form of a pair of compact binoculars. I can't think of a single girl in my class that would be jumping for joy at the thought of being the recipient of such a gift. Except Leslie Markham maybe, whose spectacle lenses are so thick as to almost qualify as binoculars in their own right.

The last few years have seen little in the way of memories surfacing. My jigsaw has barely progressed, but if I'm honest, I'm not surprised. I accepted some time ago that Loxby harbours no significant events in my life before birth. In many ways it's been a relief, freeing me of the urge to look to the past, allowing my present life to chart its own unique course.

After a few months of us returning from Denholm Water following our holiday, I'd even given up trying to recall my name from my previous life. I did manage to locate Ken, though. As an exercise in detective work it wasn't what you'd call taxing; an internet search on Halfords' branches within sixty miles of Denholm Water rewarding me with a photograph, Ken at its centre, sporting the same red glasses, and shaking hands with the area manager.

The photograph in question had been proudly uploaded to the store's website and carried the heading: "Ken Link (left) is congratulated by area manager Mike Pratt on his promotion to his new role of deputy store manager." It's a mystery as to why Keith, the store manager from my time, wasn't in the picture. Unless he has moved on. Or been moved on. Or died, like I did.

Ken, despite some alarming hair-loss and being the beneficiary of a slight stoop, looked happy to see his twenty-five years of work recognised in the form of a promotion. His gappy-toothed smile bordered on smug.

Having located Deputy Ken, I felt nearer than ever before to uncovering the mystery of my identity from that life. It prompted me to send an email to the company in which I explained that I used to be employed at the store and wanted to get in touch with my ex-colleagues with the aim of organising a reunion. Not being sure of the exact year I worked there, I gave a range of years, sat back from the home's shared laptop, and waited, naively I suppose, for a return message that would list the store's staff members from that timeframe. Surely one name would leap out as being mine? I did receive an email back, as it happened:

Dear floatersfabishaw@gmail.com
Thank you for your message. Unfortunately, our data protection policy dictates that personal details of staff members past or present cannot be made available upon general request.

We hope you understand this standpoint and thank you for your interest in our company.

> *Regards*
> *Linda Brooks*

I know what you're thinking, right enough. Why is it that every H.R. department employs at least one person called Linda? What you might also find troubling is that my parents—having decided to combine their surnames to make Aters-Fabishaw—named me Florence, full in the knowledge it would be shortened to Flo. No one, but no one, wants to run the risk of acquiring the nickname "Floaters", and frankly it's nothing short of a miracle I haven't been the subject of sustained bullying from my peers.

I raised the matter with them, of course—my parents. The response I received was most unsatisfactory, the gist being that if they'd switched their surnames around the other way, it would have pointed towards an irrational loathing of people named Fabishaw. Here's an idea: fuck the Fabishaw community (which let's face it must be miniscule in number) and instead consider the feelings of your own daughter. Besides, I wasn't buying that explanation, and it's far more likely Penny insisted her surname Aters was listed first. Penny is a master at getting her own way. Catch me on a bad day and I might even describe her as manipulative.

On the plus side, no other sap walking this planet will have been saddled with the same name as me, and that means I don't have to add a meaningless random number to the end of my email handle to create a unique address.

And while we're thanking heavens for small mercies, given my unwanted nickname Floaters, I've spent the last God-knows how many years consoling myself that Bridgette's surname isn't Brown.

Despite having enjoyed the break from my flashbacks and the stresses that accompanied them, as the end of the first two years of my present secondary school grew nearer, I found my thoughts returning to Denholm Water, to my dad, to Tom and Candy. But mainly to the water, the motorboat with its missing name, and the mysterious hillside house on the opposite side of the lake. I spotted the house moments before my "mate" the carrion crow decided to frighten the living daylights out of me. It struck me that the house on the hill sat ill at ease in its surroundings, swallowed by the trees it nestled within. But more than that, I had the distinct feeling that very house was watching me, and that is the reason I requested binoculars for my birthday.

I needed to take a closer look.

30

On holiday, unpacking is one of those things adults feel the need to do straight away. It's imperative for their mental wellbeing to see their room acquire a semblance of order as soon as possible. Kids, on the other hand, will first enter the Wi-Fi code into each of the ten devices they've brought away with them, give the television remote the once over, then hurtle off to find the swimming pool, leaving behind their parents who by now will be remarking on the hotel's thoughtfulness in leaving a disposable sewing kit. Pants will be folded in half and placed in drawers with no runners, and a meeting will be convened to decide the most suitable surface upon which sun creams, toiletries and jewellery should be lined up for the duration of the holiday. Mainly though, they'll be fretting over the lack of coat hangers.

We're not on holiday this time around. From now on we're to live at Lakeside permanently so to my mind there should be even less urgency to get things ship-shape. What's the rush? Penny told me I wouldn't understand. I don't think Bridgette was quite on board with Penny's unpacking itinerary either, the securing of a gin and tonic topping her to do list. Bridgette is definitely drinking more these days, something Penny wastes no time in pointing out to her.

Our possessions from Loxby have, in the main, been sold. A fresh start needed, according to Penny. Anything deemed unsaleable, or unfair to swamp Laura's home with, has been put into storage or binned. Bridgette hired a van and brought some of the essentials here a week ago. There's a white mark on the gatepost at the head of Lakeside's drive where Bridgette misjudged the length of the van as she swung it in from the road. Remarkably, the corresponding brown mark on the van wasn't picked up by the rental company when Bridgette returned it. Clumsy as fuck, lucky as fuck.

Penny and Bridgette have taken the master bedroom, the one with the balcony and lake view. It seems to me a concession too far on Laura's part to give up the best room in her own house. Laura brushes it off, explaining she prefers a smaller room.

I reach the lake's edge, binoculars slung around my skinny neck. I warily eye the mooring posts and scan the immediate vicinity for an errant crow harbouring a grudge and with four years' worth of pent-up aggression under its wings. The water isn't quite as calm as I remember from our last visit and as a result, the motorboat with no name or provenance gently bobs and rocks to the tune of the water as it kisses the shore's edge.

There's a shout from behind and I curse the interruption to my moment of solitude. With a sigh, I turn to face the house. Can those women not leave me alone for five minutes?

I peer at the figure skipping down the lawn towards me. It's an adult alright, but not one who'd prioritise unpacking over... I dunno... *living*. And for that reason alone, Candy is a welcome sight as she weaves and giggles her way over the immaculate lawn, arms waving above her smiling face as she draws nearer.

I return the smile with interest and I'm nearly knocked backwards into the lake when Candy launches herself at me. If we were still on the rugby pitch from four years ago, she might well have received a yellow card for dangerous play.

There's that kiss again. It's the gentlest, sweetest kiss you can imagine. When Laura, Penny, Bridgette, or, God forbid, one of their distant relatives plants a kiss on me, it's more mechanical, delivered as if going through the motions. Except Uncle John. I haven't quite worked out what kind of affection lies behind his kisses which always fall in that no-man's-land between cheek and mouth. I shudder, which fortunately jolts me back to the present and to Candy who's withdrawn her lips but stands no more than a foot from me with both arms draped around my neck.

'Hi Candy!' I say, not entirely sure if I'm laughing out of nervousness or because of Candy's infectious grin.

'I'm SO pleased to see you Flo!' Candy squeals. 'We can spend so much time together now.'

I study her face. It should look four years older like my own, but somehow Candy's child-like aura renders hers less.

'I'd really like that,' I reply, meaning every word.

'I still have the giraffe you gave me,' Candy says, bouncing from foot to foot, still with her arms around my neck. 'Joyce, remember?'

I laugh again, not in a condescending way, but with a warmth that's easy to bestow on this curious woman. 'I remember. We were in trouble that day weren't we?' I add.

'Nah. No one could be mad at you, Flo. My dad thinks you're great. He likes Laura lots too.'

This news surprises me a little and I wonder if there's an affection between the pair I haven't picked up on. Something from years ago, the last time Laura saw this place as home, maybe? I don't have much time to reflect on this because I'm aware of Candy looking down my top.

'What are those?' she asks, not looking up.

Oh Lord. This is déjà vu, I think, my mind immediately switching to the incident in the woods when Candy asked the obvious about the giraffe. I decide to go down the route of frank honesty.

'Tits. Though some people call them boobs, baps or wabbers. Vanessa Black refers to hers as sweater puppies. I'm surprised you noticed mine; I'm still waiting for them to emerge.' I realise I'm gabbling and urge myself to change the subject, something which I spectacularly fail to do. 'Yours are better than anyone's I know. Bigger, I mean.'

What am I doing? I'm only thirteen (almost), and I'm fairly sure I'm at least a year shy of the point in a child's development where such themes would be considered normal conversation between friends. What's more, the woman hanging off me is considerably older than me.

'Thanks,' Candy says casually, withdrawing one of her hands from behind my head. 'I mean, I was talking about those, but thanks anyway,'

I lower my chin to find Candy pointing at my binoculars. Shite. I feel my face burning from embarrassment. Candy begins to laugh. She removes the remaining arm from around my neck, steps back and clasps her hands together, laughing so hard now that it forces her to double-over. I can't help but follow suit, our laughter erasing any awkwardness I felt to this point.

Candy flops to the ground to rest from the exertion of running and laughing, so I sit beside her, remove the binoculars from my neck and invite her to take a look.

'I don't want you to think I'm silly,' Candy announces, her expression becoming more serious now. 'I mean, I know what binoculars are, it's just that I've never seen a pair so small as these,' she adds, examining the binoculars and placing them in one hand as a method to gauge their weight.

Candy eventually lifts the binoculars to her face and swings her head left then right before settling on a spot directly ahead. I ease backwards and dip my head behind hers to get a sense of her line of sight. She must be looking somewhere near the house on the other side of the lake, I think.

'What do you know about the house over there?' I ask, easing myself upright once more, and being careful to keep my tone light and casual.

'The wooden one?' Candy asks without removing the optics from her face.

Her question confuses me since it's the only house within view on the hillside. At least, I think it is. Candy could well know better than me. I let it slide.

'Yeah, that's the one. Who lives there, do you know?'

Candy lowers the binoculars from her eyes, lifts the strap from around her neck and without dropping her stare from the house opposite, hands them gently back to me.

'Mr Crane,' she says in something approaching a whisper.

'Do you know Mr Crane's first name,' I ask, switching my gaze between Candy and the house in question.

'No, I don't think so.'

I notice Candy is almost trance-like as she stares across the water.

'That's OK,' I say in an effort to bring her back to the here and now.

'People round here don't talk to Mr Crane. My dad says they're frightened of him.'

'Frightened? Why?' I ask, leaning around in an attempt to get Candy to divert her stare from the house to me. I want to see what's behind her eyes as she talks.

'My dad says it's wrong to be frightened of him and that people should be nicer to one another.'

The more I hear of Tom, the more I'm glad he's around. Not only does he talk a lot of sense, but it seems he was the person instrumental in making Laura feel she could return to live here permanently again. And I so desperately want to be here. I've longed for this move ever since we took our vacation here four summers ago. And though I've only been back for a couple of hours, already I feel a thirst to uncover details of my previous life. A thirst I thought had left me a long time ago. That said, I have the uneasy feeling anything I've lived through before will be significantly less interesting than the life Laura has lived to date.

Right on cue there's a shout from behind. It comes from the direction of the house and delivered as a signal for Candy to return to her dad. It stops me from pressing Candy on the subject of Mr Crane and the wooden house he lives in.

Candy stoops, presses her lips to my cheek, and begins her sprint back up to the house, shouting her goodbyes as she goes. Tom waves to me from the terrace. *Did I just call it that?* I wave back and follow Candy's progress until she reaches her father and bear-hugs the man. If you didn't know better you'd assume the pair had been separated for years; a prisoner released back to the safety of a loved one after decades in exile. Candy shares a closeness with her father that I'm convinced I also shared with mine. There's a tenderness, yet also a mutual respect between two people who've come to rely on each other. I wonder briefly about Candy's mother. If she's part of their lives.

I wait until final waves have been exchanged before turning back to face the lake. Raising the binoculars to my eyes, I scan the hillside until I lock onto Crane's house, a place that from a distance I previously thought looked unsure of itself, with its tiny windows, dominated by the surrounding trees. On closer inspection I realise my first impressions were inaccurate and unjust, the place utterly comfortable in its alliance with nature rather than at odds with it as I'd first thought.

At the periphery of the lens, there's movement. I give a tweak of the focusing dial and shift my hands a fraction of a degree to my right. I've overcompensated and edge left until the source of movement I initially detected hits the centre of my field of view. A man. He carries a two-feet long section of a tree branch with a diameter so substantial it surely warrants another pair of hands to help move it. He continues with the piece of timber for another twenty yards until he reaches a small clearing to the side of his cabin. He doesn't drop the log to the ground, rather lowers it gently, and the process is akin to laying an old friend to rest. He steps back and removes his cap, as if paying his respects to the fallen.

Long, straight grey hair reaches the man's shoulders, the lower half of his face hidden by an untamed white beard. The reach on my binoculars is such that I can clearly see his weather-beaten face, but he doesn't remain still long enough for me to establish an age. Fifty, perhaps. He slowly lifts his head and he's looking directly at me; at least it appears that way. It's enough to make me recoil a few inches, and enough to provoke a slight tremble in my hands. More importantly, it's enough to cause him to disappear out of frame and it takes a few anxiety-riddled seconds to retrain focus on him once more.

I find him in the same spot, still staring straight ahead. Is that a frown on his tanned, lined forehead? Did his eyes narrow slightly? Eyes that lack laughter lines and lustre in equal measure. He still looks straight ahead. Did he see a reflection I wonder? Sunlight mirroring off my binoculars, catching his eye, giving me away? Or is that the stuff of films? Either way I'm convinced he's looking my way, though he certainly won't be able to distinguish my facial features from that distance. Maybe he's simply surprised to see signs of life in the back garden of a house that's seen virtually none for the last thirteen years.

All of a sudden it feels intrusive to be trained on this man and his home. I lower my binoculars and let them hang so they rest on my torso once more. And while I've never met Mr Crane, I'm inclined to disagree with Tom, and be wholly terrified of him.

31

Earlier that day, after my flirtation with espionage, I trudged back up the garden, and with each step felt sillier for having felt unnerved by Mr Crane. After all, he's just a man with wild hair and a beard, I reassured myself. A strong one, mind. A man who, if given the choice, you'd prefer to try and outrun, rather than fight. By the time I reached the house, the bearded man held no fear for me at all. Actually, that's not quite true. The man was wearing a pair of dungarees, and as I opened the back door, an image formed in my head of Penny a few years down the line having neglected to wax her top lip or visit a hair stylist.

***

Tom and Candy are joining us for supper. Penny's words. As an announcement it delivers happiness and dread in equal measure. Happiness because Tom and Candy will bring an extra dimension to the family table, but dread because we're now apparently calling our evening meal, *supper*. I briefly wonder if it will be conducted on the terrace. Penny's impromptu relabelling of an everyday activity smacks of a woman with delusions of grandeur, seeing Lakeside as the mansion in *The Great Gatsby*. What will be next? Servants circling us carrying small silver trays laden with Martinis?

Don't get me wrong, Lakeside is impressive but tonight will hardly qualify as a high society ball if the guest list amounts to a bloke with his daughter, a thirteen-year-old kid, and three flappers.

'Shall we take supper on the terrace?' I ask, a picture of innocence, already wearing the dress Penny has picked out for me to wear. Penny looks out the kitchen window by way of a brief weather check, then nods furiously in agreement. Bridgette knows I'm taking the piss.

One thing's for sure, the evening ahead appears to hold great significance for Penny. Her determination to make sure it passes off successfully is hard to rationalise—unless she's forgotten she's a practising lesbian and is now trying to bed the lovely Tom. A thought occurs to me, and I bat it away, but it returns like a game of Swingball, the ball circling around the metal post, passing my head every second or so. And like that bastard ball, the thought insists on returning, no matter how many times I give it the heave ho. Could Penny be attracted to Candy? She's undeniably an attractive woman with a body I'd kill to have when I'm her age. I shake the thought free, partly because Candy has limited capacity for the kind of intellectual conversation Penny craves, but mainly because I don't believe her to be shallow enough to use the woman for a meaningless fling. Add to this the logistical problems of arranging clandestine meetings with a woman who lives with her dad, throw into the mix Candy's kind nature—a woman who's more likely to want to *share* details of amorous dabblings rather than keep them secret—and I dismiss the notion out of hand.

Bridgette winks at me and turns to address Penny. 'After supper, at what point will the womenfolk retire to the snug for an hour of needlework while the menfolk discuss business, and drink scotch in the billiard room? I only ask because I was wondering if there might be time for a recital on the pianoforte.'

Judging by Penny's facial expression, she considers Bridgette's ribbing unfunny, and the conversation most definitely over.

'Just make yourself useful and get the side plates, Bridgette,' Penny snaps, adding an unnecessary layer of tension. Laura places a hand on Penny's arm and aims a slight frown her way, though one that's accompanied by warm, reassuring eyes.

'Christ, I was only joking,' Bridgette mutters as she opens the wide, deep drawer next to the range cooker. 'Do we even own side plates? I've never seen any.' Penny hears the jibe but ignores it, instead flicking her attention between the paper napkins she's folding to make swans and the *You Tube* video that's coaching her through it. If she takes much longer, Tom and Candy will be coming round for breakfast, not supper. Except Penny will call it brunch and serve-up granola laced with wild berries, drizzled with manuka honey.

I realise I'm being harsh. It's nice Penny wants to make a proper occasion of our first night here. She's changed in the last couple of years, though. Her light parenting touch eludes her these days, replaced by a tension and an irritability with either Bridgette or me, depending on who's within verbal striking distance. She means well, something that's not lost on any of us, especially Laura who I've noticed does a sterling job in finding subtle ways to remind Penny that it's OK to see the funny side in things.

In the lead up to our move there was palpable excitement within our family, and we often talked of little else. *A new adventure* was a popular way of categorising it, as was *new beginnings*. As our moving day drew closer, however, those phrases gradually disappeared, replaced by an undercurrent of trepidation radiating from the adults. It seemed to me it had dawned upon Laura and Penny that it wasn't a new beginning at all, more a continuation of a life that existed over thirteen years ago. A life that holds bad memories for Laura, one that must now be kickstarted very carefully indeed, surrounded by the right people and avoiding the gossipers, the scandalmongers.

Bridgette picked up on the change in mood and assured the two of them that those who remain in Denholm Water will have surely got on with their lives. What passes for hot news one day is old news the next, she explained. And she's right, of course, since people, on the whole, tend to be selfish in their expectations from life. A devastating flood in some far-flung corner of the world will raise an eyebrow, a sympathetic shake of the head, maybe even a 'those poor people' aimed in the direction of the television. Hit that same person with the news that a local road will be closed for three hours to allow a charity fun run to take place, and you'll be met with a white-hot rage, a barrage of expletives, and a hollow threat to contact the local MP.

The point is, people move on, fight new battles. Just as we're doing now as a family. And I for one can't wait.

Our supper on the terrace progresses nicely, despite Tom congratulating Penny on her napkin aeroplanes. Bridgette explains they're actually Pterodactyls, and Laura saves Penny's blushes by asking Candy what she thinks they are.

'Swans, obviously. God, Dad, you're hopeless,' Candy says aiming a dig at her father's ribs. It's possible Candy's napkin was one of the last to be folded by Penny after she'd got a few under her belt. If Candy's was the last then mine was certainly the first, looking as it does like a giant melted marshmallow.

'Thank you, Candy,' Penny says chuckling. The laughter spreads around the table, each person catching the eye of the others in turn. Candy chooses that moment to blow her nose on her swan which prompts another round of uncontrolled giggling, except from Candy that is, who can't understand what's taken place that's so amusing.

Holding his now unfolded napkin aloft, Tom recounts the time his wife had packed him a face cloth in lieu of a bath towel when he took Candy on a camping trip. It was deliberate, he explains, and for the first couple of nights, until he could get to a shop, he had no choice but to use it to dry himself after showering. Apparently, Candy point blank refused to lend him hers, a fact she confirms when she interrupts Tom's story.

'Dad would have got hair all over it. Mum always used to complain about his chest hair blocking the shower drain. Yuk! I don't want that all over my towel. Who would?'

To the amusement of everyone around the table, Candy's account of events is delivered with a stoic seriousness at odds with the frivolous nature of the anecdote itself.

It doesn't escape my attention that father and daughter exchange a look at the culmination of the storytelling. It's a look intended to confirm to each other the love still held for a wife and mother who remains locked within their hearts. An acknowledgement of happy times that will never be forgotten. I see Candy reach for her father's hand, him grasping it with a squeeze. I guess there are many moments like this between the pair of them as a result of a memory being jogged. I'd like to know what happened to Tom's wife. It's clear she died, but how, I wonder? I sense now is not the time to ask.

So I ask about something unrelated.

'Why are people scared of Mr Crane?' I ask. I direct my question at no one in particular because I want to see the reaction of each adult around the table. I know from my previous life that children get told off for swearing, staying out on bikes later than agreed, leaving a table without permission, buying sweets with pocket money. What they generally do *not* receive a bollocking for is asking questions, showing an interest in events around them, engaging with adults.

Despite this, Penny does her best to give me a dressing down but is interrupted by Tom.

'It's alright, Penny,' Tom says, holding a palm out in front of him and passing her a weak smile. He takes a moment to mentally compose the words he's about to say, and it's not until the first ones tumble from his mouth that he lowers his hand and places it palm-down on the table in front of him. Since I was the one who posed the question, he turns and directs his answer to me.

'Mr Crane is what's known as a recluse. Is that a word you're familiar with, Flo?' It is, of course, so I aim a nod in his direction. I can tell Tom isn't sure whether to believe me, but he accepts my response as an honest one, gives me the benefit of the doubt, and continues.

'Mr Crane didn't used to live on his own. He had a wife and a child who tragically died in a car accident. Mr Crane was behind the wheel the night of the crash. The weather had been terrible that day and deteriorated further that evening when Mr Crane and his family were heading back from visiting his wife's parents.'

Tom nods in the direction of the end of the garden. 'The water in the lake couldn't have been more different to how it looks now. It was brown, all churned up, large tree branches lurching around in it. High winds had whipped up waves that reached parts of the lake's banks that had never before been touched by its water. The weather was so severe, visibility so poor, that people were trapped on hilltops, unable to navigate back to the valleys. The Mountain Rescue teams had a hell of a time of it, that day. It's a miracle we didn't lose more people.'

Tom shakes his head, lost for a moment in his memories. 'The rain grew heavier, bringing mud and rocks from hillsides, blocking roads. Driving conditions that night were appalling. Everyone had been warned not to venture out, but Mr Crane…' Tom stops himself in order to choose his words carefully, '… is… well…he's a stubborn man. Always was, always will be, I guess. He's also pretty fearless, and to him the storm was something that wasn't going to get the better of him. He said he'd seen worse. Fact is, no one had seen worse, and the reason we didn't lose more lives is because most people took the advice given and stayed home that day.'

Tom scans the faces around the table, unsure if he's said too much, and seeking permission to continue. Penny gives him the slightest of nods with a face that's about as impassive as is humanly possible. Tom nods back and lifts his eyes to the hillside on the opposite side of the lake. 'The track to the Cranes' house became almost impassable, his car must have had virtually no grip, leaving them completely at the mercy of the gods that night.'

Tom catches himself, realising his account is almost certainly too graphic for a child's ears. He addresses his next words to Penny and Bridgette, parent-to-parents. 'Are you sure you're OK with me telling the story as it was, in all its detail? I've deliberately left nothing out because I want Flo to hear the truth, and not the kind of nonsense that was bandied around at the time. People round here like to gossip, make up their own versions of events. I don't know why they do it, maybe it's because they need a better explanation for what happened.'

'So what did happen? The accident, I mean?' I press.

Tom looks to Penny and Bridgette for their approval for him to carry on. When he's satisfied it's been granted, he continues. 'Mr Crane lost control of his car. We don't exactly know why, probably slid on mud, maybe hit a tree branch. Whatever the reason, the car left the track not a hundred yards from their home, careering down the hillside taking small trees with it as it went, and ending up in the lake. The poor man's wife and daughter died. Drowned. Somehow, Mr Crane was able to free himself and swim clear. It's said he dived into the lake several times to try and reach his family; dived until exhaustion got the better of him and pinned him to the shoreline. The man was too spent to climb the hill and raise the alarm so it was hours before he was found, rescued by a crew who'd been tasked with touring the lake to look for signs of anyone in difficulty. When they first spied Mr Crane from the boat, they believed he was dead, lying motionless as he was on the bank. After clambering ashore, what they actually found was a man without the energy to even wipe away his tears. Utterly broken.'

Tom's voice betrays him, I detect a slight shake to his voice. I take it as my cue to speak.

'But why are people so frightened of him?' I ask. I've now heard the story but that happened years ago from the sounds of things. It doesn't explain Candy's comment to me earlier.

'You need to understand, Flo, that before any of this happened, Mr Crane was seen as *different* from most others round here. Still is. He's viewed as aloof, crotchety, short tempered even. His own child excepted, he dislikes children, finding them rude and disrespectful. He's sort of an eccentric…' Again, Tom looks my way to make sure he's used a word I understand before continuing. '… Yeah… eccentric… that's Mr Crane. And people were uncomfortable having someone so… different around; someone who wouldn't return a friendly smile or make small talk in the post office, someone who rarely attended village functions. His wife home-schooled their child to a very high standard, it's said, but one week his wife was spotted with a bruise on her face while she shopped for groceries, and inevitably rumours spread about the cause of it. Most people, despite having no proof whatsoever, decided Crane had been knocking her around. It was hugely unfair. There'd never been any evidence of wrongdoing before that time or since. Mr Crane was many things but I don't believe he was a bad man. He simply didn't want to fit in. And he didn't have to. Neither he nor his wife needed to work owing to the sale of a company he'd owned in his younger days.'

I notice Tom hasn't once used the Christian names of any of the Crane family.

Tom takes a breath and a swig from his beer before continuing. 'If you ask me, Mr Crane wanted solitude for himself and his family, and he found peace in the form of that shack.' Tom doesn't need to indicate the house on the opposite side of the river. He's guessed I know who it belongs to.

'The car still sits on the bed of the lake, you know?' Tom continues, gazing across at the house now. 'It should have been lifted, disposed of, but after the bodies of his wife and child had been recovered, he insisted it remain where it was, as a hidden reminder to him of what he'd done. A punishment if you like.'

A silence hangs over the table. One which seems to stretch all the way to the water and the hillside beyond. Eyes drop to table level, those who know the story contemplating it once more, me upon hearing it for the first time dissecting the detail. All of us, however, replaying Tom's words in our heads.

I'm the first to look up. 'Tom?' I ask.

Tom lifts his head and turns to face me. 'Yes, Flo?'

'How do you know so much about it?'

Tom purses his lips, his eyes that moments ago were windows into the past, now dark, and shuttered.

'Because I was the detective who arrested him for murder.'

32

As if taking its cue from Tom's story, the evening air developed a chill, prompting the six of us to move inside. Bridgette risked Penny's wrath by asking if we should retire to the drawing room, but lessons had been learned on Penny's part and through a grin she mumbled something about Bridgette getting back to the scullery.

Gradually, following our fascinating—but let's face it slightly depressing—alfresco tales of murder and tragedy, the atmosphere thaws. There are a few minutes of head tennis between Laura and Tom, with each asking the other how they're doing these days, both saying fine and bouncing the question right back. Just as it seems that particular loop of banality won't be broken, Tom switches tack.

'Oh Laura, here's some news I think you'll like. Candy's landed herself a part time job at the florist.' Tom looks across to the opposite sofa and there's no mistaking the look of pride aimed his daughter's way.

'Oh, Candy, that's brilliant!' Laura trills, turning to the woman beside her and wrapping her arms around her in something that almost resembles an embrace, but is more akin to a special forces killer bear hug. Either way, Laura can't conceal her delight at Candy choosing to follow in her own floral footsteps.

I wonder if Laura sees herself as a mother to Candy, picking up the reins where possible from Tom's wife. They certainly seem close.

'This calls for another drink,' Bridgette announces, before zigzagging into the kitchen via a shoulder-dunt to the door frame as she passes through. As she disappears, we hear the sound of something smashing, a plate perhaps, followed by Bridgette swearing. Candy puts her hand across her smiling mouth as if it's the naughtiest thing she's ever witnessed. In a cringeworthy move where I attempt to emulate what an adult might do in a similar situation, I aim a wink in Candy's direction. I tried to stop it happening, even as my brain processed the thought, I screamed at it to see reason, stop the madness, perform a U-turn, recalculate a new route. But the mind is fast and a one-eyed blink even faster, the transaction between brain and palpebral orbicularis passing the point of no return. What am I thinking? I've already managed to weave my tits into an earlier conversation of ours. The woman will surely find sub-text in my wink and think I'm besotted with her.

Candy gives me a wink right back, and I'm unsure if this is a good thing or not. In return, I settle on a smile that's not too big and not insultingly small. Candy's wink was a thing of beauty too, smooth, playful. Mine will have been a clumsy thing, my non-winking eye not remaining fully open, rendering one side of my face a featureless, slack, melting Dali clock. When Candy's next words don't include Bell's palsy or stroke, I breathe a considerable sigh of relief.

'Come on, Flo.' Candy jumps up from the sofa. 'Let's go outside'. She thrusts a hand my way, and I have no choice but to accept the invitation and grasp it. She entwines her long fingers between mine and I stiffen, my senses fighting to straighten themselves out but losing the battle to a memory that fills my head so abruptly I have to shoot my free arm to the back of the nearest wing-back chair for support.

That's how my dad and me held hands. I remember it so clearly now. It's how he led me from the rugby pitch that day. And I can see other clips which show us hand-in-hand too, of us crossing the road together, of dad walking me through the school gate. The images come thick and fast. We're at a race meeting—motorbikes not horses—and I'm scared of the noise as the assembled grid waits for lights-out. I have a memory of my dad grabbing my hand, locking his fingers with mine, as Candy is now, and making me feel safe, protected from the noise, the smell of fuel and burning rubber, and the threat of what might be to come in the form of twisted metal and broken bones. Yet still his face eludes me.

'Are you OK, darling?' I hear the words but they arrive slowly, muffled, hard to process. 'Flo?' Penny says, louder this time, enough to snap me from my visions. I reclaim one hand from Candy and the other from the back of the chair next to me. I run a hand through my hair, conscious of my fingers still spread apart, a hangover from Candy's grasp. Or my dad's.

'Sure... yes... I mean that'd be nice,' I stammer, assembling my words into something approaching a sentence.

'Well, I'd rather you didn't go near the water now that it's dark,' Penny adds.

I wonder if Candy, as an adult, finds this insulting, the insinuation that she's uncapable of supervising a child. For all we know, she might well entertain the idea of having kids of her own one day. Would that work? Maybe while she's living with Tom it could. In that moment, a sense of protectiveness wells up inside me, and the fact it comes from a child, directed towards an adult seems wholly irrelevant, a role reversal without the slightest weight of irony.

We make our way down the lawn, Candy and I, and I'm conscious there'll come a point where one of us will have to decide how close to the water is too close. I dispel any thoughts that it might be me. I'm not a child. Well, technically I am, but I'm wise beyond my years, having two lives from which to draw to enable me to spot danger and react accordingly.

'Candy?' I say, careful to take my time after wink-gate. 'Did your mum die?'

Her response isn't instant and I feel the urge to reach for her hand, to protect her from my intrusive questioning. I resist, and instead look from my feet to study her face. She nods once.

'Cancer,' she says solemnly. 'In her wabbers.'

Candy smiles. I don't. Her smile is one solely for my benefit, I realise. A smile which is telling me it's OK, that she's past the point of heart-twisting, unabating grief. She's in a place now where memories fill her heart with joy, not anger. It occurs to me that Candy will cling onto these memories for the rest of her life, whereas mine of my dad will fade to nothing in no more than a few years from now. I'll gradually forget his strength when he lifted me, his smell when he held me. The thought cloaks me with sadness until another thought spins around my head regarding Candy. With her restricted mental ability, frozen at a level typically found in a person in

131

their early teens, will she be able to retain details of her current life in a way that I'm able to with my previous life? To cling better to memories? At some point in the future, when information-clutter decides to elbow out older stuff from *my* head to make room for the here and now, will Candy continue to be blessed with clear memories and sharp images? And as a natural progression from that, if she's a person capable of recall from a previous life, like me, will she never lose the ability to remember?

'It was fifteen years ago. I was sixteen,' Candy says gently, her voice the only sound other than blackbirds going about securing their last feed of the day. 'My dad was sad for such a long time. I was too,' she says, coming to a stop just shy of the decking and staring straight ahead at the water. 'But my mum and dad got married when they were quite young so they had lots of time together before my mum got sick.'

'You had sixteen years with her too,' I add, keen to reassure my new friend, to stress the positives.

'I know. I'm grateful.' Candy says the words with a maturity, a glimpse of the older woman it's easy to forget she masks.

'What was her name? Your mum?'

'Greta.' Candy's voice wobbles but she recovers. 'She was from Finland. She came to England when she was a girl. That's when she met my dad... at my dad's school... and they were together ever since.' Candy wipes a tear from her eye with the back of her sleeve. 'It broke my dad's heart when she died. But he's a lot better now.'

This time I do reach for Candy's hand, and make sure to ease her fingers apart with mine, then squeezing them tightly shut, making our two hands into one fist.

'We used to come to the lake a lot,' Candy says, giving my hand an extra squeeze. 'I'm glad we can come here again.'

'Me too,' I say, unsure if the moistness in my eyes is for Candy, her dad or myself. Because, having left this planet at the age of sixteen, I too was deprived of the opportunity to grow old alongside my parents, deprived of receiving a card from them for the driving test I never took, deprived of dancing with them at the eighteenth birthday party I never had, deprived of seeing their joy at watching me step over the threshold of the first house I never bought, and deprived of seeing the pride in their faces at the wedding I didn't have.

Candy wheels around to face me. 'Will you be my best friend?' she asks.

'Yes,' I say chasing off an imminent tear. 'I will. I'd like that very much.'

Candy loosens her grip on my hand, stoops to fumble around in the dirt where the lawn meets decking and straightens up holding two small stones in one open palm. She passes one to me and at her request, on the count of three, we throw them as far as we can and wait for the *plop... plop* as they break the surface of the water.

I imagine them sinking together to their watery grave. Like Mr Crane's wife and child. Tragedy binding them together for ever.

'Child of light.' I'm brought to my senses by three words that make none. Candy is swinging her arms, grinning.

'Er... right... OK?' I say it as a question to ensure she knows I'll need more to go on.

'Child of light. That's what Greta means in Finnish.'

And Greta's daughter is both of those things, I think, as I hold hands with my friend and we stare across the water.

33

The first day at my new secondary school as a year nine pupil is a predictably anxious affair. In the week leading up to today, I've been flooded with memories of my first day last time around. At least I think they were memories. They could well have been nightmares since they all seemed to take me unawares whilst I was lying in bed.

Last time around, the lucky children were the ones who pitched up with friends made in primary school, they made the transition more easily.

The kids who arrived from out of town with no mates in tow struggled, unable to break into existing peer groups reluctant to let outsiders in. In time those same peer groups expanded, of course, and adopted new members; the girl who was good at tennis, for instance, or the boy who was dropped off at the school gates in the coolest car; those and others deemed worthy were eventually welcomed with open arms.

The really tough gig was for kids who relocated, arriving at the school mid-term or at the start of an academic year having not been a pupil in the previous one. Like me today.

I figure if you have a talent for something, you'll be OK (except if it's chemistry, then you'll just be seen as a complete parasite). Generally though, people are drawn to talented or gifted individuals. The trouble is, I'm not sure I have a gift, a skill, a magnet to draw others in, assuming, that is, we exclude my powers of recall from previous lives. I won't be bringing that up in a hurry as a means of gaining acceptance. That's the sort of thing that sees you plummet horribly in the popularity stakes, though looking around me now in the assembly hall, with an empty chair either side of me, I haven't got far to fall.

The assembly is conducted by the headmaster, a Mr Hole. A ridiculous name for a ridiculous man. He carries sweat rings the size of dinner plates under his arms, speaks through a voice box pinched from Kermit the Frog, and even accounting for his Cuban heels, is no more than five feet tall, which would be fine if he didn't overcompensate by being rude to those around him.

This morning, in separate incidents, he was hell-bent on undermining the authority of both a school secretary and a female teacher. It reeked of a small man with a complex, creating a scene for the benefit of the pupils queuing at the entrance to the main hall. His reasons for the dressing-down of each member of staff were tenuous at best, though I suspect he vents his anger at Mrs Peacock on a regular basis on account of her being a good foot taller than him. I dislike him instantly.

Why is it that school pupils always choose the summer holiday period in which to die? In my previous life I have a memory of a boy in my class not reappearing in September because he'd become ill. Meningitis, I think. I remember the sombre atmosphere in the school on our first day back, his class teacher announcing his death from the stage. Most kids had heard the tragic news over the summer break, those who hadn't were hunched over, disbelieving, unable to rationalise what they were hearing.

In those days, if a tragedy occurred, people were appropriately sad about it; the closer the friend the more upsetting it was and the longer it took a person to straighten themselves out. But they did. In the end.

There's a sombre atmosphere here, now. Some kid one year younger than me has croaked it following an accident on his electric scooter outside the Co-op. I mean, there's never a good time or a good way to go. But a scooter? The Co-op?

Mr Hole is barely three sentences into his eulogy when the snivelling starts around the hall. Even the new starters in year seven, most of whom can't possibly have known the poor sod who's died, are at it. Mr Hole raises his voice to climb above the sound of weeping.

The next thing to happen is even more predictable as mobile phones start pinging. It'll be pupils wanting to be first to post the news on Facebook, getting on there early to secure as many *likes* as possible. Phones slip back into pockets. Message posted. Grieving done.

We're told by our vertically-challenged headmaster that counselling is available. Sounds like a box-ticking exercise to me; a procedure suggested on a child safeguarding course that Mr Hole won't have attended himself, but rather sent a deputy in his place.

I wait for Mr Hole to conclude his sad news by offering up his wisdom in the form of a moral. There's always a moral to even the blandest of assembly narratives. It'll go something like this: *don't fuck about on scooters in car parks.*

Mr Hole takes a deep breath. Here it comes, I think.

'So, what I'll say to you all is this… you might think you're safe from harm… you might think you're invincible. I don't know, poor Michael may have thought the same. But we're left mourning the death of a boy whose life has been tragically cut short. So I'll ask you to stop and think about that. To think hard when you're about to do something you know could be dangerous. Think of Michael.'

I won't be thinking of Michael. How can I? I don't know him. I don't even know what he looks like. Fact is I'm in a bad mood. The summer holidays are over, the last two weeks of which I didn't even get to spend with Candy because her and Tom went to somewhere in Greece so they could get stomach bugs and sunburn. And now I'm in a strange building with people I've never met before, being patronised by a performing meerkat.

We file out. A leaflet is thrust my way by a woman stationed at the exit door. She deals them like a croupier at a blackjack table.

'What's this?' I ask.

The woman looks less than happy that I've thus far not taken it from her hand. And even less delighted that a newcomer has deigned to ask her a direct question. She fans the leaflet up and down, side to side, like she believes there's a chance this way I might better see it and take it from her. I follow it with my eyes, just to make sure she knows I'm aware of its presence.

'It gives details of where you can get help,' she says sniffily, and in a way that couldn't be any more lacklustre if she tried.

'Help with what?' I ask, partly curious, but mainly to enhance my standing as an arsehole of a teenager.

'Help with your loss,' she fires back, irritation rising with each word.

'Right,' I say, conscious of the queue building behind me. The woman indicates for those behind me to come through to clear the bottleneck. I inch to one side, not really far enough to let them pass, but the gesture has been made and that's what's important. I notice that every pupil without fail takes a leaflet. I find it puzzling.

'I don't think I've lost anything,' I continue, as the final stragglers bump past me.

'Nonsense,' she barks. 'We've all lost something today. We've lost… we've lost—'

'Michael?' I help her out.

'Yes. Michael. We've lost Michael,' she snaps.

I look at her quizzically for a second or two. She glances at her watch, looks over my shoulder. Behind me I can hear Mr Hole getting shirty with someone.

'Did you know Michael well?' I ask.

'What? No. He wasn't a pupil in my class.' Another glance towards the stage.

I can tell the woman isn't used to being questioned like this, and she's unsure how to react. She's wary because I'm new, an unknown quantity, and if she flies off the handle she might be inadvertently showing aggression towards a child with a diagnosed behavioural problem. I could have the letters A.D.H.D. after my name, stamped in capitals on my file. A symptom is curiosity. She'll know that.

Some foot-tapping starts, her left leg shaking like a shitting dog. The woman looks like she's weighing up whether it'll cause problems if a student doesn't go home with a leaflet.

'Will *you* be taking a leaflet, Miss?'

'Manson. What? No. I don't know.' The woman is mistaken in thinking I was asking for her surname. I wasn't, but it's useful information all the same. Miss Manson's head turns a nasty shade of crimson, radiating a level of anger more commensurate with someone who's found out their Wimbledon tickets are to watch Andy Murray not Rafael Nadal, rather than the refusal of a thirteen-year-old to accept a leaflet.

But I'm not a normal student. I have a confidence acquired from knowing what I can and can't get away with. And what's more, I'm as angry as Miss Manson. When I lost a loved one, I was broken, weighed down by my grief, suffering loss on a scale no human can be prepared for. I wasn't passed a fucking leaflet with a phone number to ring then, so I sure as hell don't need one now.

'You should, you know,' I say, returning some warmth to my eyes.

'I should what?' Miss Manson shoots back, more uncertainly now.

'Take a leaflet. You might need counselling. There'll be someone kind to help you through it all.' I nod. Pleased with myself for a point well made.

Miss Manson snaps. She's had enough, and even I can't blame her. I feel her warm breath as she shouts over my shoulder.

'Mr Hole. We have a child refusing to take one of our "good grief" leaflets.'

Jesus, have they really called it that?

'Do we now, Miss Manson?' Mr Hole hollers back from the stage behind me.

140

I turn around to see Mr Hole pushing a piece of paper into the chest of a man who looks like he might be the caretaker; scruffy, world-weary, and carrying the haunted look of a man who has to be around kids all day, unarmed, and with no authority or license to lash out.

Mr Hole marches towards us. I say, *marches*; that gives an overly flattering description of the length of his stride pattern. His shoes squeak on the parquet floor adding another layer of ridiculousness to him that makes me smile.

'What's so funny?' he demands, coming to a stop and bringing his feet together in a final shrill squeak.

'Nothing, sir,' I say, flattening my face out.

'This girl won't take a leaflet, Mr Hole.'

'Is that so?' Mr Hole barks, choosing that moment to fold his arms. 'Well you can explain that to me in my office. Come with me. Name?'

'Florence Aters-Fabishaw, sir.'

Mr Hole strides past Miss Manson, snatching the leaflet from her and casting a look her way which implies he has better things to be doing with his time.

I'm led into the headteacher's office. There's a good deal of dark wood panelling, no doubt stuck on to present the image of a solid, princely, nineteenth century institution providing unparalleled excellence to all who pass through its imposing doors. The fact that the panelling isn't wood, is about three millimetres thick and glued to flimsy plasterboard walls thrown up in the nineteen-seventies when construction standards were at an all-time low, seems to have escaped the notice of the man lowering himself into his leatherette swivel chair. He lifts a bum cheek, then pulls on a lever to make sure

141

the gas-powered chair post is set to its highest position. That done, he places both hands palm-down on the heavy desk, and in what is plainly a well-practised operation, he uses his hands to pull the chair closer to the desk. Most people would perform this manoeuvre with their feet. Mr Hole isn't most people.

While he revs himself up to deliver the bollocking that will inevitably come my way any minute now, I glance around the room. On top of a cheap bookshelf sit five even cheaper-looking trophies. At a guess, I'd say he's received them for some sort of sporting achievement. The exact nature of the sport eludes me. Limbo, perhaps. I squint at the trophy placed far right and can see a tiny plastic golf club perched on its lid. So, not sport then.

'Right... Er...' Mr Hole scans the desk around him, then clicks his fingers twice. He's forgotten my name despite me giving it to him less than two minutes ago.

'Florence,' sir. 'You can call me Flo.'

'Well, Florence. Listen up. We have rules in this school. Rules that pupils are expected to adhere to. And when a pupil steps out of line there are consequences. I suggest you do not make yourself that pupil.' Mr Hole tries to recline his chair by leaning back into it, but he lacks the required mass to make it happen.

I opt for silence.

'Well, girl. Do you understand what I'm saying?' He's dialled-up both his volume and the colour of his face; the latter, while needing to go some way before catching up with Miss Manson's shade, is making a valiant effort to achieve parity.

'Not really, sir, no.'

'Did you or did you not pass an entrance exam to gain entry to this school?'

Oh Lord, the man sees himself as detective now, with me as his suspect. It crosses my mind to reply with *no comment* but I put that one back in its box, for now.

'I did, sir.' It was a stupid question since I wouldn't be here now if I hadn't. I wait for his follow up. It'll contain the word *intelligence* at some point. Or *brains*.

'Well that tells me you have at least a modicum of intelligence, so I insist you apply some of those brains during your time here…'

Bingo.

'… So, starting today, I want to see that you have the capacity to follow simple rules. Understood?'

'Yes, sir. Of course, sir.'

'Good. Well let's consider the matter dealt with.'

Mr Hole bends himself double in order to push the leaflet across the desk. His diminutive frame prevents him from completing this task successfully, and even with a final nudge, the pamphlet comes to a stop a good eighteen inches from me. It's debatable whose jurisdiction it now falls within. I look first to the leaflet then to Mr Hole.

'I'd rather not take the leaflet if it's all the same with you, sir,' I say, with the result that Mr Hole's face reaches a shade of claret normally only seen in vintage years. Before he erupts, I begin to speak from the heart—a speech that I could have delivered ten minutes previously if only someone had given me the chance.

143

'You see, sir, I lost someone close to me once. It's hard for me to find the words to describe how it affected me. Because it did, sir… affect me… badly. For months I was only ever one cry away from self-destruction. One cry from giving up on a life that at the time I couldn't see the purpose in going on with. I felt… I felt a sadness so crippling, it couldn't be fought off, no matter how hard I tried. So… in the end I didn't fight it, instead I allowed it to live within me until I realised I didn't *want* to be free of it, because… because…' My stomach knots, my throat tightens and I remind myself to breathe. 'I'm sorry, sir… I just need a second…' I bunch my shoulders up and angle my face to the ceiling. I'm unsure if I do this to regroup by focusing on something featureless, or to slow the progress of the tear that's escaping. I drop my shoulders, force them back and face front once more, ignoring the tear that accelerates until it settles at the corner of my mouth. '… because if I chased the pain away, I knew I'd be left with a void. And there's no refill, is there, sir? So what was I to do?'

Mr Hole opens his mouth to offer some pearls of wisdom in response, but I don't allow him time to interrupt.

'I'll tell you what I did, sir.' I take a deep breath. Swallow hard. Visions start to flood my head. I'm remembering again. 'After the funeral, I started by doing things I took little pleasure in… taking the bins to the end of the drive, selling raffle tickets at the church fete. I was still… still *hopelessly* weighed down by grief, but at least I was functioning on a basic level. And I was lucky because those close to me helped me along the way, and in return I helped them back, until I was able to… you know… like… converse outside a shop without bursting into tears on hearing a word or phrase which jogged a precious memory. I was able to see good in things where I could previously only see bad. So I guess one way or another I regrouped... yes, regrouped... and my brain... or maybe my heart... told me in no uncertain terms that I needed to carry on with my life.'

I pause, the images filling my head, consuming me, slowing me up. Yet in an instant they retreat and I take a couple of deep breaths. 'So if your rule is that I should take a leaflet and grieve, it's a rule I'm going to break, because there were no rules for me... for grieving, sir. And there won't be any in your leaflet either. There'll just be help, should a person need it. Which I don't. I never knew Michael. I feel sad for him and his family, of course I do, but I won't grieve for Michael, and so have no need of someone to help me through it.'

My mouth feels dry, and a pressure clamps my temples. But I'm nearly done.

'Please keep the leaflet, sir. Keep it for someone who needs it more than me.'

I remind myself I'm thirteen years old. I had an approximation of what I wanted to say, but I had no idea I could speak with such composure, such authority. Mr Hole, on the other hand, has completely lost the power of speech, so I don't wait to be dismissed. I rise slowly to my feet, tuck my chair under the desk, and make for the door.

'Er... Florence?'

'Yes, sir?' I turn around to face the room.

'I'm very sorry for your loss.'

I nod once. 'Thank you, sir,' I say and turn to face the door once more, my hand reaching for the handle.

'When did they die?'

With my body still facing the door, I turn my head around, not fully, not so it's facing my headteacher, just so I'm looking into space with unfocused eyes.

'I'm not sure, sir. I can't remember. No more than twenty-five years ago.'

34

I'm led to my classroom by the school secretary, the one who'd been on the end of an earlier tongue-lashing from Mr Hole. My class teacher, a rotund man, young compared to his colleagues, welcomes me, and indicates a spare desk towards the back of the room.

Something has happened in my absence, I'm sure of it. The air is too still, the atmosphere too heavy. I can't discern if it's tension or anticipation. I begin the long walk to my desk, aware of heads swivelling, twenty-eight pairs of eyes tracking my movement.

And it's then I realise. Word has got around that I was hauled into the headteacher's office within minutes of assembly finishing. It'll be a school record. Twenty-eight pairs of eyes probing for answers. *What the hell did this girl do that so royally pissed off the headteacher? And how is she managing to look so nonchalant about it?*

I've discovered my skill, my magnet for pulling my classmates towards me with every step I take.

I'm the girl from out of town who's going to have no problem fitting in.

It's time to slow my pace, milk the moment.

I arrive at my desk, drop my bag to the floor and sit myself down. Only after I take the time to brush the desktop with my hands do I look up and eyeball my new classmates.

I've arrived.

Mission accomplished.

35

It's a ball-achingly long journey to and from school. Two buses, each smelling of oil, diesel, and something else I'd rather not put my finger on. One of the drivers seems nice, always taking the time to say hi to all the kids as they board. He's in stark contrast to the other regular driver who looks as if he should be on some sort of register; one that precludes its list of members from being within three miles of kids. It's not just his greasy hair and stained tracksuit bottoms, it's the fact he looks like he hates being a bus driver, which begs the question what's keeping him here?

It's Friday. The house will be almost empty when I return. I say 'almost' because Bridgette will be in residence, working as she does for herself now. It'll be a couple of hours yet before Laura's back from the hotel she's taken a part-time job at, and Penny has had to go into head office for the day. She's still toying with the idea of teaming up with Bridgette. The reason she hasn't isn't due to a lack of work, there's plenty, according to Bridgette. I think it's more to do with Penny and Bridgette not getting on so well these days. They argue more than they used to. A few years ago you'd categorise any spats between the pair as playful joshing, only very occasionally spilling over into something more venomous. Nowadays, words traded are harsher, looks exchanged more spiteful, and there seems to be less concern shown for each other's wellbeing.

As I walk up the drive, I look to the upstairs window where Bridgette will likely be working. And sure enough I can see her on the phone, reclined in her chair, tapping her pen against her chin, laughing. I hope my mums don't work together. There'd be way too much posturing, an unquantifiable amount of sulking, and a fight to the death over who gets the window seat.

I was bought a bike for my birthday. That wasn't so much of a surprise. What was, however, was that I received the one I asked for. I was expecting a cheap alternative, like always happens when my parents buy me trainers. I'm under strict instructions to confine my bike rides to the length of our lane outside, but that's become monotonous and I'm Flo—I need adventure. I grab a flapjack and a few things for my rucksack, shout a back-to-back hello and goodbye to Bridgette, then retrieve my bike from the garage.

As a family we've only been living at Lakeside for a short time, long enough though for me to take note of the road network around here. It's mostly single-track lanes lined with tall hedgerows, and right now as I prepare to push off, I have a rough route in my head of the journey I'm about to take. My main problem is I have no clue how long it will take me to ride it.

What I haven't factored in are the gradients. In a car or bus, you aren't aware of such things. Hills are flattened out when riding in a vehicle, but on my bike, every turn of the pedals so far has been to push me up horrifying inclines, and not to put too fine a point on it, I'm fucking knackered. I'm starting to think whoever came up with the expression 'what goes up, must come down' was taking the piss. I've been flat out for about twenty minutes now and I'm as sure as I can be that I'm not even halfway. The reason I'm not totally sure of distance travelled is due to the tall hedges either side of the roads that don't allow me to get my bearings. I may as well be riding blind.

Occasionally there'll be a break in the hedgerow, like the one now to my left, so I stop to gauge progress. A landmark or two would help but there's a sad lack round here with one field looking pretty much like the next. There is, however—in the field I'm currently looking into—the grumpiest-looking cow I've ever seen, and I make a mental note to remember it for next time, or indeed my return journey later. It's on its own for some reason. I take in all four corners of the field for signs of a herd but there isn't one. They'll have all topped themselves, I reason. I would if I had to spend all day alongside this grouchy bastard. I decide to name it, and conscious that I should pick a female name, I settle on Alan— the name of my equally narky bus driver.

I think I'm getting closer to my destination. It's mid-September but there's still a warmth to the air come early evenings, so much so that I feel a trickle of sweat run down my spine, caused in no small part by my rucksack blocking the airflow to my skin. Thankfully though, my pack is light since it contains only water, a flapjack, a banana, and my binoculars. I pause to eat the flapjack before continuing on my way.

Rounding a corner, I'm nearly taken out by some spanner driving a Vauxhall Corsa, but I manage to keep both wheels on the tarmac and roll to a stop at a junction which gives me a choice of two equally narrow lanes. I take the one to my left, which even to the most generous of spirit can at best be described as a track. It's potholed, narrow, and dark, with trees arcing themselves over its entire length, presenting the road as a cramped tunnel. A strip of moss and grass in lieu of a painted dividing line sprouts from the centre of the track. There's little clearance between dirt and canopy which leads me to believe it's been a considerable amount of time since any vehicle larger than a car took this route.

There's something foreboding about it, claustrophobia claws at me. The brimming confidence I set out with nearly an hour ago has been replaced with trepidation, and suddenly I long to be back at Lakeside.

But I have a fearless tag to uphold, earned from my week at D.R.E.G.S and I'll be letting my classmates down if I turn around now.

The noise of the bike's tyres as they scrabble through the dirt is too loud and risks giving me away, an incongruous racket alongside the gentle soundtrack of birdsong and the rustling leaves of the hunched branches overhead.

A clearing lies ahead. I can see small pieces of rusting machinery dotted about, joined by narrow strips of long, dried grass untouched by vehicles. If viewed from above, the assortment of objects would give the illusion of a constellation—a new astronomical discovery that some poor bearded pipe-smoker would have to come up with a name for. "Pile Of Shite (Minor)" would be a good starting point, I think.

What I'm looking for—if my bearings are correct—should be to my left-hand side. Viewed from Lakeside, to the naked eye, the Crane residence gives little away. But look more closely, and with Tom's tale in mind of the night disaster struck, and you can see a slight transformation in the tree line. The scars to the landscape—that would have been obvious years ago when created by Mr Crane's car as it ploughed through the undergrowth—are now, when viewed from Lakeside, so subtle as to almost render this particular section of landscape indistinguishable from the rest of the hillside.

Close up though, as I step through brambles and nettles at the side of the road and look down the slope, there's better evidence of the route the car took as it carved a path to the water below. The slope is steeper than it appears from Lakeside. Stumps remain of the small shallow-rooted trees that clung to the slope before they were ripped from the earth, trees that would have *slowed* the car's progress, no more. New trees have been planted alongside the fallen. Pillars of new life, though I don't imagine Mr Crane will see it that way.

I'm not sure what I was expecting to find. I suppose I wanted to see the place for myself, not out of morbid curiosity, more to connect myself to the story, be touched by Mr Crane's grief. I put this down to my heightened sense of mortality that most kids my age wouldn't understand. Kids my age don't think they'll ever die. Dying is what people who are extremely old do. It's not relevant to kids. Doesn't apply. But I know it does. I'm living proof that death can take you at any age and I'm only aware of a previous life because I can remember snatches of it. If I couldn't, I may as well still be dead because I'd be unaware of both my life before birth and the possibility of one afterwards.

A shout comes from the direction of the wooden house, jolting me to my senses. The voice is gruff and clipped.

'Who's there? What are you doing on my land?'

I stiffen. The voice can only be from one person. I turn slowly, giving myself time to chase the apprehension away that I'm feeling.

'Mr Crane?'

'Did you hear me?' the man yells.

He edges forward, squinting, his eyesight from that distance not good enough to see who he's dealing with. He reaches a point where his focus sharpens, no more than seven or eight yards from where I stand, and upon seeing me he seems startled, and if I'm not very much mistaken, alarmed. He drops the toolbox he carries to the ground, though his eyes don't track its fall and he makes no move to pick it up. I take a step towards him and he instinctively shuffles backwards. I'm no longer sure this can be the fearsome Mr Crane, the one the villagers are wary of, the man people go out of their way to avoid. All that considered, the poor man looks no closer to speaking so I try again in an effort to engage him.

'Mr Crane,' I say, starting to feel unnerved by his silence and unswerving stare. 'I didn't mean to startle you.' I wipe a hand on my jeans and hold it stretched out in front of me. I'm hoping he'll close the gap between us but my olive branch is one he appears unwilling to take. Left with little choice, I allow my hand to flop to my side once more. 'Um... I like your house,' I say, nodding in the direction of the structure that sits thirty or so feet behind the yard. And I do... like it, I mean. Don't get me wrong, it's in a poor state of repair, strips of mismatched wood nailed-on where previous ones have perished, the chimney lacking mortar between most of its bricks. It's the kind of place some eejit in a shiny suit working for an estate agent would describe as 'having potential'. And it does—if the buyer happens to own a bulldozer.

That said, I'm drawn to the place, a humble yet proud home, crouched beneath the tree canopy. It has a warmth, a cosiness, and a view to die for. Even as I say the last few words in my head, I regret the choice of them immediately. It occurs to me that the man standing in front of me must be torn between staying and leaving this place. If he stays, he won't free himself of the constant reminder of the accident that killed his family. If he leaves, he relinquishes his grip on the happy times, of memories made between the four walls of his house, and out here in the yard.

When Tom told this wretched man's story, he left one crucial detail out. Why was Mr Crane arrested for murder? Everything about Tom's account of what happened that night pointed to an accident, nothing more. Tom and Candy are visiting tomorrow night. Not for supper—that pretence has been dropped in favour of 'dinner'. I intend getting some answers from them tomorrow night.

'My name's Flo. Pleased to meet you, Mr Crane.' I iron out a slight wobble in my voice. 'I have a new bike. Well, it's my first, actually.'

Mr Crane nods at my bright red bike that I've propped up against a tree. 'It's a fine-looking bike,' he says, his eyes narrowing. 'Be sure to oil the chain every few weeks. That'll keep it running well.'

I look to my bike then back at Mr Crane. 'I will, thank you.'

'You look all hot and bothered. You want a glass of water?' It's said matter-of-factly, like my throat's need for lubrication is comparable to a bike chain's need for oil.

Still, at least Mr Crane has recovered his composure, I think, though I'm still puzzled by his initial reaction at seeing me.

I'm not sure what my next move should be. I'm thirsty, that's for sure, having swigged all of my water rations in riding this far. But I shouldn't go into this man's house, it feels too dangerous. I know nothing of him. Out here I can run if needs be. Having said all that, I don't feel scared by this man. He looks more wary of me if anything. Physically he looks strong but his eyes project a weariness, a man for whom life ceased to give him joy a long time ago.

'You wait here... OK?' he says.

I nod.

'You wait here while I fetch a glass from the house.'

'Thank you,' I say, partly relieved that he's made the decision for me not to enter his house, yet partly disappointed I won't get to see inside the house where he and his young family spent their days. 'Oh, Mr Crane. Could you fill my bottle for me, too?'

I wait until he nods before reaching into my backpack. The distance between us will need to close now if he's to take my water bottle. I make the steps necessary to reach him. His eyes never leave mine. And I can see beyond the weariness in them now, to a tenderness. There's even the merest hint of a twinkle, in the way a person's eyes light up on receiving a precious gift or seeing a particular species of wild animal for the first time. Or seeing an old friend.

With Mr Crane in the house, I get a better look at his yard. The first thing I see, or more accurately what I *don't* see, is a car. Hardly surprising, I think. You'd need the constitution of granite to pluck up the courage to get behind the wheel after a life-changing episode of the sort this man's had. While there's no car, there is however a very second hand-looking quad bike, parked in front of one of three timber outbuildings; barns that, somewhat incredibly, are in an even worse state of repair than the main house. One of the doors to the largest barns is ajar and I edge closer to get a better look inside. My heart aches when my eyes fall upon a push bike. Pink. Slightly larger than mine. Was this his child's bike? Its colour and shape suggest a girl's bike, and its presence in the barn after all these years tells me her dad must feel unable to bring himself to remove it from the property.

There's a shuffling of boots behind me, I swivel around. Mr Crane eyeballs the open door then hands me a glass and my bottle, and, without saying a word, walks to the barn and pulls the door shut. It sags on its hinges, its lower rail scraping a channel through the earth meaning he's made to lift it in order to secure it in position. It looks extremely heavy but he makes light work of it.

He padlocks the door and shuffles around to face me. I expect to be told off for snooping, or asked to clear off, but neither of these things happen.

'Do I know you? You say your name's Flo?' he says, studying my face.

'Yes Mr Crane, it's Flo. But I don't believe we've met.' He gives a stroke of his beard and a shake of his head.

'My mistake,' he says. 'Could have sworn you look familiar, though.'

'I'm new here,' I say, sending a wide smile his way.

'I don't mind the new ones,' he says, before finally shifting his eyes from mine and aiming them somewhere across the water. 'It's those that've been here for years. They're the ones I've no time for. Those who can't accept that a man like me lives his life differently.' He looks back in the direction of his house, then for reasons that escape me lifts his eyes to the sky. The change in body language is completed with him thrusting his hands into the pockets of his dungarees and letting out a heavy sigh.

'They see me as someone who doesn't fit in, see. But I do… fit in… just not to their way of doing things. Just because I catch my own food where I can, and I don't mow my lawn on a Sunday, they label me as an oddball.'

A quick glance left and right confirms the complete absence of any lawn and I wonder if he is in fact an oddball, or delusional, or if he simply landed on a bad example.

'Oh, there used to be a lawn here,' he says wistfully, having registered my confusion. 'Over there.' He points to an area between the two smaller outbuildings. And we grew vegetables in front of the house. He looks to each place in turn, no doubt remembering how his land used to look in happier times. He'd used the word 'we', too, I notice.

'It was you and your wife and child.' For some reason I don't feel the need to pose my words as a question.

He looks at me, a flicker of something in his eyes. Could be anger, or shame, or regret. Or something else entirely. I find this man hard to read.

He removes his cap and turns it over in his dirt-ingrained hands.

'Sienna.' That was my daughter. His eyes moisten and it rips me apart to watch him continue to suffer. 'Beautiful, she was. Like her mother, Hettie.'

I swallow. I'm not sure I can handle this. Mr Crane talks of his family with a sadness that fills me with guilt, since I have nothing but happy memories of my childhood.

And those memories choose this moment to swim through me now, displacing my conscious thoughts. They arrive as snatches in time, viewed through a Vaseline-smeared lens, our features fleeting and indistinct.

I'm aged five and, as if filmed by a third party from behind, I see my father and me pulling carrots from the ground, tiny things mostly, us laughing when a comically misshapen one is freed from the earth.

I'm aged nine, my dad hugging me after the two of us became soaked when erecting our tent somewhere near the coast. Him holding me tight, running his hands up and down my back to warm me.

I'm aged twelve, go-karting with friends for my birthday, looking for my dad each time I start a new lap, waving despite not being able to pinpoint him.

I'm fifteen, my dad picking me up from a party, waiting outside so as not to cramp my style, looking straight ahead, the disappointment palpable as I stagger to the passenger door. Him not once looking my way because he knows I've drunk alcohol, his silence leaving me in no doubt that there'll be a discussion, but not tonight.

I'm sixteen. I'm taken from this world. I no longer see my dad.

'You OK, Flo?' It's Mr Crane, looking concerned that I disappeared temporarily.

I sway and put a foot to the earth but it doesn't connect, simply keeps on travelling like it's swinging loose in a bottomless pothole. The scene I'm looking at shifts, the treetops in the distance are now at eye level, greens bleeding into the greys and whites of clouds. I feel nothing for a while. Weightless, falling down a hillside but not in pain. Then as suddenly as I'm falling, I'm not. A strong hand wraps itself around my arm, a second one grabs my shoulder. Strong hands, but gentle. The branches of the indistinct trees become sharp again, the sound of water in my ears replaced with birdsong, Mr Crane lowering me onto a rusty piece of farm machinery. He leaves me and I'm scared to be alone, unsure of myself without his support. He retrieves the glass of water and takes my hand, opening my fingers like Candy and me do. I take it from him, my eyes never leaving his. I'm not scared anymore. He seems to relax when he sees me drinking. I'm unsure where I went, but I'm back now, sitting up, greedily taking the water on board. And my first thought, after thanking Mr Crane for catching me, is to wonder why, in my flashbacks, I never see my mum.

But that's not the only thought I have, there's one that's troubling me more. Because I've not been honest with myself. And I've not been honest with Mr Crane. Because I lied to him. I told him we'd never met. I look into his eyes now, and I know that's not true.

36

The journey back from Mr Crane's is the best one I've had in my present thirteen years—plus my previous sixteen (as far as I can remember, anyway).

Mr Crane had been concerned about me cycling home after my temporary blackout. He told me that if he'd owned a phone he would have called my parents to come and collect me. It seemed alien to me that a person wouldn't own a phone of any kind, whether it be a mobile or one connected to a landline. But then, Mr Crane in his own way is a kind of alien himself. I've certainly never met anyone like him before. I watched him look between me and his quad bike as he weighed up his options. He shook his head, dismissed the idea, and slumped next to me on the indeterminate piece of machinery that I had pegged as farm equipment but which the villagers would likely conclude to be a medieval instrument of torture. He glanced back to the quad bike and it was painfully obvious to me he hadn't driven with a passenger since the accident, let alone with a girl.

I got to my feet, conscious that I'd been away from home too long, worried that at least one of the other adults would have made it back. I think Mr Crane would have been prepared to overlook the slight sway as I stood, but when I faltered after taking only a few steps, he settled on his course of action.

'Right young lady,' he said, reaching for my arm. 'You're coming with me.' He walked me to the quad bike, though we stopped short of it, both staring at the machine, both simultaneously aware of a problem to be overcome. Two people. One seat.

A man more in touch with the world we live in would have rejected the idea out of hand, terrified of recriminations of wrongdoing. But Mr Crane isn't a man who sees duplicity where there is none. He's a man who, when presented with a problem, sets about solving it in the best way he knows how. And if that means getting a young girl safely back to her parents, then that's what will happen, regardless of where his passenger is seated. Point out to Mr Crane that his actions are likely to draw criticism, not to mention a questioning of his motives, and the man would be genuinely baffled.

And as I climb onto his lap, I know the man beneath me sees no significance in the action other than it being a necessary first step in getting me home.

With my bike strapped to the rear of the quad, we sail down the lanes. I'm wearing a crash helmet, one that Sienna might once have worn—or, given its age, a world war two tank driver. I'm giggling. I can't help it. What a sight we must be. We're made to stop to wait for a handful of sheep who have decided the vegetation at the roadside is preferable to that on offer in whatever field they've escaped from.

'They're Bill Sanders' sheep,' Mr Crane says. He has to shout to guarantee he'll be heard through my crash helmet and above the idling two-stroke engine. 'I'll get them back to where they belong, on the way back.'

There's one straggler. A stubborn-looking bugger, smaller than its mates who've decided not to hang around. It stares at us, jaw in perpetual motion as it chews a sheath of something green.

'Looks like my headmaster,' I shout. A second later, the sound of Mr Crane chuckling reaches me.

I have to ease myself to one side so Mr Crane can see the lanes ahead, and I twist my body to see his long white hair flailing about in the turbulent air. He carries a look of concentration that, now and then, gives way to something else: contentment. I smile to myself as we pass the miserable cow, and my smile becomes a laugh when I elbow Mr Crane in his ribs in order to point it out.

'That's Alan!' I shout.

Mr Crane looks first to the cow, then to me, then back to the cow again. It's a comedy double-take.

My only wish is that our thrilling ride could have been longer, but Mr Crane slows the quad bike gradually and pulls it into a farm entrance just a couple of bends shy of Lakeside. He'll have his reasons for stopping short of the house, and if, as I suspect, he's done it for my benefit, I'm glad. I don't want him to feel uncomfortable around 'those that've been here for years', which surely must include Laura and Penny.

Mr Crane untethers my bike, lowers it gently to the floor and hands me my rucksack.

'Thank you Mr Crane,' I say. 'That was really kind of you.'

'You're welcome Flo,' he says climbing back into the driver's seat.

'Can I visit you again?' I plead.

Mr Crane's face falls, his eyes drop their sparkle. 'I don't think that's a good idea, Flo. It'll get us both into trouble. Best not, I think.' He must register the disappointment on my face because he adds some crow's feet to the corners of his eyes and allows his mouth to give the merest hint of a mischievous grin. 'Of course, if you should happen to bump into me when I'm fishing on Sunday mornings, that's an entirely different matter.'

I can't stop the smirk from spreading over my face. He starts the engine and straps on the pair of goggles he'd insisted I wore for the journey down.

'Where do you go to fish, Mr Crane?' I shout over the rattle of the engine.

Mr Crane considers his response. 'You'll have to use those binoculars of yours to find out.'

And then he swings the bike back in the direction of his house, raises a hand and yells, 'By the way… It's Marcus.'

As I walk towards Lakeside, it occurs to me that it's not just bad *memories* that will remain lodged in Mr Crane's head as he grows older. There are other things he won't be able to shed; his house, his grounds, others' perception of him, even his name—the name folk still recoil at. The name that will have left Tom's lips, in the line of duty all those years ago.

'Marcus Crane, I'm arresting you on suspicion of the murders of Hettie and Sienna Crane. You have the right to remain silent…'

37

Dinner was a fun affair until I was reminded that I'm now of an age where I should help with the dishes. During our meal, I didn't ask about Mr Crane for two reasons. Firstly, I didn't want to show too much of an interest in him for fear of creating suspicion. Were this to happen, it would make it extremely difficult for me to visit him in the future. And secondly, the evening was proving to be a happy one, filled with laughter, corny jokes, and Tom telling embarrassing stories of Candy when she was a toddler. It just didn't seem right to risk changing the mood. Instead, I decide to wait until I can get my hands on Bridgette's laptop so I can do research of my own about Marcus Crane.

After the dishes are cleaned and put away, the adults reach for Jenga and gin. Not a good combination. Candy and I are invited to play but I have a better idea.

'Candy, let's go explore the garden.'

'Keep away from the water,' Penny says and is immediately scolded by Bridgette.

'Oh, they're alright. It's not like they'll be jumping in!'

'All the same I'd rather—'

'Christ, let them have fun.'

Penny shoots Bridgette a furious look, and I know I'll overhear an argument about it later.

'Candy will take care of me, won't you Candy?' I say the words to Penny, keen to stress how patronising the lack of trust in Candy might seem to my friend.

Candy beams at this, at being handed the reins of responsible adult.

'Oh, don't worry Penny, Flo will be safe with me. We'll be extra careful,' Candy says.

Before any of the adults have a chance to respond, I grab Candy's hand and make a bolt for the door that leads to the garden. We hare down the lawn and it's Candy who trips this time, almost dragging us both to ground as she stumbles. More squeals of laughter. Again, I look back to see what might have snagged on her foot but can see nothing obvious.

We reach the jetty, giggling and breathless. And hot. It's a warm evening, the sun shining its last on the lake before it disappears behind the hillside that frames Marcus Crane's house.

I tell Candy about the previous day, my ride on the quadbike, swearing her to secrecy which I can tell sits uncomfortably with her. She promises anyway, and I tell her of Mr Crane's sadness, and how I don't think he could ever have been deliberately responsible for the deaths of his wife and daughter.

'Were you best friends with Sienna?' I ask. 'I mean, before *we* were best friends.'

'No,' she snaps.

Her abrupt response takes me by surprise, so out of character for this gentle woman. During the stillness that follows, each of us return our stare to the Crane house on the opposite shoreline.

'You shouldn't really see him, you know,' Candy says, gently now, untwining her fingers from mine and dropping her hand. 'My dad tells me to be careful around him.'

'Why?' I ask, feeling irritation towards Tom for adopting the same stance as the rest of the villagers. I realise my voice is sharp and make sure to lend a softness to it when I add, 'He was found innocent wasn't he?'

'Well, yes, I think so. I don't really know much about it,' Candy says, looking out to the water, keen to avoid my gaze. 'There was some other stuff, too.'

The 'other stuff' will be gossip, I decide. Trivial tongue-wagging from adults who should know better. But I'm not ready to make Candy uncomfortable. That wouldn't be fair.

'It's OK,' I say. 'Candy?' She takes her time, lost in her thoughts somewhere, so when she eventually turns to face me, I move to reassure her. 'It's OK,' I repeat with a smile. I look up to the hillside to see the orange glow of a lightbulb escaping from one of the small windows of Marcus Crane's house. A shape slides in, silhouetted against it now, a man looking out into the twilight. I wonder what he does with his evenings. I doubt he owns a television; he'd be a man more likely to turn to a book or listen to a play on the radio, I muse. Or perhaps he doesn't stop working, mending a floorboard here, a kitchen cupboard there, anything to distract him from the past he's lost. I know how that feels, it's what I tried to explain to Mr Hole the other day.

I think of the two men for a second, each so different from the other. Mr Hole with his high income, swapping out his many headteacher hats daily depending on whether he's crawling to school governors or placating an unhappy parent.

Marshalling his team in a way that makes him feel superior, fretting about all sorts of targets he's promised to deliver within the school prospectus, chewing Mrs. Hole's ear off in the evenings about his useless deputies.

Contrast Mr Hole with Mr Crane, a man whose prospectus promises and delivers nothing. A man whose mission statement is to toil to exhaustion during daylight hours in order to better see him through the lonely night times when his own thoughts are at their loudest.

One man with an eye to the future, one who'd rather be blindfolded to his past.

'Flo?'

I hear my name but have to wait for the time it takes for my thoughts to retreat from Marcus Crane's house, over the lake, back to me and my friend standing on the jetty, and back to the present.

'Earth to Flo?' Candy raps her knuckles softly on the top of my head.

'Sorry,' I say. 'Miles away.' I choose not to tell Candy where those miles took me.

We sit side by side on the jetty, our legs dangling over the edge. It won't be long before moonlight kisses the lake, taking the nightshift, relieving the sun of its duties for the day. It's beautiful here, I think. Despite everything that's happened, it's still beautiful. And maybe that's what keeps Marcus Crane going.

I glance at Candy. It's her that's lost in her thoughts now. Over her shoulder, the motorboat bobs and gently tugs on its ropes.

'Candy?' I say tentatively. 'Do you know what the name of the boat is?'

'No.' Candy says. Her response is too quick, too firm. There was no thinking time applied, no consideration given to whether it was knowledge she possessed, or not.

I stand up, move to the boat, and kneel at the jetty's edge. Then, using the method I perfected last time I was in this position, pull the boat towards me until I can reach the tarpaulin.

'Look,' I say, glancing over my shoulder. Candy doesn't turn around, continues to stare across the water. She tenses at hearing my voice. 'The boat used to have a name but it's been removed. Do you know who removed it, Candy?' Candy still doesn't turn. 'And why they removed it?'

Candy whips her head round. She carries a pained, confused expression and I can tell she's conflicted. She doesn't want to let me down, but something's stopping her from involving herself in the conversation. And just as I think she isn't going to speak, she does.

'I'm not allowed to talk about it,' she says, returning her gaze to the water. She carries the look of someone who wants to let me in, I'm sure of it, but something is stopping her. Or someone.

We spend the next half an hour talking about school and Greece. Candy shows me photos on her phone of her and Tom. I wonder what the hotel staff, or beach goers, or taverna waiters made of the two of them. Would they see a father and daughter holidaying together? I'm not sure they would. Candy's inner child makes her very tactile, and in more than one selfie, she's draped off her father's shoulder. In another snap, taken by a third party, she's seated on Tom's shoulders, her legs around his neck as he tries to keep his balance in the hotel's swimming pool. It's not something you'd normally witness between a father and a daughter in her early thirties. They'd surely be seen as a couple, and an ugly image rushes me—of others nudging each other across their sun-loungers, making comments about the man who's clearly punching above his weight, or the man who's paid for his young girlfriend from a catalogue.

I tell Candy about my first days at school. Remarkably, Mr Hole was employed at the time Candy had a short spell there. It's no secret that Candy had short spells at a lot of schools until one was found that both Candy and Tom had confidence in, one best placed to help Candy thrive.

'Mr Hole wasn't headteacher when I was there, though,' Candy says, smiling at the memory. 'He was a religious education teacher so there was a lot of talk about various gods. I remember one day Julianne Tasker asking him why God made some people shorter than others. He handled the question quite well, deflecting it by suggesting Julianne talk to Miss Railton, the school's biology teacher.'

The pair of us snigger like primary school kids. 'What I don't understand,' I say, keen to stay on the topic of Mr Hole, '… is why he wears trousers that are two inches too short for him. I mean, how is it even possible to *buy* trousers that short? You'd think, if anything he'd end up with ones that are way too long, meaning he has to turn them up.'

'Dunno. Could be that they're long shorts.'

I burst out laughing and swap looks with Candy to find that she isn't, and I realise that Candy is genuinely troubled by a person's inability to buy clothes that fit. Her serious expression causes me to laugh even harder. Eventually Candy grins and the sound of our happiness slices through the still air that hovers over the water.

A shout from the house announces there's cake to be had, so we clamber to our feet, dust our bums down and saunter in the direction of the house. Before heading back, I give Marcus Crane's house one more look. It's in darkness now.

After cake, I'm told to say my goodnights to Tom and Candy who'll be leaving soon. I'm not mad about leaving them all to their private chatter, wine and second helpings of cake, but I toe the line and trudge upstairs.

With teeth cleaned and pyjamas on I climb into bed, leaving the door ajar in case there are any hot topics being discussed downstairs worth listening in to. There isn't. Well, not unless you count Candy telling the room about a colleague of hers, who earlier that day at the florists, attempted to make an imprint of her boobs in a block of oasis. The idea was to pass it to her boyfriend as a birthday gift. According to Candy, it didn't turn out well, the young woman unable to generate sufficient pressure to make an impression. I wonder if they made an impression on Candy. Somewhat narked by the fact Candy hadn't seen fit to tell me the story personally, I roll over, before scolding myself for such irrational thoughts.

My gaze falls on my rucksack and I smile remembering my four-wheeled adventure with Marcus Crane from yesterday. I frown as I remember him discouraging me from coming to his house, then smile at his suggestion that it would be OK if I were to 'bump into him'. There was just one problem, he hadn't told me the location where he likes to fish. I assume it's somewhere local to him, and by extension, me. Instinctively I reach for my rucksack, keen to retrieve my binoculars, ready for tomorrow morning when I'll use them to scan the shoreline for Marcus Crane and his fishing rods.

As I rummage inside, my fingers brush against an object that feels unfamiliar. Having deposited the banana and water bottle in the kitchen, I'm fairly sure the only item remaining in my backpack should be my binoculars. I locate the optics, twirl the neck cord around my fingers, lift them free and set them on my bedside cabinet. I reach back into the bag and feel around for the mystery item nestling at its base.

It's cool to the touch, rectangular in shape. I can't fathom what it is that I've inadvertently left in there. Something from school, perhaps. Having got a decent grip, I start to tease it from my bag. It snags a couple of times but eventually I lift it clear. Turning it over in my hand, a smile creeps across my cheeks because it's not something left in there by mistake at all. It's been placed there quite deliberately. By someone else. By Marcus Crane. What I'm holding in my hand is a small, slightly rusty oil can. And right here, right now, it seems like the best gift I've ever had.

38

Sunday took an absolute age to rear its head, but it did, eventually. With the first two jobs of the day complete, namely breakfast and hiding my newly acquired oil can, I'm asked if I want to go with Penny and Laura to an antiques market at a local airfield. It's a bit like asking me if I'd like to chop my own head off. Of course I wouldn't. Why would I? I'm thirteen. I've sat through that programme on TV countless times. What's it called? Oh, yeah, *The Antiques Roadshow*. It's cult viewing in our house. Dusty items of shite hauled to some dusty old stately home, and pored over by even dustier old people who, frankly, given their unparalleled ability to fake excitement at the objects dumped in front of them, should have pursued a career in acting. As if that's not bad enough, that Bruce woman always rocks up halfway through with a collection of objects championed as having historical significance but which are worth fuck-all.

The only reason I'm allowed to refuse to accompany Penny and Laura is because Bridgette needs to work again. I haven't been able to work out if her job is driving a wedge between her and Penny or whether Bridgette's using it as an excuse to spend less time with her. I've not completely ruled out Penny and Laura choosing activities that preclude Bridgette from joining in, either.

Last weekend, the pair of them attended an art class. Life drawing, which apparently involves a model whipping their undies off and reclining on a chaise longue for an hour or two. A female model in this instance, meaning Laura's loss was Penny's gain. So, Bridgette was left behind. Bridgette hates art, whether she's making it or looking at it. She admits she's rubbish at drawing. And trust me, she really is. Back in Loxby, for a laugh, we asked her to draw Penny. The end result was so bewilderingly bad, Laura had to ask Bridgette to point to where Penny's face was meant to be. A lot of suggestions were put forward that night as to what Bridgette's piece of art resembled. After much debate, a turd in a sombrero was settled upon as being the most accurate.

There's another reason I'm permitted to stay in while largely unsupervised; two days ago—despite it looking highly unlikely—Mr Crane managed to get me home *before* Laura and Penny returned from work. Bridgette, being Bridgette, hadn't even noticed I was gone for almost two hours. That woman must think I have a high boredom threshold if she thinks I'm happy to ride one hundred yards in each direction for that amount of time. The more I think about it, the more I'm put out that she didn't think to glance out of her study window at least once to check I was OK. Neglect. That's what it is. There are phone numbers kids can ring for just this sort of thing. I decide to put that particular course of action on the backburner... for now.

There's a double garage as part of Lakeside. Calling it a garage is a stretch, mind. Traditionally, a garage is somewhere you store cars. You'd be hard-pressed to get anything with four wheels in this junk-filled space. Unless it belonged to

Noddy. Seriously, what *is* all this stuff? Every object that has ever existed is in here; cardboard boxes, bags of compost, a lawnmower, a bag which at first glance seems to contain… well… more bags, old tools, a spare tyre, a trug full of leaves, two stacks of firewood, a few sheets of warped plywood, and more… lots more. And that's just what I can see from near the door opening where I keep my new bike. The tools will belong to Scott, I reason. I'd be telling him to get his arse down here to collect them or else they'll be chucked in a skip. Not that he'd turn up. That man's useless, and like his tools, he should also be sent to landfill.

Given the spikey atmosphere at mention of his name, that break up must have been one miserable chapter in their lives, so it's no wonder he's not quick to show his face round here. His name is rarely mentioned, and when it is, it coincides with a shift in Laura's mood, the woman's mind often retreating for hours on end before the Laura we know and love returns to us. Of course, I'm only seeing the destruction from one side. Scott probably has a different version of events to tell. Perhaps one day I'll get to hear it.

For now though I flick my bike's kickstand and start to wheel it outside when my peripheral vision spots something glinting in the far corner. It's hard to make out due to the presence of a large sheet of plasterboard in front of it. Curiosity gets the better of me, and after leaning my bike against the door frame, I carefully pick a route through the myriad of dross, aiming for the rear wall. My foot snags on an old desk fan causing me to lose my balance. I would have recovered if I hadn't overcompensated, banging my knee on a crate which resulted in a polished wooden box falling to the ground, scattering its contents on the concrete floor to the accompaniment of metallic-sounding clangs and plinks. Cutlery. A whole set. The sort of thing an expert on *The Roadshow* would raise an eyebrow at before delivering the news that it was worth cack-all.

Honestly, I'm gonna make my feelings known on the state of this garage later. It won't all belong to Laura, some of it will have travelled with us from Loxby, no doubt. Not the tools though. Throughout my life I've never once witnessed my mums, or Laura for that matter, attempt any kind of DIY. I can forgive Laura; there would have been a time when her husband might have assumed that role. It sounds old fashioned but it's a division of labour that still works for many. My mums have no excuse though. When they've had a drink—which is always—they love nothing better than to champion women's rights. I'm cool with it, it's important, and I'm more than conscious that many of their attitudes have rubbed off on me. Show me a lad at school who tries to impress his mates with a "kitchen" gag, and I'll introduce my boot to his shin.

My mums will sit there for hours talking of injustices and the measures required to address them. I smile when I hear them, since they're each preaching to the converted without seeming to realise.

A year or so ago, in Loxby, in the dead of night, the curtain pole in my bedroom came away from the wall. Frightened the shit out of me, it did, as the metal pole clanged on the radiator during its descent. I spent almost four months with a piece of cardboard gaffer-taped across the window as a makeshift curtain. In the end, having grown fed up with living life as a mole in complete darkness, I dropped our drill and screwdriver set onto the breakfast table. Both women looked from the tools, to me, and back again. Then to each other.

Penny snorted. 'What are these for?'

'The curtain pole in my bedroom. I'd like my curtains back please.'

'Someone's got out of bed the wrong side this morning,' Penny said. Bridgette sniggered causing my irritation levels to ratchet up another notch.

'So, are you going to fix it?' I asked, eyeballing each of them in turn.

Both women looked at me as if overnight I'd developed special needs.

'Us?' Bridgette asked.

'Of course you. You're feminists right?'

Penny and Bridgette swapped glances, their lawyer instincts kicking in, erring on the side of caution by invoking their right to remain silent.

'So... grab these tools and fix the curtain pole. If you don't know how, there'll be a video on *You Tube*.'

'We'll get someone in, honey,' Bridgette responded on behalf of both of them. Penny nodded her agreement and returned to her cereal.

'You'll get a *man* in. That's what you'll do,' I pressed.

'Well, we're busy working women, darling,' Penny protested.

'Not in the evenings and at weekends,' I snapped.

In unison, the two women regarded the tools in front of them, well aware that their argument thus far—when you considered both women's legal acumen—was thin, petering out before it had even begun. Flawed, ill-thought-through, weak.

'You could have tackled it yesterday if you hadn't lay on the sofa all day with a headache. The headache that was actually a hangover,' I pressed, looking directly at Bridgette.

Bridgette picked up the drill and examined it as if laying eyes on one for the first time. It was a battery-powered model. She squeezed the trigger causing the drill to burst into life. Panic-stricken, she immediately dropped the alien piece of equipment on the table, spilling some orange juice in the process.

'You're rubbish you two. You talk a good game but…' I wasn't sure how to finish my sentence so instead blurted out, 'even that piece of carboard isn't window shaped. Well, it might be but not for *my* window.'

I remember storming out of the kitchen feeling pretty pleased with myself. I'd struck a blow in favour of the women's movement and humbled two of its most seasoned campaigners in the process.

I hovered just around the doorway in the next room in order to hear how the pair would resolve the situation.

'She's got a point,' Penny mumbled.

I heard the drill being picked up from the table again, no doubt receiving a second inspection.

'We could have a go, I suppose,' Bridgette muttered.

There followed a silence so long I started to question whether I was hearing impaired. Penny spoke next.

'We'll get a man in,' she whispered.

***

The garage is dusty, making me sneeze, but I'm nearly at the back wall and even from here I can confirm the nature of the object I saw peeking from behind the sheet of plasterboard. A bike. Silver. It looks to be adult-sized, considerably larger than my own at any rate. Upon reaching it, I run a finger along its top frame, forming a line through the thin layer of dust. I can't see the whole of the bike but what I can see tells me it's in immaculate condition, like it's hardly been ridden.

It'll almost certainly be Bridgette's. She's the sort who buys something on a whim, declares it to be the best purchase she's ever made, then discards it within a week, like a piece of mouldy bread. I look around me. Odd if it turned out to be Bridgette's though, given its position in the garage. She'd have had to manoeuvre it past an awful lot of existing junk to get it to its current resting place. Two sneezes later and I decide I've had enough of this space, so pick my way through the clutter back to fresh air.

That done, I scoot around the side of the house and leg it down to the jetty, binoculars swinging wildly around my neck as I run. I park my bum at the furthest end of the jetty, to give myself the best possible view along the lake in both directions. Before I lift the binoculars to my face it occurs to me that I have no idea what time Marcus Crane likes to do his fishing. But don't fishermen start early? It strikes me as being a hobby men adopt to spend as much time away from parental duties as possible. Start early, home late. Like golf. That game goes on forever, rotund men destroying perfectly nice grass with a new club they've invested hundreds in in the mistaken belief it'll turn them into a better golfer. And when it doesn't, at least they've had six hours with their mates talking about cars they aren't going to buy and women they'll never have. I hear lots of women play golf too, which must really piss off the blokes. A boys' club infiltrated, and to add insult to injury, now getting beaten at their own game.

The sun is behind me which gives me crisp images through the lenses. I locate Marcus Crane's house. He's not in his yard. He could be in his house, of course, but Marcus Crane doesn't strike me as a person who'll be indoors on a day like today. He'll be out, distracting himself with chores, like catching his supper.

In my peripheral vision I spot movement and swing the binoculars to my right. Water and hillside flash past in a blur. I've moved my head too quickly and lower the binoculars to get my bearings. I see the movement again and, keeping my head still to preserve my line of sight, carefully lift the binoculars to my face once more.

I smile. For there he is, Marcus Crane, scrambling down the hillside at a spot maybe half a mile from his house. His progress looks vaguely comical, with him taking tiny, careful steps which gives way to a few yards of bum-sliding after a loss of footing. He doesn't carry much, a rod and a small metal box for his bait, no doubt. I think I can work out the spot he's aiming for; there's a small beach upon which a tree has fallen perpendicular to the shoreline, its trunk projecting well into the shallows of the lake, and I'm certain the end of this stricken tree is the place he'll fish from.

I sweep to my right a little more in an attempt to get a fix on where I'll need to ride in order to get close to Mr Crane's perch—I afford myself a smile at my unintentional pun. If I'm not mistaken, the junction where I turned left to make my approach to the Crane house should be about the right spot. A short distance back from the junction there's a break in the hedgerow and I earmark the location as an easy route for me and my bike to descend from. Easier than Marcus Crane's route to the shoreline, at any rate.

I fix on Marcus Crane again, and smile as I see him picking his way along the trunk of the fallen tree until he reaches its end. He stands for a while, hands on hips, lifting his head to the heavens to feel the morning sun on his face, then easing himself into position, placing the bait box on his lap.

It's time for me to get going.

39

I arrive at what I think is the spot that I'd zoomed-in-on back at Lakeside. The physical exertion of Friday's journey lingers in my legs, worrying really considering I only cycled one way that day. Reassuringly, in getting to this point, I'd passed my landmark, Alan—though in the two days since we last met, she'd seen fit to turn one-hundred-and-eighty degrees to give me the benefit of her considerable arse.

Having dismounted, and temporarily leaned my bike against a small tree, I step through the gap in the hedge and peer down. Earlier, from my vantage point at Lakeside, I may have been deceived when I'd identified this access point as an easier route down to the shoreline than the one Marcus Crane took. Looking down now at the mixture of scrub, shale and rocks clinging for dear life to the steep hillside, I wonder if I shouldn't ride further on to find a better spot at which to make my descent.

A small tree sits halfway down the slope, currently blocking my view of the small beach area where Marcus Crane has settled. If I can reach the shoreline here though, it looks more than possible to complete the short scramble around the lake's edge to reach him. I return my gaze to the terrifying slope that my toes peer over, and any ideas I had about completing the descent while wheeling my bike are instantly dismissed. I'll need all my limbs working in tandem to help me get to the bottom.

The first ten yards or so prove to be heavy going but pass without incident. The small rocks aren't loose as they first appeared, rather the tips of larger rocks beneath the surface, conveniently placed to provide me with a pattern of protrusions I can brace my feet against. Each one gives me the time I need to plot my next few yards. The small tree is only about fifteen yards away, but annoyingly—given the effort I've expended thus far—is still closer to the summit than it is to the shore. My plan is to reach the tree and use it as a resting place to catch my breath before tackling the bottom two-thirds of the slope. If I'm lucky, I'll be able to sit with my back to its trunk with my feet pointing in the direction I've come from.

The sun climbs higher in the sky, and a sheen of sweat clings to almost every inch of my skin. When I reach the tree it will afford me some shade, and I should be able to peer around it and see Marcus Crane. I smile at the thought of meeting up with him again, with his no frills, easy manner. He's the sort of person you can sit in peace with, neither one feeling under any pressure to make conversation. Yet, I also caught a glimpse of a more mischievous side, the other day. Don't get me wrong, it's buried deep in there, locked away with happier, more carefree times. But it's there; there in the man's eyes, in his step, in the lines on his face. It flickers, no more, before retreating to the safety of the depths it rarely allows itself to escape from.

I'm jolted back to the here and now by the squawk of a bird overhead. Close. My next move is an instinctive one, snapping my head skywards and shielding my eyes against the sun. It's enough for me to lose concentration, my focus diverted from my feet, from the route I'd planned in my head to complete the short distance to the tree. My left foot slips, then to my relief grips once more, but the short slide has the effect of twisting my body, and as I plant my right foot to brace myself, it too slips, whipping my body around even further, leaving me off-balance and side-on to the slope. Both feet are sliding now, and I put a hand down in a desperate attempt to slow my descent. Small stones graze my palm but I keep my eyes firmly on the tree, now no more than a few yards away. I'll make it, I think. It'll hurt when I hit the trunk but it'll halt my slide and give me the chance to regroup.

But then something happens. A small rock happens. One that looks innocuous, loose, part of the scree I'm skating down. Except it isn't loose. It's the tip of something bigger below the thin soil. I'm no more than a few feet from the tree when I feel my right leg stop dead, tripping me, launching me headfirst towards the tree with such force that I brace myself for the impact. But thankfully, the trip skews my body to the left, and I'm no longer on a direct collision course with its trunk. And then it dawns on me, I'm not on a collision course with any part of the tree. I'm on a collision course with nothing, sky, fresh air.

Yet… looking up, there's a branch just above head height. My body flies forwards at speed, a rag doll bouncing between rocks, twisting to the extent I'm beyond the point where I have eyes on the branch. In the split second before I lose visuals I plot the position of the branch, stretch my hand to the sky as far as it can reach, and wait for the touch of bark on skin, the touch that will be my cue to wrap a hand around it and brace my arm to prevent me plummeting to the rocks below. Last chance.

It feels too long a wait. The impact must be imminent. Any second. I don't know why I process these thoughts. Perhaps it's my way of surviving this, telling myself it'll all be OK. I feel the wind on my arm, wind not wood. A useless periscope held aloft as the scree hurtles up to meet me. I winch my arm in but it's too late, and the last thing I see before my skull connects with rock is the blue of the water below, and, in the distance, the sun glinting off a long single strand of cobweb in the form of a fishing line.

40

'Flo, can you hear me?'

I recognise the voice, of course.

'I'm here now. You're safe.'

I don't open my eyes. Can't. The pain is pinning them shut. Sometimes it comes as a sharp but short pain, though I can live with that. Other times it arrives as a blunt, long-lived type, the sort you get no relief from, the kind painkillers hold up their hands in surrender to. That's the worst kind of pain. Like the one pushing on my skull now. Even through the blackness it's like a vice, relentless, not for moving, hell-bent on wearing me down.

'You've had an accident, Flo.'

I know that much. I'm aware on a basic level that something has happened but I haven't the strength to look deeper, to look for the cause. What's more, I'm frightened to wake up and see the damage.

There's a period of quiet, and more pain takes the opportunity to rush in. I don't want silence. Silence means I might be alone with my agony. A hand takes my own, caresses it gently, its touch enough for me to briefly divert thoughts away from my suffering.

'I'm going to pick you up now, Flo. Is that OK?'

If I manage a nod, I'm unaware of it. It's possible the decision has been taken out of my hands because strong arms lift me clear of the rocks and water. Sharp pains now, spearing through most of my body causing me to gasp, enough to force an eyelid open in response. The water's clear, a tiny black fish darting back and forth seemingly at random, swimming off when its home turns red. I see the drops falling from the side of my head, and they hit the water like the stones Candy and I threw far into the lake that night.

'Flo. Can you talk? Talk to me, Flo.'

I can't. I'm worried about the fish. Will the whole lake turn blood-red? Will it be able to swim to cleaner waters quickly enough?

I try to move my dry lips, to form them into a shape to allow me to speak. And when I do manage a word, it's breathy and weak, and I barely recognise my own voice. 'Fish,' I whisper.

'Fish... did you say fish, Flo? The fish will all be alright too, Flo. They'll be OK on their own.'

And I'm relieved, my body hurts a little less because of it, clearing a path for my thoughts, allowing my brain to process the accident. I'm not able to recall all of it, just the rocks and water rushing up to me, then me waking, water lapping around my ears, making the world around muffled; the sounds of water stroking the shoreline, a tractor in the distance, all pin sharp then fuzzy as the water rises and falls around my face. Then comforting words from a man whose voice I know well.

'Let's get you back to the car, darling.'

I nod, wince, then scream from the pain of being lifted. 'Dad!... Dad!... It hurts... Dad, no!'

'Flo?'

I must still be in the water. I'm shivering and my dad's voice seems different, somehow. My head lolls to one side and I see the stream I was playing in with my dad. Us jumping from boulder to boulder, laughing when the other missteps, then scooping up freezing cold water in our cupped hands and splashing the other before they have chance to climb out of the rushing water back onto a rock. It's our camping trip, except it wasn't rain that soaked me through that day. I'd failed to recall properly, taking scraps of information, and assembling them into something that made sense at the time. He was warming me from my accident in the stream at the campsite; later the same day telling me that my chipped tooth would be made perfect again, my broken wrist strong again. My dad always keeps me safe and warm. I love my dad.

'I love you, Dad,' He doesn't respond. I so badly want him to know. And I want to hear his voice telling me the same as he carries me to safety. 'Dad?'

'Flo?'

There's that voice again. The noise of the water recedes, and I'm aware that I'm no longer shivering. Warmth closes around me, pain smothered. The natural sounds I heard moments ago retreat, replaced with man-made tones, an alien chorus made up of random chimes that mean nothing to me.

'Flo, darling. Can you hear me?'

My eyelids flutter, then open a fraction, but shards of harsh light tunnel their way in, forcing me to close them again.

'Flo? It's me, Laura.'

'Laura?' I manage, barely able to hear my own voice. I blink twice, allowing just enough time between each to allow my eyes to adjust to the harsh, fluorescent light.

Her face is no more than a few inches from mine. Another person stands to the right of where I lie, a nurse, I think, and I side-eye her, even though doing so makes me groan with pain. Both women offer up smiles they know won't be returned, not for a while, not yet. Not until I've been delicately revived to full consciousness.

41

Three weeks is a long time to spend in hospital. For one of those I didn't have my own room. For two of them I wasn't even conscious. An induced coma is what the doctor called it. He'd explained the process and potential long-term health consequences to Penny and Bridgette. Then, when I was well enough, he had to explain the whole thing again to me, poor bugger. They were waiting for the metrics to fall within the right range, before reviving me, he explained. It's crucial apparently not to act too soon, or worse still, too late.

The day I was helped back to consciousness it was Laura's turn to sit with me. How mind-numbingly boring must that have been, each of them taking shifts to look at my lifeless body, seeing a twitch where there wasn't one, becoming frantic when the beeping from my heart monitor changed time signature.

I'm told Penny flipped after visiting me one night after a particularly difficult day in the office. She was asked for the umpteenth time by Mrs. Grantham—a busybody with a bowel condition who'd taken the bed opposite—if there was any sign of me waking up. Penny, by all accounts, had shown remarkable restraint in the week leading up to this point, but when Mrs. Grantham followed up with, 'Well, you start to worry they won't, don't you? Some never do. You see it all the time.' Penny had told her to, 'Shut the fuck up', then marched off to see the ward sister to demand some changes.

Quite where Mrs. Grantham acquired her medical knowledge was a mystery, although Penny assured me she smacked of a woman who was likely at her happiest when in hospital, chewing the face off anyone who happened to be within range, coughing out her extensive medical history at will. Ultimately it was me who made the move, not Mrs. Grantham. Moved to a private room with a tiny TV and no Netflix (again), though seeing as my stay in the room was mostly spent in a coma, I had no right to be prickly about either of those things.

I was glad to be rid of the gown, though. A nice nurse by the name of Charlotte told me I'd feel better if I was wearing my own pyjamas. I didn't like to tell her my pyjamas had been bought for me by Bridgette, who at that time still thought it was acceptable for a thirteen-year-old to wear anything *Disney*. Instead, I placed an order with Penny to find me something suitable. She did OK, ignored the pyjama theme completely, and returned instead with plain, black tracksuit bottoms and a black t-shirt which bore a picture of a white cat and the caption, "I do what I want."

It was a slightly odd purchase given that Duncan died a few years back, and I've never personally owned a cat. That said, the gesture was appreciated and considering my mums' chequered history when it comes to buying clothes for me, things could have been a lot worse.

I'm relieved to have my own room, too. Sometimes my door is left ajar and the ward chatter reaches me in the form of beeping machinery, squeeze boxes to help patients breathe, cries during the night from the disorientated, and Mrs. Grantham's farting. I'm grateful for the peace.

My injuries were explained to me first by a doctor, and then by Charlotte in a vocabulary I could understand. It was quite a list, comprising—but not limited to—fractured skull, severe bleeding on the brain (hence the induced coma), broken collar bone, one broken wrist, four broken ribs, and a dislocated kneecap. Oh, and a chipped tooth. There was also the loss of dignity at having to shit through a tube but we don't dwell on that. Just like we don't dwell on Bridgette knocking the medicine trolley over while playing charades across the bed with a fellow visitor. I wasn't aware of this incident, of course. Not until a fellow patient had mentioned it after I regained consciousness. I asked Penny for more details but she was reluctant to elaborate, so one day, after Charlotte had administered my pain killers, I prised some more detail from her.

'Not much to tell really,' she said, turning in the doorway on her way out. 'Caused a hell of a scene, mind. Pills everywhere. Sister was fuming, I remember that much. Oh, and the pharmacist had to be recalled to sign-off on any meds that hadn't been administered up to that point.' Charlotte puffed her cheeks out at the memory.

'Oh God, how embarrassing,' I said through a smile I was struggling to suppress.

'It was Daphne who was doing the rounds with the trolley. First we knew of it was when we heard the crash as it tipped over. Sister was livid for days. Still, it's done with now, and it gave us nurses a good laugh.'

Charlotte chuckled to herself and turned to leave when a thought occurred to me.

'Was it a film?'

Charlotte wheeled round. 'Eh?'

'Or a book… or song… the charades? What was Bridgette acting out?' I asked

'Oh, a film,' Charlotte replied before raising one eyebrow. '*Dumb and Dumber.*'

42

Two days after waking, a detective came to see me. Not Tom. He was deemed too close to my family to 'discharge his duties impartially.' Those were the words quoted by Detective Harry Field, a dishevelled-looking man who needed to ease up on the hair dye. After reassuring me there were no right or wrong answers—which is something I'll ask him to repeat to my maths teacher when I'm back at school—he asked for my account of the accident.

I was under the impression I'd summarised it nicely with, 'I fell down a hill and banged my head,' but that didn't cut it with Detective Field, so I was asked to elaborate, to give a full account of my actions that day, from the time I left the house to the time I lost consciousness.

It seemed straightforward enough, until it wasn't. The detective would take my answers, dismantle them, and present them back to me, but reworded in such a way that the amended answer didn't quite fit with the original question. Connotations were added where I'd suggested none. I told Detective Field that I'd visited Mr Crane a couple of days before my accident.

'Did you arrange to meet again?' he probed.

This to me implied we'd arranged to meet the first time.

'No. Mr Crane said he thought it was best if we didn't,' I replied.

'But you *did* meet him again, didn't you Flo? On the day of your accident.'

'Yes, but… that wasn't… that was me—'

'How did you know Mr Crane would be fishing that day, Flo?' Detective Field attempted a smile to put me at ease but it was a wholly insincere one, and his thin, dry lips only served to further irritate me. 'Mr Crane told you it was best you didn't meet but then told you where he could be found fishing. Is that right, Flo?' His smile had already disappeared. 'It sounds to me like he wanted you to meet with him after all.'

'No… he just told me that he fished on a Sunday. He didn't tell me where.'

'Did you tell your parents about your *first* meeting with Mr Crane, Flo?' Detective Field asked.

'No.'

'Why not? Did Mr Crane ask you to keep your meeting secret?' His questions came thick and fast, and I was increasingly confused, unsure of the answers I should give.

'No!' I cried. Detective Field recoiled at the ferocity behind my answer.

'Alright. But presumably you told your parents you were going to meet him on the day you had your accident, right?'

'Penny and Laura went to an antiques fair,' I said, hoping that would suffice as an answer.

'But Bridgette is your mum too, not just Penny. That's right isn't it? And she was at home wasn't she? Why didn't you tell her, Flo? Were you scared to? Why did you keep it a secret?'

After this latest round of rapid-fire questioning from the detective, a woman seated in the corner of my room, who, to that point had remained silent, decided to interrupt.

'Detective, that's a lot of questions. Can I suggest you keep to one at a time, for Flo's sake.'

The woman had been introduced to me as Sue. I remember her name because I distinctly remember thinking she looked nothing like a Sue. Definitely more of a Wendy, or at a push, Pam. Sue was the only reason Detective Field was allowed to talk to me at all. She was from Child Services, or something like that.

Detective Field looked unhappy at his ticking-off, but nodded politely, and started again. 'I'm sorry Flo, my bad. I—'

You shouldn't say that,' I interrupted. Detective Field's eyebrows lifted an inch, as he tried to replay in his head what he'd said and how it could have been construed as offensive.

'I'm sorry?'

'"My bad." It's cringeworthy when adults say that. "Cool"—there's another word you should steer clear of. Bridgette described my bike as "sick" the other week... month... whenever it was. The point is, don't ever, ever use that word either.' Out the corner of my eye I saw Sue, staring, unblinking. 'Anyway, what were you asking?'

'Er... right... yes... why didn't you tell your mum you'd arranged to meet Mr Crane?'

'Because I hadn't arranged to meet him,' I said.

'But you went to see him and didn't tell either of your parents. That's right isn't it, Flo?'

'Yeah.'

'So why didn't you tell them about meeting Mr Crane?' he began. 'It's OK to be frightened, Flo. No one is going to be mad at you. None of this is your fault.'

'I know it isn't. It isn't anyone's fault. I had an accident, that's all,' I protested.

'Why didn't you tell your mums, Flo?' he urged again.

'Because everyone around here thinks Mr Crane is bad, but he isn't. He's nice. He was nice to me.' The words are out of my mouth before I can stop them.

'Nice? In what way, nice?' Detective Field dives in, shifting forwards in his chair, feeling closer to getting the answer he wants to hear.

'Well... he saved me when I fainted at his house. He caught me. And he gave me a glass of water,' I said, the words tumbling out in my haste to defend Mr Crane.

'Did Mr Crane give you the glass of water before or after you fainted, Flo?'

'What?'

Detective Field repeated his question.

'I... I... Before. And after. It was the same glass, I think.'

Sue took that moment to rise from her chair.

'I think that's enough now Detective, don't you?' She cast him a look that told him it was, no matter what ideas he might have to the contrary.

Detective Field did have ideas to the contrary, but he also knew how easily a case could be jeopardised by pushing too hard, especially where minors were involved.

'Yes... well I think we're done, Flo. Thank you so much,' he said as he rose from his chair. 'You've been a big help and you've been very brave. Goodbye, Flo.'

The detective left. Sue followed shortly afterwards after having a brief word with me to explain what I could expect to happen over the coming days.

As I sat there sobbing, tears streaming down my scratched cheeks, I felt anything but brave. I did feel angry though, because the sum total of what I'd been told to this point was that I'd been rescued after falling into the lake. And I'd been awake for two whole days now. Two whole fucking days.

43

Candy is allowed to visit. I wanted to see her as soon as I awoke from my coma, but my doctors were insistent on limiting the number of visitors I received. They needn't have worried; I've been sleeping through most of my days and nights. Half of Cumbria could have stood at the end of my bed and I wouldn't have noticed.

I'm tired today too, but the sight of Candy nudging the door open, peering in, frightened of what she might see, gives me a new lease of life. I shoot her a huge grin and begin the lengthy process of propping myself up. It's an operation I take in stages, and very slowly. One limb moved at a time to limit the pain. By the time I'm upright, I'm breathing heavily, and Candy takes this as her cue to help, picking up a pillow, plumping it into shape and sliding it behind my back. As I lean forwards to allow room for this to happen, I wince when my ribs remind me they're not fully healed.

She picks up on my discomfort immediately and I'm rewarded with a Candy kiss, her lips remaining pressed to my cheek for longer than normal, with more firmness. When she finally withdraws her face, it bears a tear.

'Hey. What's the matter?' I ask, reaching for her hand, instantly wishing I hadn't when my collarbone protests at being moved.

'Nothing,' Candy splutters. 'I'm just so happy to see you. Happy you're going to be OK.'

'Glad to hear it,' I reply. 'And anyway, if anyone's gonna be crying round here, it's me.' I shoot Candy a reassuring smile.

'Oh, God, you must be in so much pain,' she says, looking my body up and down. I can tell it's killing her to not be able to give me a hug.

'I've been better. But it's alright, there's a nice nurse here, Charlotte.' I nod towards the tall stand beside the bed. 'She loads that bag up with morphine and the pain goes away.'

Candy looks at me from head to toe and back again. 'You've done this to get out of school, right?' She laughs at her own joke and I can't help but join in.

'Yup,' I respond, a thought occurring to me. 'Hey, I bet Mr Hole has done an assembly about me. I wonder if more leaflets were handed out.'

'Leaflets?' Candy says, confusion etched onto her face.

'Long story. Doesn't matter.'

'When will you be allowed home?' Candy asks.

'Not sure, but I think it'll be at least a week yet. I need to have scans on my head every few days.'

'What will happen with school?'

'I think Penny and Bridgette have contacted the school to let them know it's unlikely I'll be back before Christmas. Seems like a long time. I bet I won't be able to get out of schoolwork though, but it beats being stuck in a classroom.'

'Oh, that reminds me, I brought you something.' Candy delves into her rucksack and retrieves a laptop. It has various stickers on its lid, the most prominent among them being a photo of the cast of *Friends*. 'I thought this would stop you from getting bored. You can use it for schoolwork too, if you like.'

'What? No, I can't take this. This is yours, Candy,' I say, genuinely touched by the gesture.

'I'm only lending it to you. I won't need it for a while. I finished school yonks ago.'

'Yeah, I know,' I protest. 'But you'll need it to keep in touch with friends and stuff.'

'Exactly. You're my friend so I'll be able to keep in touch with *you*. You can add your email account. I have my phone so we can chat by email,' Candy explains.

'That's really nice of you, Candy,' I say. 'Give me a hug.' She leaps to her feet and before it's too late, I quickly add, 'a gentle one!'

And it *is* gentle. I barely feel her hands through my t-shirt, hardly notice her head when it rests on my shoulder. I feel another shot of morphine and exhale deeply as it cools my veins. I'm living a strange existence right now, one I'm lucky to be living in at all. I need to look to the future, to good times with my family, with Tom and Candy. Especially Candy.

I inch my mouth closer to Candy's face, preparing to speak. I've forgotten to thank her for the laptop, to say how grateful I am, and right now it feels like the most important thing in the world that she knows. I realise all too well, of course, that what I'm really thanking her for is for being my friend, for the kisses, the hugs, the closeness. I feel heavy, yet light at the same time, the painkillers counteracting my bodyweight, dulling my lucidity, and threatening to rob me of this chance to tell Candy what I need her to know. My lips part to form the first word but my eyelids flutter, one of them brushing Candy's hair. I'm so close to sleep, I don't even hear the words that fall from my lips.

'Thank you, Dad.'

44

When I wake, my room is in darkness but for the ambient light from the machine I'm tethered to. Soft light spills in as Charlotte opens the door and pops her head around the frame. 'Are you OK, Flo?' she whispers. 'Do you need anything?'

'No, I'm fine thanks, Charlotte,' I manage in return, my voice weak and dry.

'OK lovely, I'll pop back in a couple of hours,' she says, making her exit.

'Oh, Charlotte. When did Candy leave?'

'Oh, the tall woman? Blonde hair? Was that Candy? You've mentioned her before,' Charlotte says.

'Yeah, that's her. Do you know how long ago she left?'

'Oh, hours ago, darling. She said she'd left you the laptop so I locked it in your cupboard while you were sleeping. Candy asked for the Wi-Fi code before she left. Paid for a week, I think. So that was nice,' Charlotte says, checking over her shoulder to make sure our conversation isn't disturbing other patients. 'Oh, your mum and her friend came too but you were sleeping for most of the day. They asked me to say hi.'

'Thanks Charlotte. And thanks for looking after me.'

'Oh, don't be silly, Flo, it's my job. You're no trouble.' Charlotte pauses. 'Well… most of the time.'

'Oi!' I cry. Charlotte's eyes widen as she puts a finger to her lips and shushes me.

'It's funny,' Charlotte begins, 'Your mum's friend... I'm sure I recognise her.'

'Yeah probably. She used to live round here. Years ago,' I mumble, feeling sleep taking me once more.

'That's what I thought, so I asked her. She said we couldn't know each other because she'd never lived here before. Oh well. And there was me thinking I was good with faces. Turns out I'm not. Anyway, night Flo.'

'Night,' I whisper.

I lie flat, my gaze fixed on an unremarkable ceiling tile, and I wonder why Laura lied to Charlotte.

Charlotte didn't need to tell me that my 'mum and her friend' came to visit. I knew they had. Because I saw them. It's why I had no need to ask Charlotte *which* of my mums had visited. Because I saw it was Penny.

I don't know why I pretended to be asleep when they arrived. I'm not proud of myself. Perhaps it's because I was too tired for a visit. Or perhaps it's because I felt I'd had a lovely day to that point, one that couldn't be improved upon.

They didn't see my eyes open a fraction when they got up to leave. They didn't look my way when they stood by the door. If they had, they might have seen clues of the guilt I was feeling for the pretence; my chest rising and falling a little faster under my t-shirt. Had they paid attention they might even have heard my heart monitor singing a faster tune.

But they didn't pay attention. But I did. And the guilt I was feeling evaporated as I watched them console each other with a long, tight embrace.

***

I come round, unsure how long I've been sleeping. I know it's still night-time because my room carries the same depth of darkness, and through the small pane of glass in the door, the ward beyond remains washed in its earlier tone of grey. I'm feeling more alert, my body grateful for the downtime I've given it. I allow my head to loll to my left, in the direction of my bedside cabinet. Seeing as Candy has paid for Wi-Fi, I may as well use it, I think.

I know it's going to hurt—the process of extricating myself from this bed. It's only yesterday that I made my first trip to this room's bathroom. Even then, I didn't manage the journey unaided. A substantial woman by the name of Becky helped me out of bed, then fairy-stepped me to the toilet and back. Each shuffle taken was agony, every one of my injuries teaming up to torture me. Halfway across the room I wasn't sure I'd make it, but Becky held me upright while I paused, and she waited patiently with me until I'd gathered the stamina to try again.

I won't have to travel nearly so far for this journey, just a couple of feet, but at the end of it I'll need to bend down to the cupboard in order to retrieve the laptop. Bending down is almost unbearable as I found out yesterday when lowering myself to the toilet, every bone and nerve-ending in my body screaming at me to stop.

I'm not about to give in now though, so I begin the performance of gingerly moving my legs to the edge of the bed. I'm holding my breath as I move, a soft whine rattling about somewhere at the back of my throat.

'What on earth are you doing?' It's Charlotte standing in the doorway, hands on hips, looking particularly displeased.

'Oh, hi. Was… just going… to get the… laptop,' I manage, breaking between words to take in oxygen through my clenched teeth.

Charlotte is at my bedside in a flash, lifting my legs back to where they came from.

'You shouldn't be walking alone. Not yet. What if you fell? What if you fell and hit your head? It could be really dangerous you know? Any sort of impact to that thick skull of yours before it's fully healed could be really bad.' Charlotte bends to the cupboard, unlocks it and retrieves the laptop. She places it on my lap and skilfully eases me into more of an upright position. 'Besides, you've got the call button. That's what it's there for, to call for help. Use it next time!' Charlotte looks at me now, gradually dropping the stern face and fixing me with a smile. 'Alright?'

I nod and contort my face into a grimace, my mouth turned down at the corners, lips pushed back from their gums, upper and lower teeth perfectly aligned and clamped shut. In short, I've turned myself into the *Creature Comforts* tortoise aimed at giving Charlotte a look which says *Sorry!*

Charlotte laughs. Wags a finger at me and says, 'I mean it, Flo.'

With us both grinning at each other, she leaves the room and I open the laptop.

Normally, a laptop comprises a keyboard and a screen. This one is no different other than it also carries a pink Post-it-Note. I recognise Candy's beautiful handwriting immediately.

"I hope this gives you the answers you're looking for."

Candy has added her name and three kisses.

It's a puzzling note.

I don't have to switch the machine on, because it springs to life as soon as I open its lid. I don't know why, but I expected to find a chaotic desktop, a muddled space filled with rarely used apps, rogue documents, and a nagging message urging me to perform ten years' worth of Windows updates. Basically, like Bridgette's laptop.

In contrast, Candy's desktop is sparse, the few loaded app icons just the right size and neatly arranged. The wallpaper is what really stands out though, to me anyway. It fills the screen corner to corner as you'd expect, and because the desktop is a largely clutter-free space, the photo is revealed in all its glory. It's a photograph of Candy and me, our arms draped around each other's shoulders, laughing, a filter-free selfie taken of us sitting on the jetty, with water and hillside as its backdrop. The kind of photo that best friends upload to *Instagram* but usually with less smiling and more pouting. Because Candy has taken the shot, her arm looks huge, something I'll want to rib her about next time she visits. I smile as I look at the two of us beaming straight into the lens, though my smile drops as my eyes fall on half an inch of motorboat at the very left-hand edge of the screen.

A click on Alt-Tab reveals that a single application has been left open: Google Chrome. Given Candy's highly organised desktop, it seems odd to me that she wouldn't have closed it down. The pink Post-It Note winks at me from the bedsheet: *"I hope this gives you the answers you're looking for."*

There are two tabs left open on the browser's top bar. It must be a deliberate move on her part, to leave the content active. I click on the first tab. To begin with, the page starts to buffer, and I wonder if Candy has activated the hospital's Wi-Fi correctly, but after a few seconds the screen snaps into focus and what I'm looking at is a newspaper article.

MAN HELD OVER DEATH OF JOSEPH NEWMAN

To begin with, I try and scan the article, keen to get a handle on its content as quickly as possible, but I'm not getting the gist of it. I need to read it properly, absorb the detail. So I do, and when I finish, I fall back against my pillows, conscious that the beeping machine next to me has upped its tempo.

And it's only after reading the article properly that I understand Detective Field's line of questioning, his constant probing, him manoeuvring me to where he wanted me to go, guiding me back on track when I meandered away from his preferred narrative. I hold the key for Detective Field and his colleagues, this broken thirteen-year-old girl who everyone seems gobsmacked to still be alive. I'm the one who can confirm their suspicions, give the answers they seek. And that's why I know he'll be back.

Joseph Newman was a young local man who lost his life in our lake's waters. Fishermen reported seeing a body being dragged from the water by a man who subsequently discarded the deceased on the shoreline. The man then left, seen climbing the hillside alone. He was identified by the fishermen as Marcus Crane.

With a trembling finger hovering over the laptop's trackpad, I click on the remaining browser tab:

JOSEPH NEWMAN
FIVE MONTHS ON - FURTHER LAKE DEATHS
MAN CHARGED AND RELEASED FOR A SECOND TIME

Things become a little clearer upon reading the second article. It comes five months after the first. It recapped and added detail by way of explaining that police were still reluctant to accept Marcus Crane's version of events in which he explained he'd first seen the teenager's bike as he descended the hillside from his home in order to fish. Worried at seeing a bike minus its rider, he'd picked his way the short distance around the shoreline to where the bike lay a few yards up the hillside. It was only then, according to Mr Crane's testimony, that he'd found the body of the young man in the water. He told detectives that having pulled the body clear of the water, he'd tested for a pulse, and when he found none, scrambled up the bank to the road where he hoped to find help. As it transpired, the fishermen had already contacted the police who intercepted Mr Crane before he could raise the alarm himself.

The article concluded with reference to the more recent arrest of Mr Crane in connection with the death of his wife and daughter after the car they were travelling in plunged into the lake. It summarised the case for the reader by explaining that having been charged with his family's murder, Mr Crane was subsequently released and all charges dropped. Suspicion had pointed his way due to a substantial life insurance policy taken out less than six months prior to his family's deaths. Mr

Crane's argument all along was that the life insurance policy was purchased in order to provide for their daughter Sienna, in the event of his or his wife's deaths. The coroner was unable to prove that Hettie and Sienna Crane's deaths were anything other than accidental, and a verdict of death by misadventure was reached. Mr Crane was eventually charged with careless driving, a charge to which he pleaded guilty in court.

45

My eyelids ping open in panic. My groin area is hot. 'Oh, bollocks, I've pissed myself,' I mutter miserably. I'm also aware I've dribbled, my chin slick with saliva. Up until now, the days spent with my arse hanging out the back of my gown signalled the lowest point during my time here. I may need to reconsider.

Luckily, I haven't pissed myself, it's the warmth from Candy's laptop I can feel. Any eroticism I might normally attach to this is quickly dismissed in favour of getting to the bathroom in order to pee. Rather than wait for a nurse doing their rounds to assist me, I use my call button, reasoning this will make Charlotte happy. It's not Charlotte who comes to my rescue though, and I make a mental note to berate her over her abandonment of me in favour of taking time off. Doesn't she realise she should be at my beck and call twenty-four-seven?

After an agonising return trip which sees me cover ten yards in eight minutes, I'm settled back in bed, preparing myself for another long day of sleeping, eating shite, shitting-out that same shite, sleeping some more, and pretending I feel better than I do in front of visitors.

It's a simple itinerary, one I'm comfortable with right now. I'm not even pissed off that this place spectacularly fails to provide me with any flashbacks to my previous life. I'm done with all that for now. Currently, I'm more interested in Marcus Crane. I get the distinct impression the police still believe he continues to deceive a lot of people, them included. Have I been deceived by him too, I wonder? You hear of trouble following certain people around. Usually crooks. Is Marcus Crane one of those people? A magnet for trouble? Or is he a magnet for tragedy, attracting more than his fair share of bad luck. Two very different things, though I doubt Marcus Crane, even for one second, would consider himself unlucky.

There are always those who claim to be unlucky but are they, really? The person who wins a prize at a raffle and declares '*Wow. This is a shock. I never win anything,*' statistically will have been victorious the same number of times throughout their life as the next person. People feel better about themselves if they can find excuses for why they haven't done better, that's what it comes down to. For instance, the person who gets passed over for promotion will point to a whole raft of reasons why they've been overlooked but not once will they admit that it's probably because they're crap at their job, or have too many spurious sick days, or fail to get along with colleagues. They'll label themselves a victim of circumstance, someone who's just plain unlucky. Bridgette falls into this category. Well, one of its sub-categories at any rate. Bridgette would consider herself unlucky that her car rolled back off the driveway that day. At best, it was careless, but in reality it was just massively stupid.

Take me for example, in the time since I was admitted to this hellhole, three separate people have branded me as 'unlucky'. But was I? Not really. And I told them that. Was falling after tackling a 1:2 gradient wearing a t-shirt, shorts, and

212

trainers, with no climbing experience, and coming away with serious injuries, unlucky? No. If anything, it was more probable than not that I *would* hurt myself. Would I take the risk again? Maybe. Probably not. My collarbone twinges causing me to stiffen. Alright—no.

There's a rap on the door. There are only two different types of raps I've identified thus far. Three if you count the cleaning and kitchen staff who don't knock at all. During the night, the nurses win gold for having the gentlest knuckle rap, loud enough for you to know they're about to enter but not so loud for it to fully wake you if you're snoozing. The doctors, however, take the door rap to the next level. Theirs is done with little consideration for what might be taking place on the patient-side of the room. Their knocks arrive as turbulent things, loaded with irritation, fury, and, above all, a weariness rearing its head at the tail-end of a sleep-deprived fifteen-hour shift. *Doctor here; job to do. If you're naked, tough shit.*

I wonder what species will be on the end of the fist that's currently pounding the door. The knock, when it first arrived, was so weighty it gave me a start and caused sharp pains to scurry back and forth across my rib cage.

When Detective Field explodes into the room I'm not sure whether my next words are as a result of pain, or merely due to the sight of the man himself.

'Fuck's sake.'

I make sure to give a smile of apology to Sue, the Child Services worker who beetles in behind him.

'Morning young Flo,' he says brightly. I muse on the logistics of acquiring a gun while I'm a resident in this joint. Preferably one of those that shines a red dot on the person it's

213

aimed at. I'll point it towards Detective Field's bollocks, then draw his attention to it by nodding in the direction of his crotch so he knows what's coming.

The detective removes the coat that frankly I'm astonished he's wearing at all given the relative humidity in this place; a cloying, unrelenting bastard of a heat rivalling that of a rainy August night in Mississippi. He scans the room for somewhere to hang it, and when he finds none, lays it across the bedclothes towards the end of the bed. I don't feel the weight of it but I wince for effect anyway, then raise a single eyebrow to suggest he might want to reconsider. He sighs, gives the room another recce, and settles for hooking it over the portable stand carrying my drips of many colours.

That done, he eases himself into one of the visitors' chairs and opens his notebook.

'So, Flo, I thought we could pick up on where we left off yesterday. That OK with you?'

'Why do you suspect Mr Crane of wrongdoing?' I ask. By the expression on his podgy face, he's not happy that I've ignored his question, and even less happy that I've chosen to pose one of my own.

'I didn't say we suspect Mr Crane. Now if we—'

'No. But you do, otherwise you wouldn't be trying to make me say bad things about him.' I fold my arms. I may only be thirteen but I can easily manufacture an attitude a much stroppier teenager would covet. 'Mr Crane was found innocent of the deaths of his wife and daughter and also innocent of the murder of Joseph Newman. I'm not stupid, Detective Field, I know you're trying to find that elusive piece of evidence that'll shed new light on those cases. Well, I don't have anything for you. I went to visit Mr Crane. It was my choice. He wasn't expecting me. I fell and hurt myself which is why I'm here. End of story.'

'Look, Flo, I—'

'And by the way, no one has told me how I was recovered from where I fell. I can take a pretty good guess though. Marcus Crane found me, didn't he? Marcus Crane lifted me from the rocks and carried me to… where? The roadside? He doesn't own a phone so the only choices available to him were to leave me on the shore or take me somewhere safer. And since I have a memory of being lifted clear of the rocks and water, I'd say he carried me back up the hillside.'

'That's Mr Crane's version of events, yes.'

'Version of events?' I splutter. 'You're doing it again. Thinking the worst of him. Did you ever stop to think Marcus Crane might have saved my life that day. If he hadn't seen me fall, how long do you think I'd have survived with these injuries?' I sweep a hand from head to toe to remind the detective how catastrophic the damage turned out to be. I feel myself becoming upset as I think of Marcus Crane plucking me from the water, doing the very thing for me that he couldn't do for his own daughter—save her life.

'He may well have saved you, yes. But my job is to look at these things from all angles,' he says with a gentleness I've thus far not seen in him. I feel slightly sheepish for ranting at him.

'I just feel sorry for him, that's all. He lost his family, but he can't move on with his life because people continue to point the finger at him. Not just you. Everyone round here does it. I think the guy deserves a break.' I've leaned forward to add bite to my argument and the effort catches up with me.

215

I slump back so hard I feel the metal head of the bed through my pillows. 'You fucker!' I wriggle my bum further down the bed so my head finds more pillow. Detective Field looks aghast. 'Oh, God, not you. I wasn't talking about you. I just hurt my head. Sorry.'

'We can do this another day, Flo,' It's Sue who speaks, casting anxious glances between me and Detective Field.

'No, I'm fine. Thanks for asking. But I'm fine. I would like to know one thing though before we carry on. I mean if that's OK?'

Detective Field considers my request before setting his notepad to one side.

'Alright, Flo. What do you want to know?' he asks.

'After Mr Crane carried me up the hillside, how did he raise the alarm?'

'He didn't,' Detective Field confirms. 'A passing farmer saw Mr Crane with you in his arms. He was exhausted by all accounts. You were placed on a tractor's flatbed trailer and the farmer called for an ambulance using his mobile phone. So, you were lucky that this farmer…' The detective picks up his pad and flicks back a couple of pages to consult his notes. '… er… ah yes here it is… a Mr Sanders. Bill Sanders. Do you know him? He works a farm not far from where you live.'

'Not personally, no,' I reply. 'I'm better acquainted with his cow, Alan.'

46

Yesterday's grilling from Detective Field wasn't so bad. After he'd begrudgingly dealt with my questions, he spent the next five minutes asking how I'd become acquainted with Alan. Specifically, whether it was Mr Crane who'd introduced us? And when? And if we'd ever been alone in the field? (I took that to mean Mr Crane and I, rather than Alan and me). I could tell he was unsure if there was merit in pursuing the cow as a line of enquiry. He was reluctant to dismiss it out of hand though, since in his head, it was a link between Mr Crane and me. Given the number of eyebrow-raised glances cast my way from Sue in the corner of the room, it was as obvious to her as it was to me that within Detective Field's police manual, Alan would sit squarely within the chapter headed "Clutching at Straws".

The rest of our chat followed pretty much the same pattern as yesterday's. Me telling him what I could remember from those few days, him telling me I might be misremembering, suggesting alternative scenarios that I may have forgotten to mention. And so it went on, an endless loop that as an exercise served no purpose other than to take us nicely up to the point where my breakfast was delivered.

Detective Field left with his tail between his legs, mainly on account of having received a bollocking from the ward sister for using my drip stand as a coat hook.

***

I sigh. My morning to this point has been a complete waste of time. I sincerely hope what I'm about to do next will be more rewarding. My plan is to see if I can uncover the name of the boat at Lakeside. It still troubles me that someone saw the need to remove its name in such a hurry, explicitly to prevent *me* from knowing it.

Opening Candy's laptop, which I can see will need recharging before long, I research boat ownership. Between government and private websites there's a heap of information readily available. The rules governing the registration of boats differ depending on whether it's a sea-going craft, or one to be used solely on an inland waterway such as a river, canal, or lake. Sea-going vessels must be registered with the UK Ship Register, whereas powered vessels used for business or pleasure on lakes must be registered with the specific authority appointed to that stretch of water.

With a simple search, I find the organisation that looks after the lake that Lakeside backs onto. It's responsible for new registrations and renewal of existing ones. It's fairly cheap to register, and in return the boat owner must prominently display their craft's registration number, while adhering to strict rules governing the type and size of font to be used. I minimise the browser to enable me to see the wallpaper photo of Candy and me. The motorboat is partly visible but there's no registration number in evidence. It'll be hiding beneath the tarpaulin, I suppose. Like its name used to.

As if that wasn't dispiriting enough, I can't find any way of searching the site for a list of registered boats. And it isn't possible to search by owner either. As a last resort, I plump for a general search in Google Chrome, typing in Laura's name and adding the words "boat" and "name" to the search string. It returns nothing.

I close the laptop. Eating breakfast and playing detective are two tasks too far for me this morning, so I roll my head back, shut my eyes and give myself freely to sleep.

47

I'm fully recovered and find myself in the large barn belonging to Marcus Crane. Marcus isn't home. I stand just inside the threshold and let my eyes wander, forming a relief map in my mind of all the building's contents, all of which have been pushed to the perimeter walls, stacked neatly, loose items now in boxes and labelled. "Car", "Paint", "Hand Tools", "Bike Bits". My heart lurches when I spy three or four labelled "Hettie" and "Sienna".

A psychiatrist would say Mr Crane was compartmentalising his past. And it certainly looks that way. Except there's an anomaly in the form of photographs. Hung on every wall. Dozens of them. Not carelessly pinned in place at odd angles to each other, but each in its own ornate frame and hung equidistant from the next; photographs that should be inside a home, mounted on emulsion- painted plasterboard walls, not displayed here as some kind of shrine in a damp timber-built barn.

There remains only one object in the centre of the room and it stands there on the pristine floor like an actor taking centre stage, its spotlight a shaft of light from the open door. Unintentionally or not, the beam lends the object a significance. A central character in the story.

It's Sienna's bike with a chalk line scrawled around it on the floor, marking its spot, akin to the outline of a corpse at a crime scene, only this one rectangular. And as I stare at the line, I'm aware of a long, stretched-out creaking sound behind me, then a thunderous crack as the open-door slams shut, throwing the scene into darkness, but not quite—a pencil thin beam of light pierces a gap between two timber boards that have slipped over time, striking the bike's chrome bell on its handlebars. On hearing the door bang shut, I don't turn; I don't feel the need, choosing instead to be still, inclined to be mesmerised, willing my eyes to adjust better to the darkness.

There's a noise. It's mocking and brutal, *plink... plink...* the sound of the cutlery that fell to the concrete floor in Lakeside's garage, except the sound reaches me from the direction of the bell. A warning. Another bead of light enters, but settles on nothing, moving sporadically, a dancing orb-like spirit. I panic when I lose track of it until I pick up its movement once more. It heads straight for me, then stops. I lower my chin and watch it move erratically on my chest, though deviating no more than an inch in any direction. A dancing red dot. Confined to my heart. And in that instant when the trigger is squeezed, the air rushes from the building crushing my eardrums, the explosion ripping through the structure, a blinding flash of light searing my retinas. And after those forces have careered between floor, ceiling, and walls, I'm all that's left in its path, weightless and blind, the terrible aftershock causing my body to rear up; a galloping, snarling thoroughbred that's reached the cliff edge.

'Flo!'

'Flo?'

I stare blankly in front of me, unsure if I was a player in a dream or one within a flash, a crease in time to something earlier. I'm conscious, I think, but all the things I've seen and heard are still with me, gradually changing form and colour, bleeding from one shape to another: information posters where there were photographs; a bouncing red LED display instead of a gun; the sound of the bike's bell replaced by a cantering beep from the machine monitoring my vital signs. And there's no longer a bike, just my drip stand lit by a fluorescent overhead spot.

And that is my moment of clarity. The point when I realise my previous life has tipped the scales in favour of my current one. This life holds far more mysteries for me now, ones that are present and real, its players complicated within its ever-changing scenery.

'Flo?' There's more urgency to the voice now. Light switches are flicked. The ward sister summoned. 'Are you back with us, Flo?' Charlotte says.

I stare back at her, unblinking, then return to face front once more.

'Yeah,' I whisper. 'I'm back. I'm definitely back.'

48

Tom visits me, bringing with him chocolates and one of the shittest get-well cards I've ever seen. It portrays an indeterminate cartoon animal, possibly a bear but could equally be a beaver, carrying a baseball bat. There's no witty caption, and more importantly no explanation as to why a baseball-playing, talking animal should want to wish me a speedy recovery.

'It's a crap card, I know,' Tom says, pointing at it.

'It's pretty crap, yeah. I hope it was cheap.' I flex it to gauge the stiffness of card used. 'It feels it.'

Tom laughs. 'Don't tell Candy this is the one I bought. She'll be mad at me for weeks.'

'Your secret's safe with me.' I accompany the words with a small salute, and I'm sure I hear a snapping noise from my sternum.

'I'll hide it behind the others.' Tom gets on tiptoes and drops it into position towards the back of the cabinet, ensuring it's properly masked by the other cards I've received. 'I just wanted to make sure you're OK?' he says.

'Yeah. Better every day, thanks. The doctor thinks I'll be home in a week, tops. If you ask me, I think they want shut of me. Can't blame them.' I hitch myself up the bed a little.

'Have the police been treating you OK?' Tom looks down at his hands, wrings them together. 'I'm sorry I couldn't be the one asking the questions. Conflict of interest and all that,' he mumbles.

'Detective Field is fine. I can handle him,' I say. 'Weird though…'

'What is?' Tom responds, sitting up straighter in his chair.

'Well… why they should think there's a conflict of interest. I mean if I was a suspect that'd be different, but since I'm just the girl who got hurt…'

There's a shift in Tom's body language. He breaks eye contact with me, wriggles in his seat, his hands folding over themselves in rapid time, like he's washing them with an invisible bar of soap. And just as I think he's about to offload whatever's on his mind, his facial features relax, and his body and hands settle.

'Nah. It's only because I know your mother from way back.'

'But that was such a long time ago,' I press. 'I can't see why Penny being here should stop you from doing your job.'

Tom smiles and shrugs. 'It's the rules, Flo. That's just how it is. I'd be seen to be too close. Those who count—my bosses—reckon my judgement could be impaired, even just by asking you some harmless questions. Sorry.'

'I guess,' I say. 'Can you at least tell me why the police didn't believe Marcus Crane's version of events when that boy was pulled from the water?'

Tom tenses. 'How do you know about that? Did Detective Field tell you?'

'No. One of the nurses did,' I lie. 'I was curious. She couldn't remember much, not even any names, until I mentioned Mr Crane. Then she told me about the suspicion that hung over his story.' Tom looks relieved that I haven't acquired more detail. It's clear he's weighing up how much he's allowed to say, and more importantly how much he *wants* to say.

He sighs heavily. 'There were inconsistencies with Mr Crane's story. He reported seeing a boat heading to the shoreline below his house half an hour or so before he set off to fish. Shortly afterwards, a couple of fishermen arrived on the scene but swore they hadn't passed another boat as they'd made their way down the lake. We're as sure as we can be there was no other boat, and at the time we were convinced Mr Crane fabricated the account to deflect scrutiny from himself. But, we had a problem, it was a late afternoon in Autumn so light was fading fast, and the two fishermen— good, honest, reliable lads—who'd spotted Mr Crane... well... they'd been drinking for some of the afternoon. Even though we believed the fishermen's statements to be true, we simply couldn't use it as part of any prosecution. It was all a bit of a mess, really.'

'OK,' I say, struggling to think of further questions, knowing full well they'll come to me as soon as Tom leaves the room.

Tom smiles and claps his hands together. 'Anyway, you're quite the interrogator, Florence Aters-Fabishaw. I hear you asked more questions of Detective Field than he did of you?' Tom says, a broad grin finding its way to his cheeks.

I suspect Tom and his colleague don't always see eye to eye.

I chuckle. 'I did. I just wanted to know what happened after I lost consciousness, that's all. And to be fair to Detective Field, he gave me the answers.'

Tom raises both eyebrows to go with the smile that still stretches across his face. His mischievous look is back. 'Someone at the station overheard Detective Field making a call to a local farmer about some cow or other. No one quite knows what's behind it but he's never going to live it down, all the same. When one of the constables made him a coffee this morning, despite knowing that Detective Field takes his coffee black, he yelled over, "Do you take milk these days, sir?"'

I laugh, though quickly try to stifle it when the accompanying pain plucks my ribs. 'Don't,' I say, unable to prevent the first tears of laughter spilling down my face.

'Even his secretary got in on the act by asking him if he'd be pursuing any udder lines of enquiry.'

At that, I'm not sure what leaves my body first. It could be the small thread of snot from my nose but I can't discount the tiny amount of wee that escapes as I double-over in hysterics, snorting and howling with both pain and laughter. My face paints a picture of agony and ecstasy in tandem.

'Oh, God,' I splutter, taking a moment to compose myself. 'Right, for making me laugh, you've got to help me to the toilet,' I say, swinging my legs to one side, noticing how much easier the manoeuvre seems even since yesterday.

It must be a pitiful sight as we shuffle across the lino floor, but I'm glad he's here. It's nice to have a man in my female-dominated world. I'm growing to see him as the father I don't have... well... I do, obviously, but I'll probably never know who he is and I'm not sure I'll ever want to. He was a donor, nothing more. That much has been made clear to me by my mums. A man who filled a tube so I might live. Noble, in its own way.

And yet, as the bathroom door shuts behind me, I can't help but feel there's more to the man who waits patiently on the other side.

49

I'm told that as long as the doctors are happy with the scans I'm to have later, I'll be discharged at the end of the week. Today is Wednesday. I'm moving quite freely now, and mercifully I'm detached from the bedside monitoring machine. A nice man is currently seated by my side, a physical therapist called Clive. A shit name for a decent specimen of a man; a name completely at odds with his appearance. Men called Clive don't generally tend to be fit, not ones I've met anyway. And I've met lots. Well… a few. None, actually. Still, that doesn't change the fact it's a shite name, and if I were him I'd be changing it, pronto.

Clive can be no more than early twenties and I study his face while pretending to listen to details of the exercise programme he's drawn up for me. It's a striking face, high cheekbones for a man, a strong jaw that isn't too narrow and not too square, and azure blue eyes, made more vivid when offset against his near black hair. I take a second to compare him to the boys in my school who lack his aura, his assuredness, his adult frame. At school I'm surrounded by skinny tadpoles with long limbs, acne, and senses of humour so underdeveloped it seems unfair to mock them for it.

Clive is the sort of man I'm deeply attracted to. Whereas the lads at school would try and blag drinks for me at The White Horse with the rest of the chavs, Clive would take me to a seventeenth-century country bistro where we'd drink excellent sauvignon by the fireside.

'Can you do that for me, Flo?'

I tune into his sentence late, though I can tell by the tone of his voice he's asked me a question. Shit. I try and read his face for clues. I'm fairly sure he hasn't asked me if I'm free for cocktails on Saturday night. He looks to his printed sheets, his exercise plan tailored specifically to me. I take a chance.

'God yes. Definitely.' As an answer it covers most bases but just in case he's looking for something more specific from me, I nod in the direction of the planner. 'Will you leave that with me now or do I take it with me on Friday?'

There's no adverse reaction from Clive to suggest I've given an answer totally at odds with his question. I breathe a sigh of relief and admire the shape of his eyebrows.

'Yeah, sure. Take it now. I can always get another sent to you if needs be.'

'Would you like my email address?' I ask, far too hastily. What the hell am I doing? I'm being too eager. Dial it back, idiot.

'I'll attach it electronically to your patient file. That way you can request it at any time. Patient services will be able to forward it on to you,' he says, in a tone far more business-like than I was hoping for.

And with that, he ups and leaves. Leaving me with my hormones, a sheet of A4 and a sense of what might have been.

Clive disappears into the abyss that lies beyond the door of my room. No doubt onto his next patient who knowing my luck will be female, single, nearer his age, with fuller lips, bigger tits, ten times more beautiful and with fewer broken bones.

I shoot a wistful look towards the glass pane in my door— my window to the bustling ward, its characters, its noises, its smells, its deaths.

I shriek. It's almost a scream, but screams happen in films, not in real life. In real life, the terror that's in front of you shocks you so violently it instantly drains you of the energy required to vocalise your fear. The logical thing to do is to look away, protect your senses from what's in front of you. With fear, though, instinct always trumps logic, your body automatically defending itself by arming itself with the facts required to decide upon fight or flight.

Not taking my eyes from the door's tiny pane of glass, I sit straighter, pressing myself against the metal frame at the head of the bed, while simultaneously easing myself to the farthest edge of the bed. I'm whimpering now, a guttural sob, my left arm flailing frantically for the nurse call button that unbeknownst to me has fallen to the floor, out of reach. There's no help coming and I've got nowhere to run from this woman whose eyes look pleadingly at my own.

The woman's olive skin is wet, as is her long, dark hair, water dripping from its bedraggled tips onto the neckline of her hospital gown. Her breath mists the glass but I can still see her brown eyes that look beyond my own, to within me, searching, beseeching. I know this woman. I saw her that day when our family visited Lakeside for the first time. She stood by the ambulance while a body was stretchered from its rear doors. Stood there, as she does now, soaked through to the skin beneath her hospital gown. That day, her face was framed by the car window I looked through. Since then, just days ago, it was a printed image within a photo frame, mounted alongside a dozen others like it.

I'm looking at Sienna, Marcus Crane's daughter. She was part of my dream, part of my flashback, and I feel now what I felt then. This woman was part of my life.

And in an instant, her face disappears from its current frame. It doesn't exit left or right, doesn't turn, simply vanishes. I stagger to the door as quickly as my healing injuries allow, groaning with the effort, ignoring the residual pain. I yank the door open, and step into the corridor, eyes darting wildly in all directions. But there's nothing to see. No sense of panic from the nurses' station at the end of the corridor. No mystery patient. Nothing to suggest there'd been anything or anyone on the other side of the glass.

And even the orderly standing not two feet from me, doesn't look up, just continues to mop the wet floor.

50

We sit opposite Mr Hole—Penny, Bridgette, and me. Penny made the appointment on Friday. Bridgette was supposed to have done it but forgot.

I'm glad the weekend's over following my return home from hospital. Both my mums fussed and clucked around me, moving pillows when they didn't need moving, making food when I wasn't hungry, asking if I was comfortable seconds after I'd dropped off to sleep.

I'm using the sofa bed in the living room for a couple of days, purely to save me the journeys up and down the stairs. It's fine, I've got everything I need there: TV; shower room; kitchen; and as of yesterday—after I insisted the sofa bed was reorientated—a lake view, though according to Laura, its new position gives off a negative vibe and is messing with the room's feng shui. A bit rich considering the room is still playing host to that monstrosity of a coffee table. My new living accommodation is all well and good but it lacks privacy. There's always someone buzzing about with little attempt made to buzz quietly.

We're late for our appointment. Mr Hole looks at his watch twice as we take our seats. He looks a third time because Bridgette wasn't paying attention to the previous two. Mr Hole embarks on his routine for getting himself seated. I glance across to see Bridgette frowning in incredulity at each step of the process. When Mr Hole pulls himself towards the table she looks my way and smirks. I try to stop the snigger from escaping but fail. As does Bridgette. Penny scowls at us both, which makes things worse.

'Well, firstly, let me say how good it is to see you back on your feet, Florence,' Mr Hole says, not once directing his words towards me.

'Thank you, sir.'

'Yes, well, I understand you'd like to know how we intend going about schooling young Florence while she's absent from school. I gather she'll be away for some months yet?' He directs his question to Penny, the woman he's decided is our family unit's alpha female.

'That's right,' Penny confirms.

'Right, well, I've asked Florence's form and subject tutors to email her a reading list at the beginning of each week. This should keep her up to speed for when she returns.'

Does he realise I'm in the room? He should, I'm sitting directly opposite him, a child filling in a parent sandwich.

'That's not going to work for us,' Penny announces. 'How will we know if Flo's keeping up?'

I bristle at the suggestion I might be a slow learner. I'm in the top ninety percent in all my classes—well... the ones that matter, anyway.

'Oh, from what I've been told, Florence is doing exceptionally well with her studies, so I don't think we need to overly worry about her.'

Mr Hole goes up in my estimation, which admittedly isn't too difficult seeing as he's starting from a benchmark populated by microbes.

'Here's what I'd like,' Penny starts. Mr Hole twerks in his seat, inching himself taller in anticipation of the onslaught he feels coming. 'Each day, Flo's teachers will set up a *Zoom* call so she's getting one-to-one tuition. I'm not talking about much time, fifteen minutes perhaps, enough to make sure Flo understands precisely what her course work entails and to give her the chance to ask any questions.'

'I er... I don't think that will be possible. Our teachers have very busy schedules and—'

'What's more, I expect a partial refund for the period of time Flo is not physically attending lessons. You can't expect us to pay full whack when we're getting less for our money.' Penny sits back, folds her arms, daring the goblin opposite to challenge her.

'I'm afraid that won't wash with the school governors Mrs. Aters-Fabishaw. Our fees are non-negotiable.'

'Well, if that's your stance, we may be forced to withdraw Flo from your school completely.' Penny isn't ready to give up, but Mr Hole is pumping himself up to his full fighting height. Something tells me he's more scared of the school governors than he is of my mum.

'I'm afraid if you were to withdraw Flo from this school entirely you would be liable for the whole year's fees. There's nothing I can do about that.' Mr Hole mirrors Penny's body language by folding his arms. It's the world's two shittest sumo wrestlers facing off.

'Sir, might I say something?' I ask, calmly.

Three pairs of eyes lock onto mine, Penny and Bridgette then exchange a nervous glance before training themselves back onto me once more.

'Do you have equality and diversity targets, Mr Hole?'

Mr Hole shifts his eyes side to side, worried about the tangent I've taken.

'Well yes, we do but—'

'And would you say those targets are currently being met, sir?' I interrupt, keeping my voice level.

'Erm… I'd have to—'

'Let me help you out, sir. Unless your diversity target's minimum is set at two students of colour and one pupil from a same sex household, I'd suggest you're falling well short. And your situation hasn't been helped now that Harry Jenkins—your only disabled pupil—has finished his GCSEs. It must have been quite a blow to find out he and his wheelchair won't be staying on to do A-Levels, sir.'

Mr Hole's lower jaw flaps up and down, but no words come forth.

'I'm no expert, sir,' I continue, 'but I'm surmising that it won't look good for you if a pupil that sits firmly within a minority group—as I do—is forced to leave the school she loves. It's the sort of thing the press like to get their teeth into. I'll probably be interviewed, a photo taken of me on my sick bed, my two mothers behind me, their faces wracked with worry.'

I allow my words to hang in the air a while. Penny and Bridgette have been glued to me throughout my monologue, and now turn to face my head teacher in anticipation of his retort.

Mr Hole removes his palms from the desk, leaving two sweaty imprints behind. He sniffs, and when he talks it's with a conciliatory tone.

'I think we may have got off on the wrong foot,' he says, forcing a smile which doesn't reach his eyes. 'I'll recommend to the governors that, given Florence's serious accident, we as a school should pull out the stops to make sure her education doesn't suffer.'

'And my mums will see half my school fees waived for the period I'm away?' I press.

Mr Hole swallows. Twice. 'Yes,' he mutters. 'I'll see what I can do.'

I nod my thanks to Mr Hole.

'I'm feeling rather tired,' I announce, turning to each of my mums in turn. 'I think I should rest now. Thank you, sir. You've been very understanding.'

Mr Hole's confidence returns at this, his face carrying the look of a man who believes he's successfully negotiated a positive outcome for the school. A hard bargain struck. A skilled arbiter at the top of his game.

We file out of his office in a line, like three schoolchildren being dismissed. I'm pleased with my contribution, though I can't help thinking the protective skull cap I'm having to wear for the foreseeable future—while looking utterly ridiculous—lent my argument some weight. I became the vulnerable child who feared she might be let down by an education system slow to change, slow to embrace diversity.

I always knew the minority card would come in useful.

51

My head injury is what's preventing me from returning to school. My parents are too nervous about me being in an 'unpredictable environment'. So, for now, I'm at home which suits me fine.

What doesn't suit me—literally and figuratively—is my protective skull cap. Bridgette is pretty relaxed about it but Penny insists I wear it when I'm doing anything other than sitting or lying down. The other day I walked two paces to retrieve my phone (bought for me after I played the safety card) from the coffee table and was bellowed at by Penny for making the journey without my head protection in place. This could get tiresome very quickly.

Today, I'm expecting Candy to visit. There are two things that are going to happen. Firstly, I won't be wearing my crash helmet in front of her. Secondly, I'm going to enlist her help with finding something that I suspect might be in the garage: photos.

Each year I put together a photo book as a record of the previous year's events. I'm interested in photography, you see, and where possible I take my decent DSLR camera out and about with me, capturing landscapes, mainly. My camera phone only really gets used for snaps of family and friends. Collating all the shots, selecting the best ones, and discarding the dross takes a lot of time, something I have in abundance these days. I'm late creating the book this year, normally I'd have it designed and printed by the Spring, but in my defence there's been a lot going on.

I'm out on the decking near the house when I hear the doorbell. I'm watching Mr Crane go about his business, though from this end of the garden my binoculars don't quite have the reach they do from the jetty. He's making journeys to and from the large barn, the one which houses Sienna's bike, the one I dreamed I was standing within. Each time he returns from the building he carries a handful of items, then carefully places them down in his yard. In what looks like a well-practised routine, he breaks off for a minute to feed the birds, placing seed on top of one of the rusted skeletal pieces of machinery. Small birds swoop in, comfortable in his company, undeterred by his proximity to the improvised feeding table.

I'm forced to leave him alone to answer the door to Candy, where we exchange our obligatory hug and cheek-peck.

'Follow me,' I say cheerfully. 'I need your help looking for something.'

'Ooh, how intriguing,' Candy squeals.

Candy squeals a lot.

With the garage door open, we both stand hands on hips staring into the disorganised space, sunlight catching specks of hovering dust.

'What are we looking for?' Candy asks, suddenly not sounding so enthusiastic now she's seen the haystack from which we're to find our needle.

'My camera, for starters,' I begin, 'and there should be a couple of memory sticks.' I look Candy's way and pass her a look of apology for seeking her help in searching for items so tiny.

Candy rubs her hands together, presumably to generate some enthusiasm rather than heat, and starts to pick her way through the disarray.

The first thing we notice is a complete absence of logic when it comes to where packing boxes are placed, what they contain, and who their contents belong to. Because Laura had been living with us for so long in Cambridge, she had to ship a lot of her possessions back to Lakeside at the same time we did. Some boxes are labelled, I can see one that reads "Dining Set", for example, but the majority are unmarked. I take the left-hand side of the garage. Candy takes the right.

I'm distracted by a giggling to my right. Candy has unearthed a photo album from a box marked "GARDEN". The decision to place a photo album in that particular box would prompt head scratching in most. Not me. I know that Bridgette was the person responsible for most of the packing. Candy flicks through the album, giggling at the photos that chart my early life from baby to toddler. There's one of me holding a large kitchen knife which surely can't be good practice.

We both agree that given the discrepancy between this particular box's label and its contents, we'll need to methodically search every box to find what we're looking for.

Luckily, it's not long before I locate my camera, and I carefully remove it along with a tripod and a few other accessories. Maddeningly, the memory sticks aren't in the same box and it's essential they're found since they contain most of the material I need.

We're making progress, in more ways than one. Anything brought from our old house that looks destined to spend the rest of its life in one of these boxes—because it's either crap or broken—I toss onto the drive. I throw with force to ensure anything merely crap becomes broken too. It's both fun and therapeutic; a candle-making set and a breast pump the latest items to make the short journey from garage to driveway.

I hear a snigger to my right. Oh Lord, I think. What the hell has Candy uncovered now?

'Alright… what is it?' I ask, in a way a teacher might at the first signs of giggling from the back of the classroom. When Candy doesn't answer I look harder, but she's crouched over a box, her head bowed, her long curls masking her face. I'm sure she's crying. 'Hey,' I say gently, making my way over to her. 'What's wrong? What is it, Candy?'

She doesn't look at me, remains fixed on the box at her feet, with me standing over her. I want to crouch down next to her but there's no room, so I do the next best thing and place a hand on her shoulder. Her head moves a fraction in the direction of my hand, acknowledging the gesture, or else taken unawares. She takes a few seconds, a few deep breaths and wipes a tear from her face. Then without saying a word she closes the box, stands, turns, leaves the garage, and makes her way down the side of the house in the direction of the back garden.

It's all so unexpected, so out of character. I want to be with her, to comfort her, tell her that whatever's made her sad, will go away. I make to follow her but the box won't allow me; I'm at the centre of two things requiring my attention, pulling me from opposite directions.

I make my decision and squat in front of the box, its uninteresting exterior surely belying whatever lies within. Having lifted the twin carboard flaps of its lid, I peer inside, resisting the urge to touch anything. Whatever moved Candy to tears must be amongst the contents' top layer, I suppose, but staring inside, I see nothing obvious responsible for triggering Candy's unexpected emotional reaction. I can see a spice rack, some tea towels and a small magnetic chess set. I reason it's not impossible for one of these objects to hold sentimental significance for her, though for the life of me I can't imagine how. I remove the objects one by one. A few minutes ago, I'd have chucked both the spice rack and the chess set on the sizeable pile of scrap on the driveway. Not now. The only remaining items in the box are a pair of curling tongues and a can of slug pellets. I mean, why the hell isn't that in the box marked "GARDEN"?

Candy sits on the jetty, her knees brought up to her chin. As I get closer, she looks first to me, then across the lake. The breeze catches her hair, momentarily lifting it from her face, drying her tears. Taking care not to rush, partly for my own sake, partly for Candy's, I ease myself next to her, my knee complaining and ribs protesting, until I'm in place, motionless once more. I take a couple of deep breaths as quietly as I can until my aching subsides completely.

'What happened back there, Candy?' I ask.

Candy doesn't answer, instead choosing to lean her head on my shoulder. I can smell her hair. Roses. It always smells of roses. We sit like this for five minutes, maybe more, until Candy gives up her secret.

She removes her head from my shoulder and raises the hand that until now lay limp on the other side of her body, concealed from me. In it she grasps a small piece of paper. No, a photograph. Without a word, she holds it out in front of me.

It takes me a while to process the image, and when I do, I'm assaulted with a flurry of images of my own. Strong ones. Arresting. Haunting. I'll deal with those later. For now, I slip my arm around Candy's shoulders, the sides of our heads touching as we both stare at the glossy picture in Candy's trembling hand.

In itself it's an unremarkable photograph, showing Candy and a boy sitting in front of the motorboat as we are now, arms around each other. It could be us—if we were smiling. She and the boy look impossibly happy with their sparkling eyes and white grins set off against sun-blushed skin. It's the sort of photo taken at the precise moment laughter erupts, the result of a shared joke or a tickle to the ribs done immediately before the shutter is pressed.

Candy continues to stare at her image, looking for meaning she knows won't come. Not now. It's been too long. Any meaning disappeared the day the case was closed.

'What's the name of the boat, Candy?' I ask softly. I ask because the pair of them are obscuring it in the photo.

She lifts her head slowly from its resting place, turns to face me, a single tear one blink away from freedom.

'My boy Joseph.'

52

Joseph Newman.

There'll be a grave somewhere bearing this name.

There'll be a mother who stands at its headstone grieving for her boy. A mother with a different surname to his, to the one she used to share with him. A different Christian name too, perhaps?

At the hospital, almost a week ago, a stranger called after us as Laura wheeled me from the canteen. She didn't flinch at the name he used, didn't turn her head towards the voice. At the time, I assumed the man was addressing someone else beyond us. Julia was the name he called out, and I know if I delve deeper into the boxes in the garage, I'll find evidence of Laura's previous identity being Julia Newman. And in a registry office somewhere, there'll be a certificate recording the birth of a boy named Joseph Newman, son of Julia and Scott Newman. It all begins to fall into place; my nurse, Charlotte, thought she recognised Laura, but Laura denied having any knowledge of her.

At some point, Julie Newman, or Laura Pollard as I've always known her, must have felt she had no choice but to start again. And the best way to do that, as painful as it must have been, was to break ties. She'd found a new place to live within a new village. She'd put distance between herself and this place with its haunting scenery and familiar faces loaded with pity; distance from those who'd silently judged her as the woman who neglected her child, who wasn't there for him when he needed her. How could a person continue to live under that scrutiny? You could lock yourself away, a hermit between your own four walls, but you'd be condemning yourself to a lifetime view of the hillside where death took your child. Every morning you'd throw open your curtains to another gut-wrenching day devoid of the answers you crave, a day filled with a despair so toxic it would render you unable to function. You could stay, of course, find the resolve to move around the village and nod greetings at its residents as normal. Laura could have stayed and faced her demons, but not everyone is strong enough.

Penny must have had a hand in it, helping her friend to leave this place. As a lawyer, she'd have been able to complete the paperwork, process the change of identity by deed poll.

Once upon a time a person could leave for pastures new without the need for an identity switch. Not now, not since the internet barged its way into everyone's homes. A stray photograph on Facebook linked to a friend of a friend of a friend to someone living in Laura's new village is all it would take. Or an internet search by an employer, done by way of a background check on their prospective new employee.

It's clear to me that if Laura felt she needed to leave her old life behind, then she had to leave *everything* behind, including her name. I'm grateful she didn't have to face this alone, and I'm proud of my mum for being there to guide her. I think back to the evening in the hospital where I was brought round from my coma. I think of how difficult it must have been for Laura to watch a young person flirting with death. And days later, when I pretended to be asleep, when I was out of danger, with doctors having declared I'd make a full recovery, Laura looking on, unable to comprehend why her own son couldn't have been so lucky.

I think of the risks she's taken by returning here, the courage she must have needed to draw upon. Of her wondering if enough time had passed for people to fail to recognise her. Praying that juicier stories might have displaced her own; stories more current—another unexplained death, or an affair between teachers, perhaps.

Was Laura testing the waters in those couple of weeks we spent holidaying at Lakeside? A prelude to a possible permanent move? A break intended as no more than a gentle transition, with the majority of our time spent confined to the house and garden? Unwittingly, I'd dispatched any chance of Laura taking a softly-softly approach when, at my request, and on only our second day here, we attended the party on the pitch. I shoved her straight into the lions' den that day. An event that must have been teeming with familiar faces, rife with the nudging of elbows. I console myself with the thought that it also served up a reunion with Tom and Candy, two people who Laura finds joy in being around.

It must be somewhat unique, I think, for a friendship to bloom that has death as its common denominator; the unlikely alliance of grieving mother and detective, him unable to provide answers for her son's death, unable to build a case against the only suspect, Marcus Crane. For those very reasons, it can't be easy for Tom either, I suppose. Knowing him as I do now, he's not a man to easily shrug off his failings. That was evident when he recalled the tragic story of Marcus

245

Crane and his family. It affected him to talk about it, and though he kept his face a picture of neutrality, there was no hiding the restlessness in his eyes, or the distress in his voice. Tom is a man who's had to deal with his own tragedies, and it would have been easy for him to side-step Laura's grief, but he helped her face the past head on, like the good man he is.

Then there's Candy, the woman who watched it all through a child's eyes. Her mother succumbing to cancer, Joseph's life terminated for reasons no one can explain. It occurs to me I don't know the nature of Candy and Joseph's relationship. Were they two friends, or more than that?

'Candy?'

She sniffs, still buried in her thoughts.

'Was Joseph your boyfriend?' I ask.

Candy looks to the heavens, runs a sleeve across her face, and nods.

53

Before Tom collected Candy yesterday, Candy and I agreed we wouldn't reveal that I've uncovered Laura's past. It's partly for Candy's sake since Tom made her promise to keep it from me, but mainly out of respect for Laura who doesn't deserve to have the life she's trying so desperately hard to move on from, laid bare by a nosey child.

Today will be interesting. I'm currently seated opposite a man called Tony, a careers adviser, touted round to schools in this region to help pupils decide on their GCSE subject options. He's been strong-armed into doing a home visit today. My home.

Bridgette is the only adult here today. She offers the man a choice of a gin & tonic or wine. A glance at the clock reveals the time as eleven-thirty. In the morning.

'Do you have tea?' he asks in reply.

Bridgette looks at the man like he's some sort of extra-terrestrial. I'm the next face Bridgette looks towards as she repeatedly clucks her tongue against the roof of her mouth. It's a cry for help.

'Tea bags are by the toaster. Cups in the second wall cupboard from the left,' I announce.

Bridgette chuckles nervously. 'I know!' she says, rolling her eyes and tutting for Tony's benefit.

What follows next is the sound of cupboard doors being opened and slammed, proof that that not only did she *not* know the location of everything needed to make tea, but that she'd also forgotten my instructions on where to find them. Instructions I gave approximately thirty seconds ago.

The only positive to take from it is that Tony doesn't take sugar.

'So, Florence—'

'Flo. You can call me Flo,' I say, taking charge without Tony realising it.

'Great, Flo. Er… thanks. So… I'm here to help you make subject choices that best match the type of career you see yourself in. And don't worry if you don't know what that is right now, either. It might be that you only have an idea of the general sphere you see yourself working in, or which subjects you might like to go on to study at A-level. So what I'm trying to say is, there's no pressure but sometimes I'm able to—'

'Voice-over artist.'

I sit back in my chair. Tony leans forward, reaches for his notes.

Bridgette takes this moment to enter with tea. There's been so much liquid spilled, I wonder if it'd be easier to drink from the tray, and what little remains in each cup looks to be one part tea and two parts milk. Bridgette looks mightily pleased with herself. Tony is a man who's weighing up how much he'll need to drink in order to remain polite.

'Er… thank you er…'

'Bridgette,' she says.

'Well, thank you, Bridgette,' Tony says.

Bridgette folds her arms and smiles. 'No one calls me Bridge or Bridgey.'

The confusion is etched on Tony's face as he replays the last few exchanges of their conversation in his head.

'Sorry,' he says. 'I didn't think I called you—'

'Men tend to do it... when they... you know... when they want to sleep with me.'

'No. I...I er... I don't want to sleep with you,' Tony says, already fearing for his career.

'Why not?' I join in, with added incredulity. 'What's wrong with Bridgette?'

Tony's face turns ashen. The room becomes still, heavy, broken only when Bridgette and I start laughing. We stop when the colour returns to Tony's cheeks and when we're sure he realises we were only messing with him.

Bridgette sashays off in the direction of the kitchen leaving Tony and me to talk careers.

'Sorry,' Tony says, having completely lost the thread, and like as not, the will to live. 'You mentioned a career, I think.'

'I did. Voice-over artist,' I announce confidently.

Tony starts thumbing through his notes, discards those and reaches instead for a printed booklet.

'Voice-over artists are sometimes known as voice actors,' I continue.

Tony's face brightens at this. 'Ah... actors... acting... yes here we are.'

I give the man an encouraging nod.

'Right Flo... so is this something in the first instance you'd look to do a course in? At college or university, perhaps?'

'I don't know. What courses are there?' I ask.

'Yes… well…' Tony gives up on the booklet's chapter index and begins flicking wildly through its pages, his eyes hunting desperately for something he can lock on to. Anything with the vaguest connection to my dream job.

He must have landed on something because his shoulders relax and his lips arrange themselves in something approaching a smile.

'You can do a theatre course. It's the route actors take. Drama schools… yes… that's what they're called,' he says, prodding a finger at the open page in front of him.

'Wouldn't that involve dancing and singing? It'll just be my voice I'm hired for, like on the radio or a TV ad, or in a video game. That's where the best work is right now—video games… *Resident Evil.* Whoever voiced that must be coining it in with all those sequels. Then you've got Alexa. How do I become the next Alexa? What subjects should I opt for?'

Tony left shortly after, promising to do some research, which was nice of him. I'm to expect an email from him with some links.

***

Tom drops in later the same day. Bridgette is drafting his will, something he says he's put off for far too long. God, there's so much talk of death around here. The pair disappear upstairs to Bridgette's office and I head outside for some air. I stoop to collect my skull cap on the way.

'Fuck it,' I mutter, leaving it where it sits, and continuing on my way.

I'm halfway down the lawn when a squirrel bounds across in front of me and shins up a huge oak tree to my left on the garden's boundary. It's arrived from a matching tree to my right—a food source and an adventure playground for what must be the luckiest squirrels around. I watch the animal climb higher, its twitching tail, its throaty grunting splitting the still air, warning others of my presence.

I contemplate their viewpoint from the treetop, higher even than the upper storey windows in the house. They must get an uninterrupted view of the whole lake, this being a relatively small stretch of water. I wonder if their ancestors saw what happened that night, across the lake. If so, what did they see, and who? How drunk were the fishermen who'd spotted Marcus Crane dragging Joseph from the water? Could they have simply been too far-gone to notice they were sharing the lake with another boat? And there are other questions too. How did Joseph drown? Was he a strong swimmer?

I'm at the jetty now. I want to see the boat again, specifically where the name was removed. I want to see it for myself. I lift the tarpaulin and lie on the jetty so my face is alongside the hull where the lettering used to be. The residual adhesive marks the feint outline of those letters that I could partially see when the tarp was in place—the letters with curls below the line—the "y" in "My" and "boy"; *My boy Joseph*.

It's overwhelmingly sad, a teenage boy plucked from his family and friends far too soon. Sadder, in some ways that Laura should feel compelled to remove all trace of him. I hope it's not for my sake. I'd like to know more about Joseph, of his young ambitions, his dreams, his vulnerabilities.

Something niggles me all of a sudden. It's not much but it worms away, wriggling inside my head. I try to banish it, cast it to the depths of the water, but it bobs to the surface, again and again. My gaze switches to the house and then back to my feet as I tap out a rhythm on the edge of the jetty, a morse code of nothingness serving only to allow my brain to clunk and whir. I can't even quite pinpoint what it is that's needling me.

I return to my thoughts from earlier, about Laura making a fresh start, a clean break. I look at it from a different angle, one where I'm not so close, not so attached. It feels a betrayal to even allow space for the thought that's pin-balling around in my head, but I've gone too far now. And isn't that exactly what Laura has done? Gone too far? Going so far as changing your name. Is that not a step too far? Moving to a new area I can understand, to rid yourself of the scenery, to separate what you see from what you don't *have* to see.

A boy dies and to all intents and purposes it's recorded as an accident. So, what's to be fearful of, ashamed of? There'd inevitably be a period of lashing out, of apportioning blame, to someone, anyone. But by changing your name aren't you simply punishing yourself? Aren't you robbing yourself of a tie to many years of glorious family life?

I'm brought to the present by a shout from the house.

'Bye, Flo. I'm off now.' It's Tom, waving both arms above his head, like an overzealous marshal directing traffic in a stately home car park.

'Hang on,' I yell, getting to my feet, walking briskly but gingerly.

Tom starts in my direction and we meet halfway. It's akin to a hostage exchange, and I half expect both of us to carry on

252

walking past the other, me to the safe house, Tom to the speedboat that will carry him to safety; a squirrel overseeing the handover before scurrying away.

'Hi, Tom. Can I ask you some questions?'

I sit on the grass which has the effect of making my question rhetorical. Tom looks unsure.

'Depends,' he says, looming over me so I have to shield my eyes from the sun.

I pat the ground next to me.

'How did the boy die? I mean what was the cause of death?' I ask.

Tom eyes me warily. 'Well, by telling you, I don't think I'm breaking any rules. This is information that's already out there.' He parks next to me, plucks a blade of grass from the lawn, and begins to tear it lengthways down its middle. 'He died from drowning, but it's not quite as simple as that. There was a blow to the head before he drowned. The coroner decided that the head injury would have rendered him unconscious, causing him to drown.' Tom's words are melancholic, slow.

'Was it deliberate? The blow to his head?'

'If by that, do you mean did someone attack him?'

I nod.

'We simply don't know,' he continues. 'We don't even know if the blow was sustained in or out of the water, but we know it happened reasonably close in time to when he entered the water.'

'So, you're saying it could have been an accident?' I ask, my eyes pleading with Tom to fill in the gaps in the story.

Tom nods. 'It could have been. We had to make some assumptions, some of which were more far-reaching than we'd normally be comfortable with.'

'Such as?' I urge.

'Such as... we had to assume that the part of the lake where Mr Crane found him was the point where he drowned. But it's possible that he floated there from another spot. A place further up the shore perhaps where he could have hit his head on the underwater rocks having fallen down another part of the hillside.'

'Like I did?' I suggest.

'Like you did,' Tom repeats. 'When all's said and done, Mr Crane popped up too often for a lot of people's liking,' Tom says, snagging himself another blade of grass.

'And what do *you* think, Tom?' I ask.

'Honestly? I don't know. It confuses me as much today as it did then. It could have been wrong place at the wrong time for Mr Crane. But three times?'

'Two,' I remind him. 'Mr Crane probably saved my life.'

'Fair enough,' Tom mumbles. 'Fact is, people are scared of what they don't understand. Fear of the unknown if you like. That's what Mr Crane is to people round here, someone to be frightened of. To some, he's a murderer, a man who, not content with murdering that boy, went on to kill his own family. To others he's just a mystery, an old fool whose silence and solitude puts him at odds with what's expected from a civilised community.'

I take a different tack. 'What do you think of him as a *person*? Forget the allegations and past cases.'

He shrugs. 'He keeps too much locked inside for me to be absolutely sure.'

'Yeah, but if you had to say.'

'I'd say he's a good man who's trying to make the best of an unhappy life.' Tom tears his blade of grass to keep his fingers occupied.

We sit in silence for a second or two. Both considering our next plays. Tom puts both palms to the turf, ready to push himself to his feet.

'Why are you so sure there was no other boat, then?' I ask, directing my question to the space straight in front of me. 'I mean… if you think Marcus Crane is a good man, why would you think he'd lie to you about seeing a boat?

'It's not as straightforward as that, Flo,' he says. Out of the corner of my eye I catch him glancing at the lake. Still looking for answers.

'Why not?'

'Because what I think or don't think doesn't come into it. It's what we could prove, from the facts we had at the time.'

'Sounds to me like you took the word of a couple of drunk fisherman over that of Mr Crane. Sounds like his way of life and his reluctance to fit in might have coloured the police's opinion of him, just as it does the villagers'.'

'Don't think we didn't check out the properties with boats permanently moored up. We did. Every one of them. We asked all the right questions, got watertight alibis, you name it, we did it.'

I want to ask if Joseph ever drove the motorboat, but I can't. I told Tom from my hospital bed that the nurse who filled me in didn't remember any names, and I distinctly remember Tom not using either of his forenames or his surname at all. He was doing it for good reasons of course, to protect Laura from her secret. As far as Tom is concerned, he thinks I don't know who Joseph is other than being a local lad who lost his life. He certainly doesn't know that I'm aware he was Laura's son. He thinks I only have scraps of the story. And in some ways, I think I still do.

I'll need to find a different angle.

'Was Laura questioned? I mean with her being a boat owner? That must have been horrible, having to do that,' I say, more mindful now of what I can and can't say based on what I supposedly know and don't know.

'I did question Laura, but it was something of a formality since there was a party at Lakeside that day. A big one, where everyone was able to vouch for each other. Certainly no one saw the boat leave its mooring at the jetty. We repeated the door-to-door enquiries at the remaining dozen or so properties and found nothing amiss at those either. We have to accept it for what it was, Flo. A tragic accident.'

'Right,' I say. It wasn't said sarcastically, not quite, but it carried a subtext that even the most oblivious would be able to read: *not convinced*.

54

With Tom gone, the images that rushed at me when Candy showed me the photo of her and Joseph return, tugging at my brain, nudging me, reminding me not to forget.

It reminds me of a video that was played on a loop at a funeral I attended with Bridgette. I'd never met the unfortunate soul who'd died and was only there because I was too young to be left at home, alone.

I'll always remember that video, though, showing the deceased in their younger days, running, smiling, pulling silly faces. By showing the woman so full of life, it was almost as if her family wanted to impress on the mourners that the person lying in the coffin hadn't always been dead.

And even though Candy's picture was a still, my headspace becomes a living screen, host to a second showing of the film reel I saw that day. At first I could only see the back of her as I watched from the water, Sienna turning to look my way, water dripping from her hair, her skin glistening in the sunlight. So very beautiful. She threw a towel around her shoulders, stepped into a pair of trainers, and beckoned me to follow.

I pause the movie, give myself a second to think, but merely arrive at the same conclusion as yesterday, that this is real, a genuine memory.

To date, the only other person I've seen in my flashbacks has been my faceless dad, of him at the pitch party and then the time he lifted me from the camping site stream when I fell. Sienna has featured a few times, although, if I'm honest with myself, most of those were almost certainly dreams.

It's getting hard to distinguish between what's real and what's not, and I think back to Ken telling me that when a child hits their teenage years, memories of their previous existence begin to weaken, elbowed out. Time, therefore, is conspiring against me, and yet I feel tantalisingly close to uncovering so much more of my life before birth.

Though that's not the most important thing to me now. My own experiences play second fiddle to the characters who shaped my life back then, my life around these people. I feel an obligation to those who died, to complete their film reel, play the alternative ending to the audience; the correct one, not the sanitised one they were forced to accept all those years ago.

What I'm watching now is certainly not a dream, this is real. I remember watching this in real time, though now it's played in slow motion as I climb the hillside behind Sienna, following her route exactly as she picks her way through the scrub and rocks. I see her calves harden as she takes each carefully planned step, I hear her laughter as it echoes off the rocks, I see her waving to her dad, Marcus Crane, as we encroach into his yard that in this footage doesn't lay waste to old, broken, farm machinery. This is a place of happiness, of love.

The sun bakes the yard, reflections bouncing from it, drying Sienna's legs and neck, her hair clinging on to the last few droplets from her swim in the lake.

She laughs again, Mr Crane reminds her that lunch will soon be ready. There's still time for Sienna to pad into one of the outbuildings. Two bikes are propped up against the far wall, and I wonder if one of them is mine. Sienna shivers, the barn's cool air turning her towel cold and damp, goosebumps peppering one of her forearms as it emerges from beneath the towel, pointing to a spot on the floor. I'm unable to locate what she wants me to see, so I peer harder into the gloom that shrouds the floor, looking for something significant.

'Flo?' The call is muffled, like the day I was lying in the water when Marcus Crane rescued me.

'Flo! Lunch is ready.'

It takes me a moment to snap to the here and now, and when I do I feel frustration at leaving my film-showing before its conclusion.

It's Laura calling, she's responsible for making lunch today. All of a sudden I don't feel very hungry.

55

I'm back in the garage. I'm here solely to confirm something I saw yesterday. It takes me a while. I'm still not very quick across the ground, and in here I have an obstacle course to tackle before I reach the finish line.

I pass dozens of boxes we didn't even reach yesterday owing to Candy stumbling across the photograph of Joseph and her. I'll investigate those another time.

Even though the garage is cool, I'm slick with sweat by the time I reach the rear wall and it occurs to me how much fitness I've lost to those weeks spent lying still in my hospital bed. I double over, hands on knees, taking time to recover. My breathing is quick and raspy, and my head spins from the effort of making it this far, blurring the object in front of me.

'What are you doing in here?'

The voice from behind startles me, causing me to straighten up too suddenly, my vision worsening, my balance deserting me.

I take a step to my right in an effort to plant my legs further apart, for a wider base, a lower centre of gravity. But in doing so, my toe meets the business end of a car trolley jack lurking between two boxes. It's enough to tip me further off balance, and when I reach out a hand to steady myself against some boxes stacked three high, there's no resistance, and the boxes shift, then cascade to the floor with me falling in their wake.

I hear my own groan even before my head connects with the trolley jack. My injuries that have been healing so well, protest at the impact, reminding me why I'm supposed to be resting. There's a scuffling to my right, all manner of junk being shoved aside to create a path through to me.

'Oh, God, Flo!'

It's Bridgette, only here because I wasn't to be found in the house or garden. Bridgette's not one to fuss, but she'll have been worried about incurring Penny's wrath if I'd gone walkabout without my protective skull cap. Which I have. I know this because it isn't on my head, but rather in Bridgette's hand.

'Shit! Shit! Shit!,' Bridgette cries.

'I'm OK Bridgette, honestly. I just lost my balance, that's all.'

She's by me now, shoving one last box out of the way. 'Oh for Christ's sake Flo, your head's bleeding,' she says, her voice trembling.

And it is, I see drops of blood sprinkling the concrete floor, an action replay of when Marcus Crane lifted me from the water. These droplets fall from the other side of my head to my previous injury, though, which I'm taking to be a good thing. It's important to find the positives.

'Bloody hell. Are you in a lot of pain? Are you dizzy or anything? Shit! Shit! Shit!'

It's difficult to say what Penny would be more unhappy at—if she was here—my fresh injuries or Bridgette's swearing.

Bridgette needs some convincing that there's no need to pack me off to the hospital. She resists for a solid ten minutes, but in the end, after she's cleaned me up and re-installed me on the sofa, I can tell she's secretly grateful to be avoiding the phone call to Penny that a hospital visit would have made unavoidable.

'When Penny gets home, stick your hat on for Christ's sake,' Bridgette urges. For some reason she whispers even though we're the only two people in the house.

A hat is an odd choice of word for my headgear. A hat suggests something purchased as a fashion statement, something to look good in while keeping your head cool or warm depending on the season.

'It's a protective skull cap,' I point out.

'Do you wear it on your head?' Bridgette asks, rightly irritated by my need to hair-split.

'Yes, but—'

'Well, it's a hat then,' she says, folding her arms to signal the end of the debate. 'Have you got everything you need? Do you want anything to eat or drink?'

'No, I'm fine. Thanks, Mum. Oh, and Bridgette?'

'Yes, love.'

'Sorry,' I say.

'Oh, come here,' Bridgette says, stooping to give me a cuddle. 'Just holler if you want anything. I'll be in my office.' Bridgette heads up the stairs, humming something tuneless as she goes.

I still get tired, even after all these weeks of recovery since my accident, and I feel myself slipping away now, ready to be reunited with my dreams.

Before sleep cloaks me, I still have time to think about what I saw in the garage, or more precisely what I didn't see. Because when I lay on the concrete floor looking at the bike which I now believe to have belonged to Joseph, not Bridgette as I first assumed, I noticed it was lacking a couple of things. The first of these is dirt. When Joseph's bike was found on the hillside, it was deep into Autumn meaning the ground would likely have been saturated. The Lake District has one of the highest rates of rainfall in the country, it's about the only thing we've studied in Geography to date that seems relevant. It's something to do with the presence of hills and mountains causing the prevailing winds to rise, which in turn cools the air and enhances the chance of clouds forming, and hence rain falling. Admittedly, from where I lay, the bike carried the hallmarks of being cycled on wet roads. I could see splashes on the underside of the frame. This tells me it hasn't been cleaned since it was found. What's puzzling me is the absence of the mud I'd expect to see if a bike was wheeled down a hillside at that time of year. Mud that would still be evident if the bike hadn't been cleaned.

But there's a more interesting omission from the bike's frame and wheels. Scratches. I could see none. The bike looked virtually new and I fail to see how you could wheel it through the undergrowth on that slope with its brambles and rocks and leave no scuffs on the paintwork.

Even if someone could offer a reasonable explanation to me as to why the bike might be minus any mud and scratches, there's a further mystery attached to this bike. It may not have occurred to the detectives at the time, but it occurs to me, as someone who's tackled a similar slope, and it's this—you wouldn't attempt to wheel a bike down that slope in the first place. You'd do as I did, peer over the edge at the top and dismiss the notion out of hand. A bike would get away from you at some point, and Joseph's clearly didn't given its impeccable condition. I managed to fall while carrying nothing. I had both hands free and still crashed down to the rocks. You just wouldn't attempt it. Why would you? You'd leave the bike at the top wouldn't you? If you took it down to the water's edge you'd only be faced with dragging the thing back up with you. Even when Marcus Crane goes fishing, he picks his way down the slope carrying the minimum of equipment. The more you carry the greater the risk of falling.

No. The more I think about it, the more I'm convinced the bike was placed there, a few yards up the hillside. And that means someone else put it there.

In the interests of world peace, there's one more thing to do before I nod off. With some reluctance I place my "hat" on my head, then allow darkness to swallow me whole.

***

When I wake, I feel like I'm back at the lakeside with Marcus Crane, or in the stream with my dad. Not because I've had a flashback, or a dream, but because my head is wet. The skull cap is made of a hard synthetic material which, while possessing excellent impact protection, makes you sweat like a bastard.

My eyelids flutter a couple of times, then tentatively open, relieved that night-time has marched into the house. Penny has accompanied it over the threshold and she stands over me now.

'Good work,' she announces, nodding to my headgear.

'Oh, this?' I say, touching it lightly on the side of my head that carries the oldest and least tender injury. 'I went to the kitchen and back and must have forgotten to take it off.'

'Well, better to be safe than sorry. It's not for ever.'

'You're going into the office more these days,' I remark.

'Hmm, yes. It's a pain in the bum. I'd much rather be here with my two girls,' she says, stroking my arm. 'I have to go into work tomorrow, too,' she adds.

That's the news I was hoping to hear. I need to make a return visit to the garage and if Penny's around, I'll have no chance, with or without my hat.

'Right let's go and see if your useless mum upstairs has remembered to nip out to get something for our tea.'

And with that, Penny climbs the stairs, weary from another long day at the office.

The next voice I hear is Bridgette's.

'Oh, bollocks!'

56

I'm up early today, keen to get into the garage as soon as Laura and Penny leave for work. I don't need to lay eyes on Bridgette to know she's begun her working day upstairs. The unnecessary noises give it away—objects being dropped onto surfaces instead of being gently placed there, a fist coming down on a stapler that's being asked to bind a document three times thicker than its capacity, fingers jabbing at the computer keyboard like battering rams, the printer spewing out reams of paper that will end up in the bin as soon as it becomes apparent she's printed the wrong document. The symphony from the modest office upstairs is more representative of the hubbub you'd expect from a multinational's HQ.

Everything Bridgette turns her hand to is done at twice the volume considered acceptable by most people. A conversation made on the desk phone is conducted as if the person on the other end of the line is deaf, or dead. She's even worse on her mobile. If we're in public and Bridgette's mobile rings, we all dive for cover. It's bloody embarrassing.

I sneak into the garage. Technically, I'm not breaking any rules because I assured Bridgette I'd wear my hat if I left the sofa.

Yesterday, when Bridgette asked me why I was in the garage, I told her I was looking for a bike pump since my tyres had become a little flat. If I'm rumbled today and faced with the same question, I'm not sure what excuse to give, though I'll probably avoid 'proof of Laura's identity'.

I stare at the jumble of objects littering the floor, suddenly overwhelmed at the task in front of me. I decide to make a start on the next few boxes along from the one in which Candy found the photo of Joseph and her. I work my way through them in good time but find nothing of interest.

There's a box in my peripheral vision, different to the others, smaller, older, more battered. I almost miss it, trapped as it is between an old vacuum cleaner and the side wall of the garage. The word "DOCS" scrawled on its lid is just about legible, despite the ink being badly faded.

I've a decision to make. There are many more boxes to investigate but for every minute I'm out of the house, the shorter the odds become of Bridgette finding me missing. With my mind made up, I stoop to pick up the box with the intention of relocating it to my bedroom, but the moment it's clear of the floor, its base collapses, and the entire contents— paperwork in the main—spills onto the concrete floor.

Cursing, I abandon the perished box, locate an unlabelled, half-full one nearby, and decant the contents of the first into the second. There's a good weight to it, and I keep everything crossed that I won't have a repeat of yesterday's fall as I struggle towards the garage opening.

Once inside the house, I manhandle the thing up the stairs, drop it to the floor in my bedroom and flop onto the bed, utterly exhausted.

Bridgette has the bloody cheek to pop her head in saying she heard a noise. I assure her it was just the sound of the bed moving as I crashed down onto it. She nods her acceptance of this, fails to spot the box by my wardrobe, and leaves me to it.

I moved back into my room yesterday, fed up with the lack of privacy afforded to me by living downstairs. The move was also hastened in order to avoid the spinal surgery that another night spent on the sofa would have necessitated.

I spread the entire contents of the box over the bedclothes, leaving me with a small square in the middle where I sit cross-legged. I feel anticipation rising of what I might find, take a deep breath, and ready myself for the task ahead.

I decide to work clockwise from the first item that sits at twelve o'clock directly in front of me. After the earlier spillage, the contents of the two boxes have become irrevocably mixed together, meaning I'm faced with a mixed bag of documents, receipts, more photographs, and the occasional obligatory item of junk.

After an item has been inspected, I place it face down on the bed so as not to inadvertently revisit it a second time. If I think something could be worth a second look, I leave it face up.

And this is how I progress, turning my body slowly as I work clockwise around the pile, like the hands of a clock. And, like the hands of a clock, I'm passing through time, through Lakeside's different eras. One photo shows the front elevation of Lakeside, the sun low in the sky, shadows long, all hinting at the shot having been taken during early morning or evening. The trees framing the house are just coming into leaf. Spring. It's almost as if the photograph had been commissioned for the front of a glossy magazine; the sort of publication bought by people hoping for a glimpse into a lifestyle they aspire to but won't reach. The house looks immaculate, the driveway free of the previous Autumn's dropped leaves. A classic car poised for a run in the country completes the photograph, its paintwork and chrome bumpers mirror-like. The only disappointing thing from my point of view, is that the photograph is devoid of people. After admiring it for a short while, I place it face-down on the duvet and reach for the next photo.

Unlike the last picture, the one I'm holding to the light now, shows the rear of the house with a large group of people standing on the lawn posing for the photographer.

I scan the group. It's a large gathering, maybe forty people. Most I don't recognise, of course, but I can see Laura, Penny, and Tom. Candy too, crouched front and centre, beaming into the lens while waving with both hands, and sporting a jumper with a large pumpkin design. Probably a Halloween party, I surmise. Not fancy dress though unless costumes are lurking under the other guests' coats.

The lawn is an orange carpet of leaves, barely any grass showing. There's a date stamp in the bottom right-hand corner but it's too faded to read.

The house itself is unchanged in its shape, but the white windows have since been replaced with the dark grey metal ones it carries today. There's none of today's timber cladding or large expanses of glass in evidence, either. I wonder if this was part of Laura's healing process, redesigning the house in parallel to reinventing her life.

There's something about the photo that seems slightly off, but for the life of me I can't settle on what it might be. I shake my head, dismissing the thought. I might come back to it later, but in essence it's no more than a nice record of happier times at Lakeside, so I place the photograph face down on the duvet and move on.

The next object along is hard to define, but, if pressed, I'd say it's a ceramic chicken doing yoga. Whatever it is, it's far too creepy to keep on the bed so I aim a throw at the cardboard box, miss, and the bloody thing shatters as it bounces off my chest of drawers.

'Shit!' I whisper.

'You alright, Flo?' It's Bridgette's voice ringing out from her office a couple of doors down the hallway.

'Yup. All good here,' I holler back. The last thing I need is for Bridgette to wander in now to be greeted by a bedful of exhibits that even I would struggle to explain away.

I look at the smashed chicken, secretly congratulate myself for destroying it, and resolve to add it to the pile of junk in the garage—the junk I had to sweep from the drive before Penny and Laura returned on the day Candy and I looked for my camera.

Conscious of time pressures, I cast a quick glance at the remainder of the pile which I've now decided resembles a stone circle, the objects spaced around me like standing stones with me as the altar at its centre. I've reached three-quarters of the way around the circle, having examined every object thus far, when I spy an official-looking document, the top page of which is headed with Bridgette's full name including her middle name that I've always liked to make fun of: *Gertrude*.

But something further around the bed catches my eye. Another photograph. At first glance it seems to be a duplicate of the one I discarded earlier of the group of people posing in

Lakeside's back garden, but its composition is slightly different.

I reach behind me, locate the one I rejected and hold the two photographs side by side. As soon as I do this, the differences between the two shots become more marked. The second is considerably darker, taken at a later point in the same day, the sky clinging on to the last of the day's light, windows incandescent squares of orange.

I know the two pictures are taken on the same day because they both show the same group of people, albeit standing in different positions, but crucially all wearing the same clothes.

In the second photo, each person holds what looks like a stick, which confuses me until I see the date stamp in the corner, legible on this photograph unlike its sibling.

"3:52pm Nov 5".

Bonfire night. Not Halloween as I initially guessed from Candy's choice of jumper. Laura's house played host to a bonfire party that night.

I hold the photo to the light and peer more closely; the sticks grasped by each of the group are sparklers. This might be a test shot before they were lit. I can also see faint narrow diagonal lines on the image. Could be rain, I think, something I become more confident of when I scrutinise the group, their foreheads screwed up, heads angled down slightly to protect their faces from the rain. And to a person they all carry an expression which shouts, *'Just take the fucking photo'*.

I return to the first image. I don't need a time-stamp to know this was definitely taken at an earlier time, daylight still visible over Lakeside's rooftop. And it's the light that puzzles me because the group are reasonably well lit, not from an artificial source, but by the ambient light from the dwindling daylight. The foreground, however, is considerably darker, like the photographer was standing under a gazebo or marquee of some kind. But this makes little sense because if the photographer were sheltering beneath something, wouldn't the roof of it be apparent at the top edge of the photograph?

Bridgette is up out of her swivel chair in her office, I can hear her padding around. Seconds later, her office door opens and closes again and I track her footsteps along the hallway until they pause outside my door.

'Flo, darling, I'm going to make myself a drink. I'll bring you one up, you need to keep hydrated,' she says, waiting for my response.

I shoot a glance at the bed, make a quick calculation, and reply, 'Yeah, fine. Thanks, Mum.'

I then use the short time at my disposal to pack away all the items I've examined back into the box. I move it to the window side of my bed, out of view. The remaining items— which amount to only ten or so including the two photographs—I secrete under the bed for later inspection. I fire off a text to Candy:

Hi Candy. Hope you're OK?
Can you remember what day of the year Joseph died?
Flo x

Bridgette returns with a drink just as my phone pings with Candy's reply. I try to hasten Bridgette's exit by keeping small talk to a minimum, but it still seems to take an age for her to go. When she finally leaves I take a look at my phone:

Hi Flo. Yeah, all good here thanks.
I was fifteen years old so it was nearly sixteen years ago.
Bonfire night.
Cx

I feel closer than ever to finding out what happened to Joseph. But more than that, my own jigsaw is taking shape.

Since we moved here, I'm convinced that this is where I lived my life. Everything is so comfortable—the landscapes, the village, its people. I even saw my dad again yesterday. I dismissed it at first because his image appeared to me as I hit my head, so I rejected it as some sort of confused hallucination. Thinking about it now, though, I'm persuaded to believe it was no such thing. The timing was crucial, you see, and stopping the clock in a replay of yesterday's fall sees him appear in silhouette against the overhead strip lights, a split second before my head connected with the car trolley jack. His demeanour looked different yesterday, though, which made me sad. He was crooked, stooped, and looked quite unlike other thumbnail images of him that have washed over me before now. He appeared as a man who carries a burden, wanting to be free from it. A concern for himself, or me, I wonder?

57

After dinner, before I retire upstairs, I take a risk. I'm careful to wait for the right moment where I'm in position to see the faces of all three women. It's important that I'm able to gauge their reaction to what I'm about to say.

'Let's have a party,' I say, which induces the merest of glances between the women.

'Sounds like fun,' Bridgette pipes up. 'Who shall we invite?'

'Well… Tom and Candy, obviously. Then what about some of your friends, Laura?' I ask. It feels a tad cruel but I shake the sentimentality from me. I've grown tired of no one filling in the gaps, of having no explanation as to why this place holds such fear for Laura. Why come back at all? If it's to face her demons, then I wish she'd tell me. I'm thirteen years old and certainly don't need protecting from home truths. Apart from anything else, it's leaving me with a sense of not knowing who my own family really are, and that can't be right when we're such a tight-knit group, always promising to share, agreeing not to keep secrets from one another. Penny is just as guilty. By being complicit, she's enabling Laura's behaviour—enabling her reluctance to open up and to integrate. What's more, she never leaves Laura's side if there's the slightest threat of a conversation taking a tangent to subjects off-limits. I'm tired of the unpredictable sea-changes in atmosphere, of stolen glances, the steering of conversations to sterile pastures.

The look between Penny and Laura lingers for a short while only. Bridgette casts a glance their way, but it's done to canvas support for the party, her face imploring the others to get behind my idea.

In what can only be described as a low shot, Penny uses her trump card.

'I'm conscious it's Laura's house, and we've only really just got it into shape, so how about we put it off until next year when we've got our feet under the table a bit more?'

Penny's skilfully managed to fit multiple excuses into one sentence. It's no wonder she's a cherished employee at the law firm.

I look towards Bridgette who in turn looks at Penny like she's talking a foreign language. I wonder if Bridgette, like me, is having doubts over the disproportionate level of apprehension attached to living within this community.

Bridgette, picking up on my disappointment, slaps her hands on her knees in a gesture that wouldn't be out of place in a pantomime, and announces, 'Well I think Lakeside would be perfect for a party. Let's do it!'

Laura looks flushed, twitchy, a finger pulling at a loose thread on the sleeve of her jumper.

'No… I mean yes. We should have a party, I mean,' Laura says, casting a look of concern towards Penny, who in turn responds with the subtlest shake of her head. Fortunately Bridgette moves things along, and gives a strangled *whoop,* accompanied by a small round of applause. I'm unsure which of Laura or me should take a bow.

'When were you thinking?' a subdued Penny asks to no one in particular.

I pause, not for so long as to allow someone to jump in, but long enough to make sure all three faces are turned my way.

'Bonfire night!'

It takes a second for my words to register, with Penny and Laura at any rate. The pair's heads snap round and they exchange a look—one that's loaded with alarm, one they allow to soften to mere unease, before fixing their faces with neutral expressions placed there for the benefit of Bridgette and me.

'What a brilliant idea!' Bridgette cries. 'We can make mulled wine.'

'Let's not get ahead—'

'And we can keep the food simple,' Bridgette interrupts, unapologetic at cutting dead Penny's efforts to stall. 'Jacket spuds with cheese, Bolognese, that sort of thing.'

'Can we have sparklers?' I ask, determined to keep the levels of enthusiasm as high as possible to negate the chances of Laura and Penny reneging on the deal.

'It's a bad idea having a party on bonfire night,' Penny snaps. 'Our guests will already be committed to organised events elsewhere.'

'Oh, God!' Bridgette snorts. 'We don't know that. Don't be such a killjoy. It's still a couple of weeks away. No one prebooks those sort of events anymore anyway in case it pisses it down.'

I'm not done. 'I thought you two could invite some of your old school friends. By the way, you still haven't shown me where you guys went to school. Or the cinema,' I point out.

'Alright, alright,' Penny spits. 'But let's start small. A few guests will do. No need to turn it into a big do.'

Bridgette reaches for her phone and mumbles something about finding a mulled wine recipe online.

To cement the event in the household's calendar, and to ensure the offer won't be retracted, I make a speech about how, as a thirteen-year-old starting in a new, strange environment, it's important for me to integrate as much as possible even if it's not with people my own age. I even ask Laura if I may bake cookies for the event since it's something I've always wanted to do. It isn't, obviously, but the additional excitement I manufacture seems to seal the deal. Laura's face softens, and while her expression may not be a true reflection of the emotions she's feeling, my mission is accomplished. I've secured the party.

**

I feel faint, though I needn't worry about falling, since I'm lying down in my room. I've come to bed earlier than usual, an action which prompted both my mums to ask if I was feeling alright. I was fine, simply keen to get back to my photos and the remainder of the documents left unexamined.

I excused myself directly after our conversation about the party, telling the others that if Bridgette was good enough to do research into mulled wine then I should do the same and find a recipe for cookies. The three adults seemed content with my explanation for an early night.

If the three adults could see my face now, they might reconsider. I don't have the benefit of a mirror right now, but if I did, I'd be looking like an extra in a horror movie, a vampire's victim drained of their blood. I've lost the ability to move, even my eyelids refusing to budge as I stare unblinking.

I'm looking at the same two photographs as earlier, but there's something missing. Correction: *someone* missing. I chastise myself that this escaped my scrutiny the first time around. I was so fixated on the unnatural shadow that hung over where the photographer was positioned, I didn't stop to study the people in the group.

I assumed there was the same amount of people in the first shot as in the second, and at first glance it looks as if there is, albeit most of them having swapped positions. But there is one person who appeared in photo one who is no longer present in photo two. Ordinarily I wouldn't give it a second thought but these are no ordinary photographs. These were taken the day Joseph died.

I want to call Tom, but he's made it quite clear he's unable to talk about the case with me. I'd call Marcus Crane but he doesn't own a telephone. I turn Detective Field's card between my fingers, the one he left me the last time we met in hospital. I was to call him if I thought of anything Mr Crane said or did to me the day I fell down the hillside to the lake's edge.

I've punched in all the digits but need a moment before hitting the green call button. Once I call him, there's no going back. He'll want to know more, dig for details I can't or won't give, possibly speak to my parents. I don't want anyone to get hurt, so in my head I adjust my approach, make sure I'm clear what I'll say.

A man's voice answers. 'Detective Field?' His words formal, the lack of greeting, impersonal.

'Hi, Detective. It's Flo. We talked in hospital.'

'Hello Flo. Something you want to tell me?' he says unable to disguise the intrigue in his voice.

I take a breath. 'It's something I want you to tell me,' I say, unsure whether to wait for permission, or to simply plough on.

'Hmmm?' he says flatly, sounding decidedly less curious now.

'What time did Joseph Newman die?'

'What?'

I opt for silence. I've asked a question that I don't intend repeating.

'I don't see why that's relevant. Has Mr Crane said something to you, Flo?'

'No!' I yell, immediately worried in case my voice has carried downstairs. 'It's not secret information, is it?'

'Well, no but—'

'Then tell me. You wanted me to trust you. Well that's what I'm doing now. It's a big deal for someone my age to call the police,' I plead.

'If I tell you, will you let me know why you want to know,' he asks warily.

'Yes... I mean no. I will... soon.'

There's a long sigh on the other end of the line. A sigh which buys the detective time to weigh up his options.

'I don't have the files with me but the coroner's report, when viewed in conjunction with the victim's movements that day, gave us an estimated window for time of death at between 3:15 and 4:15pm.'

I hear chatter from downstairs, the adults discussing the party, no doubt. I hear the rain whipping the windowpane, the wind chasing the droplets as it circles the roof over my head. I don't hear the detective's voice.

'Flo?'

'Yes?' I manage.

'I want you to think about *what* you've just asked me, and I want you to think about *why* you've asked it. And if your parents aren't aware that you're calling me now, I need you to tell them when we end this call. Do you understand, Flo?'

I nod, unable to take my eyes from photo two.

'Flo? Do you understand? I shall stop by tomorrow, alright?'

'Yes,' I confirm, dispassionately. I hit the red button to end the call, drop the phone to the bed and continue to stare at the photograph time-stamped at 3:52pm. The photograph that is missing a guest.

Candy.

58

I slept badly last night. My mind fighting against a riptide of dark thoughts, trying to battle against them but each time succumbing, robbed of answers.

I resorted to opening the curtains in the middle of the night, the darkness too overpowering, too quick to exaggerate my thoughts, distort people into monsters that frightened me. By moonlight I took another long look at the photographs.

I wake to a reality I wish I had the power to banish, to consign to a box in the garage with the rest of the mess. Clutter that others should be untangling, sorting, rather than me. I'm thirteen years old, another year and I probably wouldn't have been so inquisitive. I'll have found boys, parties, fashion, booze. Instead, I'm poking around in others' lives on the premise they're inextricably linked to one I used to live. I was happy in my old life, just as I was happy in my current one. Until now.

But I know too much. I've uncovered most of the missing pieces that scarred this family's past. There are others that elude me, but I have a feeling I know where I'll find those too.

I want Miss Manson's leaflet in my hand, a tangible crutch, someone to call, someone to unburden me of this sadness. Because I have fresh injuries, this time within my head, ones doctors might scratch their heads at, ones with deeper wounds than before. But I'll heal, just as I've always done. And those around me will too, in time. I hope.

I take one last look at the photographs and trace my finger over the face I've come to hold so dear.

Then I make the call. Not to Detective Field. To his colleague, Tom.

I reckon I owe him that much.

59

I didn't make the call to Tom to tell him about my suspicions. I killed the call before the first ring. I should have called, but I didn't. I tried, but I couldn't. I will, but I need another day. I need twenty-four hours to come to terms with what I'm about to do. I did manage a text message, but only to request he stand down Detective Field today. When the time comes to make the call, I don't care that Tom's too close to the case of Joseph Newman. He can pass on the information as he sees fit. I want to be free of it.

My mums and Laura will be working away from home today. Penny has delayed going to work, waiting with me until I've had my video conference call with my history teacher, Mr Drucker. Having kicked up a stink with my headteacher over my schooling, she's keen to see he keeps to his word.

It's obvious my teacher isn't comfortable with having to find this extra time for me, and even less comfortable with the video conferencing technology he's seated in front of.

Penny, a woman no stranger to business meetings conducted in this fashion, drums her fingers on Bridgette's desk, and, while my teacher tries to "mute" himself in order to chat to someone off screen, Penny takes the opportunity to tidy some of the crap on Bridgette's desk.

We lose Mr Drucker temporarily, his image replaced with the front page of the school's website, a gurning Mr Hole captured in one of the most awkward poses I've ever seen, pictured shaking hands with a high-flying female student who towers over him.

Upon seeing the photo, Penny sends a smile my way and mouths, '*Oh. My. God.*' It's a shared moment of togetherness that's much needed right now.

Penny speaks to my teacher to check if he can still hear us, telling him that we can no longer see him. There's a response of sorts, his voice intermittent, smothered by static. A single thumping noise suggests his equipment has either been knocked over or hurled across the room.

Penny writes me a note and slides it across the desk. It reads:

"Do they ever let this guy teach technology?"

I scribble on the reverse side and push it back to Penny:

"Doubt it. He's not even great on what's happened in the past."

I hit the mute button and turn to face my mum.

'Jamie Wright says his dad was hired to show all the teachers how to use video conferencing. It was on the first day of term after the summer holidays—you know… that day you always get angry about. What's it called?'

'Inset day. It's short for in service training, I think,' Penny says, eyes to the ceiling, checking the acronym in her head.

'Maybe Mr Drucker got a note from his mum that day,' I say, which causes Penny to laugh.

When Mr Drucker reappears he's sharing the screen with a young male student who reaches over his shoulder. The lad, who can be no more than twelve, has taken control of the mouse, and after a few clicks he straightens up meaning we can no longer see his face. We hear his voice though, saying, 'I think you were clicking on the wrong things, sir. And you have your headphones on backwards.'

'Yes, yes, thank you Jamie, go get yourself ready for class,' Mr Drucker snaps, glaring at the lad over his shoulder, unable to hide his irritation at being humiliated in front of a pupil's parent. We see his eyes scan left and right, searching for the right icon to click.

'Right then... yes... here we are... Flo... Sorry about that. Now, I have something to share with you on screen... if you... just wait one second... while I... yes... here it is... Now, what you're looking at—'

What we're looking at is a blank screen. We don't even have the dubious pleasure of Mr Hole grinning at us. Just blackness. We can *hear* Mr Drucker though, talking us through the document we can't see, telling me which parts of it I should focus on while writing my essay. We tell him we can't see him but he ploughs on, into his stride now, him unable to hear us, us unable to see him. It's a complete shambles.

Penny grabs the piece of paper and writes, *"FFS"*. She could have said the words aloud, Mr Drucker wouldn't hear us. We could start playing some thrash metal at this end and he'd be none the wiser, but Penny doesn't like swearing.

Frustration gets the better of my mum, so she asks me to shunt across to allow her to type an in-call message:

"This has been a complete waste of time. We can't see what you're trying to share. Can I ask that you email Flo the necessary documents and make sure you're better prepared next time. Penny Aters-Fabishaw."

'Right, I need to get off,' she says, leaning down to give me a typical Penny-style kiss on the cheek. I think in that moment how different it is to the ones Candy's given me since I've known her. I've no doubt Penny's kisses are meant lovingly, but they're short, functional affairs, wholly unlike Candy's which never fail to stir your soul, warm your blood.

***

It's ten minutes or more since Penny left the house and I find myself staring at the blank computer screen. I don't know what I'm hoping for; for it to absorb my thoughts, perhaps, transfer them as a cut and paste to a new location, one buried deep within a complex folder structure, passworded, secure.

What I'm about to do next would see Penny slap me rather than kiss me. I open the garage door and retrieve my bike. I've missed riding it these last few weeks, and if I thought I could have got away with it, I'd have even settled for merely riding it up and down the lane in front of the house.

I'm going further today, though, so I trade my skull cap for my bike helmet which I slip over my head, before swinging my right leg over the saddle.

It's a strange journey. I pedal with no real effort. By rights I should be shattered, my lungs should be protesting, my muscles screaming, but they all work together in harmony, taking me up the crest of a hill, then down the other side, floating by tall hedgerows, chasing skid marks of clouds that tear across grey skies.

I pull up at the gap in the hedge where I tried to climb down the hillside to meet Marcus Crane. I calmly dismount, stand with my toes curling around the lip of the hill's crest, and remove my bike helmet, grateful for the air that bathes my skull. I see the tree that failed to stop me, see the small rock I tripped on, and see the rocks that stand on tiptoes beneath the surface of the lake, ready, waiting.

I see my dad holding my hand, fingers entwined around mine, him lifting me clear of the water. I see Marcus Crane carry me away from the rocks, briefly setting me down before his assault on the hillside with me in his arms. And I see Sienna and her mother, for whom no rescue came, lost to this stretch of water that links so many people. And then there's Joseph and Candy, their happiness proving to be as fragile as the surface of this lake.

I stare into the water and contemplate the characters as they fade one by one, leaving me behind, alone, a mere bystander to all this tragedy.

I take one last look across the hillside towards Marcus Crane's house, then to my left at Lakeside, replace my helmet and mount my bike.

60

Marcus Crane is in his yard when I arrive, as if he was expecting me. He sits on one of his rusty pieces of machinery and looks entirely at ease, like a park user on their lunchbreak watching the ducks.

Marcus Crane's vista is the contents of the barn that now lie before him in his yard. I watched him over the last couple of days as he completed his task. He looked weary by the end of it, and I was left wondering if it was a physical or mental toll that wore him out. If I could have helped him, I would.

I prop my bike against the same tree, by the same slope, and wander over to him. He scooches over, snagging the knee of his trousers on a protruding bolt. He makes no move to rub the pain away. I doubt it even registered.

'Hi Marcus Crane,' I say, making a pattern in the dust with the toe of my shoe.

'Hi, Flo,' he replies. 'Did you see Alan this morning?'

It occurs to me I hadn't looked out for him, distracted as I was, solely focused on the journey ahead.

'I didn't look, but I'm sure he will have been there,' I say.

We both stare over the top of the yard's new objects, all manner of stuff huddled there like office workers sent to an assembly point during a fire drill. Our eyes look to the lake beyond.

'Cantankerous bastard of a thing, that cow,' Marcus Crane mutters.

We swap looks, both of us reluctant to be the first to crack. I lose. As hard as I try to purse my lips together, the smile eventually escapes, the effort of holding it back causing me to explode into laughter. Marcus Crane's crow's feet crease around his eyes and his smile isn't far behind, spreading across his weather-battered face.

'You cheated,' I say, indignantly.

'How?' he protests.

'Because you have a beard. You could have been smiling first for all I know.'

'Sore loser,' he mutters, still smiling.

I make patterns in the dust with my foot once more, then lean forwards placing my elbows on my knees.

'What will you do with all these things?' I ask, without looking across. There seems to be two piles. One is made up of his tools, offcuts of wood, some roof tiles, and other items I can't identify. The other is a collection of Sienna's things. It has the appearance of a museum charting the history of children's toys.

'Most of Sienna's things will go to charity,' Marcus Crane says, gently. 'There are some items that belonged to Hettie, which I'll sort as I go.'

'I can help,' I say, hoping he'll let me, stopping short of telling him that most of his family's things are too dated now to be of much use to anyone.

'Thank you, Flo,' he says. 'I'd appreciate that.' I notice he deliberately shifts his eyes away from Sienna's pile of things; the sooner we clear the yard, the better, I think.

'What about the other pile?' I ask, flicking out a toe in its direction.

'Some of it junk, some of it worth keeping. I'll split it into two piles soon enough. I'll sort Sienna's things first before the bad weather starts to hit. Some of it's already got a bit wet.'

I look to my right, to the building that's been emptied. Its large doors are ajar, and as far as I can see, only one item remains inside. Marcus Crane picks up on my confusion.

'Can't let that go,' he says. 'Sienna loved that bike.'

I nod and let my head fall gently onto his shoulder. I know this man, his smell, his strength, his heart, his silhouette. And he knows me, though he might not be ready to admit it. Right now, in this place, in this time, me being close to him in this way feels like the most natural thing in the world. I feel him shaking slightly, a man trying to hold his tears, so I stay there, giving him the time he needs before I look at him once more.

'Cantankerous bastard,' I say, repeating Marcus Crane's words from earlier. And it's enough to make us both laugh once more.

'You're a good girl, Flo,' he says.

'You're a good man, Marcus Crane,' I say.

And we sit like this, my head on his shoulder, quiet but for the soundtrack of the fluttering wings of small birds as they swoop to peck at the seed that's scattered on the next broken piece of machinery along from us.

'Marcus?'

'Yes, Flo.'

My head remains on the man's shoulder while I ask my next question. I have a feeling it's best if we don't look into each other's eyes.

'What age was Sienna when she died'?

At first, I don't think he'll answer. But then the birds cease their chattering, and retreat to the trees, as if affording him the time and space he needs to give me the answer that I already know. I reach for his hand that lies limp on his knee, take it in my own, and close my eyes as our fingers part and lock together once more.

'She was sixteen.'

61

'Can I look inside the house?' I say, standing. He looks uncertain.

'Come on,' I whisper, encouraging him with a smile.

'Well, alright,' he begins. 'But I have to warn you, it isn't the tidiest place you'll ever see.'

The tour doesn't take long. He's right, it's messy as fuck, though something tells me it's an ordered mess.

Three fishing rods are stacked in one corner of his living room, a bookshelf completely fills one wall, purpose-made to fit the space, by Marcus Crane's own hands I shouldn't wonder. Some of the titles look surprisingly modern, fiction mainly, but travel books grace a couple of the smaller shelves. No biographies that I can see which doesn't surprise me. Marcus Crane isn't a man who'd be interested in the minutiae of other people's lives.

Marcus leads, but I know the way, know the house's layout, its cracks in the plasterwork, its knots in the exposed timber beams.

The kitchen is a reasonable size, and it's not hard to turn back the clock to a time when this small family would have cooked, then eaten together around the pine table.

My heart lurches when I'm shown into Sienna's room. Like the barn, it's been largely cleared, just some posters with curling corners left stuck to its walls along with a smattering of photographs.

I move over to take a closer look. There are eight pictures in total. A couple of them show Sienna astride a horse, flanked by her mum and dad. I count five of her with Joseph, arm in arm or holding hands, a proper teenage crush in one sense, yet two people who look so comfortable in each other's company they could pass for a much older couple who've been together for years.

I wonder how long before Sienna's death these photographs were taken. And I wonder if Joseph and Sienna would have gone on to live the rest of their lives together.

The final photograph shows Joseph in the centre of the shot with an arm around Sienna to his left and round Candy to his right. All three are laughing, at what I'll probably never know. Marcus Crane and his wife Hettie can be seen in the background, seated at a small table sharing a bottle of wine. Which begs the question, who was the photographer? Another friend, I presume.

We head downstairs, and when we pass the door to the kitchen once more, I make Marcus Crane promise to cook me a meal one day soon.

Back out in the yard, before leaving, I ask permission to look in the largest barn. I register the puzzlement on his face at my eagerness to look inside a virtually empty space, but he shrugs, asks me if I want a glass of water, and when I decline, he retreats into the house to grab one for himself.

It'd be wrong to say this is what I came here for, this outbuilding. It's not my sole purpose for coming. I wanted to visit Marcus Crane, to see how he's doing, see how he's coping with looking out onto the pile of memories stacked up in his yard. I'm glad I got to see him, to satisfy myself that he's doing alright.

62

By my reckoning I've visited this barn four times now. The first was when I met Marcus Crane and purely poked my head around the door. The second was when I dreamed about the place, with its photos adorning the walls, the shaft of sunlight spotlighting Sienna's bike. My third visit was a recall, a vivid memory of watching Sienna as she emerged from the water, climbing the hillside, across the yard and into this very building.

The dream I had of this space was a curious thing, wild, elaborate, flamboyant in its presentation. I've reflected on it many times since, becoming convinced that my dream's purpose was to draw me in, ensure I didn't overlook its significance. It tendered the room in a style that prompted me to look deeper, akin to a theatre set, where one room only is introduced to the audience, crammed full—in a way a real room wouldn't be—of everything needed to span time and action, together with clues for the audience, all hidden in plain sight. A fantasy scape, garishly pointing to where meaning might be found; the sort of meaning an actual memory might be lacking.

In my dream, the boxes and tools were pushed to the perimeter, thus directing the eye away from the clutter and onto objects of more note. The photographs on the wall, a reminder not to forget the pain and suffering of the family who walked this set, every cast member exiting, only some returning. The bike's bell, an alarm, a warning to tread carefully, spot lit to ensure focus was drawn to the floor, the chalk line.

What was the purpose of my dream if not to bring me here one more time?

I walk slowly to the bike, place my fingers around the handlebar grips as Sienna would once have done, gently nudge its kick stand, and walk the bike a few paces away from the hatch in the floor which hides like a rock beneath the water, always present, but only to those who know it's there.

I can't lift the hatch, so make my way back out to the yard to find a screwdriver or crowbar, whatever I can find to act as a lever. Marcus Crane is sitting on his makeshift bench sipping water and says nothing as I set about finding what I need. I look his way and receive a single nod, his blessing.

I watched Sienna lift the hatch that day—the day I watched her climb the hill. I watched the water spot the floor as it fell from her hair; a breadcrumb trail left to find the treasure that pirates left behind.

There's no spotlight now to pierce the gloom, so I sink to my knees and peer over the edge into the small wood-lined chamber beneath. It's only about two feet by three feet in size and maybe eighteen inches deep. Deep enough to house a small cairn, a stack of washed cobbles from the lakeshore, each stone carefully selected for its flatness, each decreasing in diameter towards the top of the pyramid.

Cairns have, over time, been constructed for various reasons, for guiding seafarers along coastlines before the advent of lighthouses, for example, or built to serve as a ceremonial marker. Sometimes they're used to mark a grave, as a way of saying *"I'll always remember you"*. Yet often they're constructed simply as a symbol of love.

This crude pile of stones in front of me was a bond between Joseph and Sienna, and the fact it remains here, intact, defiant, makes it all the more poignant.

I reach into the furthest corner of this small den, acting from memory, not needing to use my eyes, my fingers finding their way and curling around what I came here to find. If it had become lost, I don't know what I would have done.

The object is wrapped in an oilskin which I peel back, reassured to find its contents dry and undamaged. I replace the hatch, and wheel Sienna's bicycle back into position.

When I walk into the Autumn light, I don't make any attempt to hide what I'm carrying, but I keep it wrapped in its cloth.

When Marcus Crane lifts my bike onto the back of his quadbike, I couldn't be more grateful. I didn't ask him for a ride back, but I think he saw the weariness in my eyes.

The journey back couldn't be more different than the last time we navigated these lanes. There's no laughter this time, although I do get a gentle nudge in the ribs when we come across Alan, standing there with an enormously long spike of grass sticking out of one side of his mouth. Just when you thought he couldn't look any more pissed off with the world, he surprises us once more.

Before leaving Marcus Crane, I reiterate my promise to him that we're to remain friends. He says nothing in reply, just narrows those kind eyes of his and roars off back to his cabin.

I stow my bike, climb the stairs to my bedroom and lie on my altar without its standing stones. The tears I thought might come, don't.

I reach for my mobile.

And this time I place the call.

63

Tom and Candy were supposed to be joining us for supper later today, but unsurprisingly they've made their excuses. Tom calls me that evening, though. I'm in my room, jotting furiously in my notebook. I'm scared I'll forget these events now I'm growing older, though in many ways it'll be a release to be rid of them.

I wonder how it works; surely once you've recalled an event from your life before birth, you don't go on to forget it? That wouldn't make any sense. That would be like saying I'll go on to forget my tumble down the hillside and my subsequent stay in hospital. Surely it means that the chance for *further* recall diminishes past a certain age.

I quizzed Ken on this very matter once when we were queuing for the bus after our shift. I put it to him that once a second life is over, that must signal the end of any memories from the previous two being carried forward a second time. He didn't know, but he mused it would be highly unlikely for a memory to surface in a second after-life because the latest individual would have no context for the initial life event.

He placed a caveat on this, though. Based on the above, he explained that the only way an event can transcend two further lives is if there is some physical evidence with an undisputed provenance which survives multiple generations. It's why, he added, some conspiracy theorists claim NASA will never be free from the worry that the moon landings will be exposed as a hoax. The worry being that a key figure will reveal all upon their death through evidence collected at the time.

And that's what's needed over time because recall won't always be reliable. It might be incomplete, distorted, tainted by other memories merging into one. And that's what most people like me are left with; one or two heart stopping recalls orbited by fragments, slithers that may never be pieced together. But more importantly, as long as these memories are confined to your head, they will stay there, fade in time, then die with you.

You need a backup.

I have one. I used to keep it in a hatch.

64

We've lucked out. The weather is fine, clear skies, calm waters, and little in the way of a breeze. It's the perfect recipe for a fireworks display.

Everyone who said they'd be here has made it. Except Candy. Just as she went missing on this night all those years ago, she's absent again. Tom has said he'll drop by later.

Penny has hired a company to install the fireworks. It must have cost a small fortune. There were three operatives buzzing around earlier. One of them thought it was hilarious to sneak up behind me and shout, 'Bang!' I told him to stop being a twat.

The last week was spent gathering whatever pieces of wood we could lay our hands on, and for our efforts we have a small bonfire doing its thing near the house. It's debatable whether all the materials currently burning away are wood based, though. There was a sheet of something added to the pyre yesterday that looked suspiciously like asbestos to me. And more than once I had to give Bridgette a bollocking for throwing empty plastic bottles on the bloody thing. Honestly, sometimes it's hard to distinguish between the adults and children round here, and if it wasn't for me, there wouldn't even have been a last-minute check under the bonfire for hedgehogs.

We have fifteen minutes or so before the fireworks start. A large man called Barry has waited behind to light them at the appropriate time. I'm not sure I'd ever feel confident putting my trust in a person called Barry, especially one employed to discharge pyrotechnics. There's an implied clumsiness to the name, and Barry has it in spades.

There's still time for a wander down the garden. I won't go as far as the jetty because that's where all the fireworks have been staked, and Barry has declared the area off-limits.

I reach the oak trees, one to each side of me. There are no squirrels tonight. They'll be donning their ear defenders, snuggled up in their drey right at the top of the tree's canopy where the main trunk ends, creating a fork in its uppermost branches. A few days ago, I used my binoculars to find its location and watched the creatures with fascination from the balcony of my parents' room.

It's not the tree canopy, or squirrels I've paused here to look at, though. What interests me is at ground level.

I worked it out some time ago, you see. It's why I tripped those couple of times. Tripped over nothing, it seemed. Except it wasn't nothing, it never is. It was a tree root. And if you look carefully, you can see a matrix of them, lurking just below the turf, some just barely breaking the surface, just like the rock I tripped on when I fell down the hillside. It's a snakes and ladders board below the grass, too many roots to belong just to the two oaks which flank the garden either side of me.

There was once a line of trees along this spot, their species unclear, but large enough, or dense enough to cloak the photographer in shadow on this day all those years ago.

It's why none of the guests saw the motorboat leave. Add to that the rain that was visible in the second photograph, and it's highly unlikely any guests would have been outside anyway, other than for the short time it took to have their picture taken. This would mean a person would have to spot the motorboat leaving its mooring from a couple of hundred yards away, through a line of trees and from behind a pane of glass.

Guests are milling around, seeing off the last of the jacket spuds. Penny and Laura weave in and out of them, refilling glasses with something fizzy. Bridgette, unusually for her, stands to one side staring out towards the lake, snapping from her solace when she sees me heading back towards the house. She gives an enthusiastic wave before heading back into the house.

We're asked to gather at a spot about halfway down the garden, and instinctively everyone opts for the space between the two towering oaks, placing themselves on the old tree line.

It's unclear how tonight will pan out, but for the time being I'm determined to enjoy the display.

The sky becomes an umbrella of light, the space between it and the water raining colour and noise. I think I see Marcus Crane standing on the near side of his yard, but the edges of his body become blurred with the smoke that hangs in the breathless night sky, and a few fireworks later, I can see him no longer.

The fireworks that sprout a fountain of colour when they reach their maximum altitude are my favourites. They remind me of those slithers of colour I carry within me, incomplete whenever the space around them isn't filled with offerings more vivid. Clarity arrives in the form of rockets, shaking the senses, filling every last void as my sheet lightning moments do; like Laura losing her earring to the water, something precious lost. Like the time I became faint standing in Marcus Crane's yard when I remembered my dad and all the places we visited.

The guests drift back towards the house, the smoke in the sky drifting towards the hillside. They stay as long as seems polite after availing themselves of the free booze and pyrotechnics.

A pity they won't see the final display.

65

At the point in the evening where the bonfire gives off less heat than the radiators in the house, we shamble back inside. All three women are nicely drunk, red faced from the bonfire and Beaujolais. Laura had hit the booze early and announces now that she's off to bed.

It leaves my mums, me, and Tom—who missed the fireworks display but has managed to snag himself the last jacket potato which he attacks greedily. More drinks pass through blood red lips and we each slump into a chair facing the fire as it spits the damp from the first logs added to its grate.

Without saying a word, Tom rises and heads for the television.

As he does, I rise too. I don't need to see what's coming next.

'I'm going out to get some air,' I say, making my way down the garden until I reach the jetty, where I sit myself down, legs dangling over the edge as I did the first day I visited here.

This is my page five moment. It'll forever have its top corner folded over or play host to a bookmark. I look to the skies for a crow, but there's none.

I don't need to watch the video that Tom will be playing right now. I don't need to watch it because I've seen what was on the memory card that Tom has transferred to DVD.

Around about now the video will show an empty garage. Lakeside's garage. Within the video camera's wide-angle frame, Tom, Penny, and Bridgette will be able to make out a slither of dashboard, with a shiny car bonnet beyond; blue, like the bonnet belonging to the car pictured in the photograph of Lakeside, the one that belonged in a glossy magazine. The same bonnet, the same car. The sort of car that would be featured in the Classic Car magazines that still sit on the coffee table that separates the three adults from the video that plays out in front of them. The sort of car that requires an expert to maintain. Someone with the ability to make replacement parts where originals are no longer available. Someone with the patience to tinker with the carburettor to iron out the flat spots. Someone with the skills to make a coffee table out of another vehicle's boot lid.

By now, the audience will see the garage door rise, a figure standing in the opening, silhouetted against the light grey sky, before they turn to close the garage door and reveal themselves under the artificial light.

It'll be an eerie watch by now, the movie made more sinister somehow by its lack of sound. Though when you know what's coming as I do, you count this as a blessing.

Nothing is hurried. The body language of the person in shot projecting an unswerving cold calmness. All eyes will be trained on the passenger side of the car now.

And in one horrifying instant the camera lurches to one side, but it holds steady in its mount, retaining its focus, capturing the person walking idly around the front of the car to the driver's side. The person's body coils itself before releasing its energy, the camera dipping to its right this time until it settles in a near horizontal plane once more.

We don't see the leg as it connects with the two trolley jacks, kicking them from under their mounts on each side of the car, and we don't hear the screams that surely came when half a tonne of engine and bodywork came crashing down.

We do see the person who killed Scott. Who took the life of an innocent man, leaving Laura without a husband and Joseph without a father.

And as I walk back towards the house, I wonder whether Penny has any regrets. Whether the slightest trace of remorse will find its way through the crippling fear she'll be feeling right now.

66

Laura was spared having to watch the video that night. She'll be advised *never* to watch it, of course. Time will tell if she can accept what happened without seeing it with her own eyes.

The detectives were made to wait until Penny's alcohol levels dipped to a level where she was legally permitted to be interviewed. It made no difference. She wasted no time in confessing; her straightforward, no-nonsense approach making light work for the detectives throughout her interrogation.

Extracting a confession for the murder of Joseph Newman should have been more difficult. There was no evidence as such to connect her with his death, but she had motive in spades, with Joseph being in possession of the camera his father had put together using a small security camera and some electronic gadgetry.

The device operated using a motion sensor, something Scott himself must have inadvertently triggered while working on the car from beneath. It was before the days of dashcams, and in some ways Scott Newman was a pioneer of the technology that's commonplace today. They'd had a break in at the house a few months before, and Scott was taking no chances with his precious classic car.

The camera didn't save his life, but it would eventually bring his killer to justice.

It was Joseph who'd found the body, who'd jacked the car back up in the vain hope his father might still be alive. His mum, Laura, was out at work, so it was left to Joseph to call the police. A recording still exists, not heard by many, but by all accounts harrowing to listen to.

The detectives were curious as to why Joseph didn't hand the video memory card to the police at the time. Penny filled in the gaps. Joseph had told her that while he waited for the ambulance and police cars to arrive, he'd remembered helping his father construct the camera, so he retrieved it, unsure of what, if any, significance it would hold.

Until he'd viewed the footage, Joseph, like the coroner at the time, believed Scott's death to be a tragic accident—another person killed working underneath a car while using jacks instead of ramps.

Joseph had made Penny aware that he had the camera in his possession and that its footage would prove she'd killed his father. He also told her he would make sure the video ended up with the police, but not until he was sure his mother was strong enough. The woman had all but mentally shut down, crippled with grief, and Joseph dedicated himself to getting her back on her feet.

If Joseph had been older he might have understood that he could have brought closure for his mother by explaining how her husband died, but he didn't want her to suffer any more than was necessary, so resolved to wait until she was better, and in the meantime, stashed the camera and memory card in the barn at Marcus Crane's house. In Sienna's and his secret place, a place for treasure, for keepsakes.

Ultimately, it was Joseph's decision to protect his mother that cost him his life.

It was the photograph, you see. Photograph number two. I pored over it that night, searching for alternative reasons as to why Candy could be missing from the photo. I was angry at myself for even giving head space to the bad thoughts about her, for allowing them to breed, but I couldn't ignore them, could I? After all, if there is one person who wants to be captured in everyone's pictures, it's Candy. Front and centre like in the shot taken earlier that day—photograph one. Candy would have wanted to be there even if lightning filled the sky, or hail was falling. That's just Candy, and it's those little things you're only aware of by truly knowing a person in the way a friend does, from spending time with them, opening up to each other.

With her absence from the photograph in mind, I thought back to other times where she acted out of character. I remembered Candy and I sitting on the jetty, her trancelike state as she stared across the water to the Crane house, the shoreline where Joseph died. I thought back to the first time I asked her the name of the motorboat, her response in the negative coming too quickly and with an undercurrent of something held deep within. But most of all I recalled the time I asked Candy if she and Sienna were friends. Her aversion to the girl was plain to see, undiminished despite the number of years that had ticked by since her death. It wasn't beyond the realms of possibility that this was a jealousy allowed to grow unchecked. Had Joseph rejected Candy when she wanted something more than friendship?

310

I thought then what I think now—that she was in love with a boy who loved another; Sienna. Candy told me Joseph was her boyfriend because it was too painful to admit that he was not. And after his death, she still found herself competing with Sienna as both women mourned his passing.

And who would suspect Candy? Sweet Candy. But a teenage brain operating on a different level of maturity to its adult body might be a dangerous thing. Could such a person harbour an inability to distinguish right from wrong in a way an adult would, or display a lack of inhibition when it came to the crucial moment?

I sifted through all of those thoughts, and more.

But it didn't add up. I couldn't see how Candy could have got to the other side of the lake. She doesn't drive. She could have cycled but she wouldn't have been able to complete the round trip and return to the party quickly enough so as not to arouse suspicion.

But it came down to more than that, to more than suspicions, or evidence—or lack of it. To something far simpler. Because it came down to the fact that Candy *is* all of the things I questioned she might not be. She *is* sweet, she *is* good, she *did* struggle to see Joseph's name in print but only because she misses him despite him never being hers. She did nothing more than love Joseph with everything she had. She could no more have killed him than kill me. That's why I aborted my initial phone call to Tom.

I'd thrown the mobile to the bed and traced my finger over the face of a different person that I love. She wasn't with the group huddled together in the rain for one last picture but standing as an out of focus figure on the balcony of Laura's old bedroom.

And that's the moment it hit me, because at that moment some of the key scraps of memories fused, encouraged by my dream to meld together, and that is when I knew what I would find in Marcus Crane's barn. I knew it would contain a video tape that carried the face of the woman on the balcony. The woman who, by her own confession to the Cumbrian police, had slipped away that bonfire night at Lakeside. Slipped away to the jetty where she found Joseph alone with his grief, mourning the loss of his father, longing to be consoled by the girl across the water. The girl who, along with her parents, were not invited to Lakeside.

And in some ways it's fitting that this is where he was freed from his grief. His last breaths taken in the same stretch of water where Sienna, just months later, would take hers.

Penny made sure to tell the detectives that his death was quick. It's not clear why it's important to her that she said this. It could be because she wants Laura to know there was minimal suffering, or it could be to lessen her own sense of guilt; no one is quite sure.

A rock. That's all it took. It'll still be there, water lapping over its smooth, ground surface. Who knows, if you looked carefully enough, maybe you'd tell which one was used, displaced from where it had lain for thousands of years; now resting in a new position where it sits unnaturally, standing out as not having settled in the place it would have after being subjected to the planet's forces, the multiple shifts of the lake's bed, floods, seasons, land heave, erosion.

According to Penny's confession though, it took more than a mere rock to kill him, it took planning, foresight. The sheer premeditation of the act required that she secreted Joseph's bike in Lakeside's garden, behind the hedge by the water, and she'd also placed the rock and a blanket at the same spot. Everything was in place as she made her way down the garden, eyeing the back of Joseph's head as he stared out over the water, unsuspecting of what was about to happen.

Her plan worked to perfection, Joseph's lifeless body was wrapped in the blanket and bundled into the motorboat along with his bike. The boat's black paintwork ensured she wouldn't be seen by the two fishermen as she hugged the shoreline in the rain and fading light. The extra distance travelled by following the headland wasn't even an issue, she'd be gone for no more than fifteen minutes. It's easy to lose someone in a group of forty for that length of time—a long toilet break, taking empty bottles outside to the recycling bins, going upstairs to grab an extra jumper. Easy.

Dumping Joseph's body in the water at the foot of Marcus Crane's land was her final act, knowing that suspicion would fall immediately on the man the whole village had come to mistrust. The bike was wheeled a few yards up the hillside to give the impression Joseph had cycled there to meet with his girlfriend, had subsequently fallen, or been pushed down the hillside, striking his head and drowning in the process.

When asked about the present location of the blanket, Penny confirmed she'd thrown it on the bonfire as she made her way back up Lakeside's garden. She'd then hurried upstairs to change into a dry set of clothes.

When the photograph of the group was taken, Candy had been whisked away to a girl guides camping trip, something she attended every year, including this year in her capacity as a leader.

Penny appeared in the shot on the balcony because, having climbed the stairs to change, she moved outside to the balcony with the idea she'd drop her sodden clothes to the lawn below, head straight outside and throw them on the bonfire. The taking of the group photograph prevented her from doing that, but she took time later in the evening to complete the task.

All that remained was the question: why?

Infatuation, obsession. Penny used the word love, but it's not that. If you love a person, you don't strive to be with them at any cost. It's true, Penny and Laura had an affair, of sorts, while Laura and Scott were married.

I think back to their embrace in the hospital room when they thought I was asleep. It wasn't much, but it was more than two friends consoling each other. It was tight and lingering, and when they withdrew, they remained touching, eyes locked onto each other's.

I remember the time at the rugby club party where, faced with just Laura and Penny, and wanting to investigate the fairground rides, Laura said, '*We'd* prefer you didn't, darling.' There were more examples, all similarly innocuous when viewed independently of each other, but amounting to more when considered as a whole.

Penny's lingering obsession with Laura also helps to explain the tetchiness that had surfaced between Penny and Bridgette, and I wonder if Penny had grown to resent

Bridgette's presence; a barrier to Penny's hopes of a more permanent union with her old lover.

Laura, for her part, had no knowledge of Penny's plans to rid Scott from their lives. She was never asked to leave her husband, though the two women often chatted of how things might have been different if they'd met earlier in life. That said, Laura never felt a pressure from Penny to upset the status quo.

It makes Penny's actions even harder to fathom; an intelligent woman driven to murder by her own thoughts, unable to rationalise them, set them to one side.

It will always remain a mystery to us how a person could possess a side so dark yet present such a conventional front at the same time. Nobody could have begun to guess how deep her passions ran, and that's what rendered the ones who trusted her so vulnerable. By the time Laura moved in with us, Penny had seemingly moved on, having been in a relationship with Bridgette for two years.

In that time, Laura had tried to carry on living at Lakeside but it became untenable. She was the wife of a dead husband and mother of a dead son; deaths that occurred only months apart, deaths that were ultimately ruled as accidents, but not before tongues had wagged, elbows had nudged, and fingers had pointed. It puts me in mind of the time I asked about 'Mister Laura' and the reaction it drew from Laura and Penny, both flustered but for very different reasons.

Laura's move away from Lakeside now makes sense, as do the prescribed medicines I found in the bathroom cabinet all those years ago.

I can't imagine how much courage it must have taken for her to come back here.

67

Bridgette always says that something good comes out of everything. To be honest, it's a shite expression. In my experience, it rarely does. If something happens to you which is crap, it usually happens for a reason, and the chances are, the next day, things will still be crap.

I'm big enough and old enough to concede there are sometimes exceptions, though, and I'm currently eating onion soup; the posh sort where you get a small, floating, circular piece of bread covered with melted cheese.

However, the soup isn't the exception to all the shite that's happened recently, although I have to admit it's very, very good. The exception takes the form of the chef who's made it for the two of us, from his own crop of onions, no less.

We sit across from each other, blowing on our spoons like idiots. We're two of those colourful fish with big lips, puckering up with two feet of air between us instead of seawater.

'It's a bit hot,' Marcus Crane says.

'No shit!' I cry, marvelling at how my spoon hasn't melted.

'Best served hot. That's what it says in the recipe.'

'Hot, yes. But not a bloody molten lava flow. If I'd known I'd have grabbed the piece of asbestos Bridgette chucked on the bonfire and lined my mouth with it.'

'Any good?' Marcus Crane asks, waggling his spoon in the direction of my bowl.

'Dunno. Can't feel my tongue.'

The news of how Joseph and Scott died will be released soon, and I asked the police if I could be the one to tell Mr Crane the details. I couldn't bear the thought of some faceless law enforcer popping his head round the door to say, *'Oh by the way, you're off the hook, you didn't kill that lad, someone else did.'* I just know there'd be no apology, or if there were, it'd be insincere and accompanied by the qualification that they were just doing their job.

It doesn't help Marcus Crane with the grief he still feels over the loss of his family, and I feel for him. Laura has at least found a measure of closure of the type the man opposite me may never find. He has no culprit to point the finger at because it was a tragic accident that befell him and his family, nothing more. He blames himself, of course, I don't think there'll ever be a time when that's not the case.

But I know Sienna would forgive him, and I want to tell him so very badly. And even though I don't feel able to do this, to break the rules, I'm hoping the news of justice for Scott and Joseph will lighten the load a little, help him see there's a better route forward for him now.

By way of encouraging him in this direction, I remind him that I'm going to be around more, and that I'm ace, and he's lucky to have me.

He laughs at this, and clears the soup bowls before we step outside, our boots crunching on the hard frost that shrouds the yard.

'You gonna help me to my chariot, or what?' I say, grinning.

'It'd be my pleasure, Miss,' he replies, offering me the crook of his arm for me to slip mine into.

Before I leave, I turn to him. 'Oh, by the way, you're having supper with us on Saturday. Seven pm. Don't be late. Oh… and dress up a bit. Trim your beard a little, get some air to your face, man!'

And as I cast off, motor idling, rudder in hand, I turn to give him a final wave.

'Who the hell calls it supper?' he yells.

I laugh all the way back to Lakeside.

68

We had our supper. I showed Marcus Crane our terrace, too. Not for long, it was fucking freezing.

As days went by, the overriding feeling I had was one of waiting. Waiting to return to school, waiting for the scorched grass to regrow from the bonfire, waiting for my next visit with Marcus Crane. I guess what I'm really waiting for is things to settle down. For the next few months what I'd like is for all of our shredded lives to recline in an armchair, not be tottering on a bar stool as they have been for so long now. There are a lot of adjustments to make. For everyone, not just me.

Bridgette has lost her partner, and I've lost a mother. Laura melted my heart the other day when she said, 'Having three mums is greedy. Best to have just two.' She gave me the most enormous hug and for the first time since my accident, I realised my ribs and collarbone no longer hurt.

We had a group chat, the three of us, which ended up in a slightly unnecessary group hug at the end. We'll be staying at Lakeside. Living our lives here, for now anyway. I look forward to spending more time with Candy and Tom, who I've quickly come to see as part of our extended family.

The relief Tom felt at the clearing-up of the mystery surrounding Joseph's death was obvious to see. At first he blamed himself for not having unravelled it himself. But how could he? The key to Scott and Joseph's cases lay in finding the dash camera which he couldn't possibly have known about. Indeed, the footage in itself has no relevance to Joseph's death and without Penny's confession, we'd still have no justice for him.

There are no secrets any longer, no suspicions hanging over Laura and the house. Laura is to move back into her old bedroom, the view from its balcony something she says she'll now see as a backdrop to the happy times she and Joseph shared, rather than the painful, dark conduit to his memory it once was.

I asked Laura about the earring she lost that day on the boating lake. She told me they were bought for her by Joseph and I could see how much it hurt for her to lose that small fragile connection to him.

Bridgette lightened the mood by telling us that going forward, we will be three women holding their heads high. Once upon a time, such a pronouncement from Bridgette would have been delivered with a gin and tonic in hand. Whether her abstinence is due to the realisation she's effectively now a single parent with double the responsibility, or whether it's due to the closure of an increasingly unhappy relationship, I'll likely never know, but the change is welcome.

There are a lot of things I wonder about. I wonder if I would have worked out the existence of the now-missing treeline in Lakeside's back garden if I hadn't tripped or paused to watch the squirrels. My notebook still has the scrawl from the day we picnicked under an oak tree, where I was told to keep an eye out for squirrels that might pinch our food. It was something at the time I felt compelled to jot down, something which resulted in a connection to the past.

There are other connections, too; some more robust than others. I've learned that Scott was killed on his birthday and it takes me back to my own birthday, when I blew my eight candles out to make my wish, beating back the terror I felt even though I couldn't explain its origin at the time. I think of the time my head struck one of the trolley jacks which killed Scott. Not just a collision with an inanimate object, but a recall, a message to look deeper, perhaps?

The night Joseph was killed, Lakeside played host to a bonfire night, held in honour of Scott's memory. The irony is too painful to contemplate. And with the Crane family accident, this stretch of water witnessed three tragedies in less than twelve months.

I know that at some point I'll miss Penny. Not yet. I'm too angry to feel loss, but I know it will come. When it does, I have no idea how deep it will run, or whether it will last. Or whether I'll visit.

Penny, for now, will be one of those memories that gets edged out by new ones. I've stopped referring to her as mum, at least for the time being. Fortunately, as a family I was always encouraged to use their Christian names or 'Mum', depending on how I felt. I tended to interchange.

I asked Laura if I could call her 'Mum'. Because that's what she's always been to me. She flung a hand to her chest and shaped to give me a bear hug, so I told her to back off and told her I'd be taking her tears as a 'yes'.

Marcus Crane did have a tidy up of his beard. You can see his lips now, and they're quite red, like he's been sucking a raspberry lolly for the whole of his life. He also had a tidy up of his yard, with my help, I hasten to add. I came into my own whenever he dithered over whether to bin an item, or not. There was one tool in particular that caused an unnecessary amount of beard stroking as he pondered whether it would be wise to let it go.

'When did you last use it?' I asked.

He puffed out his cheeks. Did some mental arithmetic.

'Christ's sake. Was it even this century?' I cried.

As it turned out, Marcus Crane couldn't be sure, so I threw it on the pile destined for the tip.

I call him that, by the way: '*Marcus Crane*'. Somehow, I can't call him Marcus and I'm too old to call him Mister. He's neither of those to me. He's so much more. He calls me Flo Fabishaw in return.

I told Marcus Crane about Laura's boat. About how she'd removed the name so it wouldn't lead to me asking questions about the past she'd tried so hard to forget. Bit by bit, she's learning to cherish those memories now, rather than bury them. Photographs have appeared in the living room. Only a couple. But it's a start. There's one of the three of them seated in Scott's classic car, and there's one of a smiling Joseph sat cross-legged by their motorboat.

Earlier today, I found Laura by the jetty. She was crying and smiling at the same time, her gaze directed at the hull of the boat. To the lettering that had found its way home, hand painted by Marcus Crane after he'd hired a rowing boat to make the short trip across the lake.

I think that's it for now, except to say we've dropped Penny's surname for obvious reasons.

Wait, maybe Bridgette's right, something good does come out of everything. I'm not *Floaters* anymore!

EPILOGUE

It's almost Christmas.

I ride the bus. A gift sits on my lap wrapped in paper from last year. It's been a tough decision, to make this trip. The landscape looks unfamiliar as it labours by, every mile taking me further from Lakeside, from the peace that has finally been allowed to settle there. Marcus Crane, Candy, and Tom are joining us for a games night later. Amongst other things, Bridgette has compiled a quiz, and some idiot (me) suggested boys against girls. I feel a trouncing coming on.

It's only recently that I've finally felt able to put everything behind me. I've even been interviewed at the local police station. It was routine, really; Detective Field asking me how I came to be in possession of the video camera, me telling him we came across it while having a clear out of Marcus Crane's barn.

Apparently, before my interview had even finished, police were ordered to his house to check out the account I'd given. They found the yard full, and the barn empty—but for one bicycle. My story was corroborated without Marcus Crane needing to utter a word.

When I said I felt able to put everything behind me, that's not quite true. That's why I'm making this journey today. I need my own closure. I want to be free to enjoy my first Christmas at Lakeside, surrounded by my family and friends.

It seems a long walk from where the bus drops me, but I finally reach the building just as it begins to rain. I wrap my coat around the gift I'm carrying to protect it from the weather. I didn't know what to write on the gift tag. I had four goes on a scrap piece of paper, each attempt spectacularly failing to say what I really wanted to write. I've left it blank.

The level of security is about what I expected. I'm one of about a dozen shuffling through, keen to get out of the cold. The others look like they know why they're here. I haven't got a clue what I'm doing, so I stand for a while.

A man in uniform must sense my discomfort, because he approaches me and asks if he can be of help.

I'm not sure if he can. Help, that is. I realise I've made this journey but have nothing to say. I suppose it's my own fault. I was warned against doing this, making this trip. Warned that it rarely gives the closure people think it will, and I think the man opposite me can tell I'm having second thoughts.

I desperately need him to speak now because I can't. If I try to, the words will get stuck in my throat. I can't even prevent the single tear from running down my cheek, warm against my chilled skin, slowing then holding its ground halfway down.

And still there's nothing to break the silence.

But he knows. What he's looking at isn't new to him. I can tell in his eyes. And that comforts me, makes me smile.

I hand my present over, turn around and make for the exit.
'Wait.'

I turn slowly, fix my eyes on the man, willing him to speak, see his dilemma, see him struggle to find the right greeting for the teenage girl who wears a drying tear on her cheek, standing in front of him by the car air freshener display stand.

He replaces his red spectacles, straightens out his stoop, gives a slight nod of his thinning crown, and allows his eyes to smile, before saying, 'Merry Christmas, Joseph.'

THE END

Acknowledgements

I thought carefully about who I should acknowledge. I won't lie, it's the section of my books I find most difficult to write. The prospect of sitting down to compile it can leave me with a sheen of perspiration, palpitations and a level of anxiety so pronounced I'll be pressing forefinger to wrist to check I'm not clinically dead.

I'm lying, of course. It's a doddle to write on account there's no one to acknowledge. Who would I thank? I did everything myself. Alone. On my tod. Locked in a dark room for days on end with just a grumpy cat and a case of fine wine for company.

I'm lying, of course. I'm not rich enough to buy a case of wine, fine or otherwise. So, I've decided to use this space to thank myself. To acknowledge my efforts. If you could see me now you'd see me patting myself on my back, shaking my own hand, and with the sincerest of nods, telling myself "well done, son."

(PS Thanks to Sue for proof-reading. You're ace.)
(PPS Thank you, the reader, for buying and getting to the end!)

Other books by M.D. RANDALL

<u>SEE YOU ON THE ICE</u>. Jack relocates for work and takes his love of the 80s and his boxer shorts with him. He reluctantly leaves behind his body dysmorphic friend Chloe, and less reluctantly three other oddities who answer to the names of Katie, Mike, and Connor.

SEE YOU ON THE ICE

NEW START. NEW FRIENDS. NEW JUMPER.
(just mind the thigh gap)

M.D. RANDALL

Jack and Chloe should probably be a couple, something they would rather die than admit to (out loud at any rate). Katie and Mike *are* a couple, but probably shouldn't be, and Connor tows along somewhere in the slipstream.

Separated by hundreds of miles, all is not lost; Jack and Chloe have that priceless commodity that the 80s didn't – mobile phones. And what Jack and Chloe are good at is the flinging of sarcasm, insults, metaphorical excrement, advice (whether sought or not), and occasionally a little tenderness, back and forth across the void between them.

PAINTING WITH FRIGHT

The question is at what point do you hand yourself into the police? When you're a link to one murder? Two? When you find yourself in possession of thirty thousand pounds belonging to one of the victims? Exactly. Better to go on the run. Into hiding. Like Audrey Harding. But you need a cover, a suitable place to lay low.

It's winter at Longacre Hall, a stately home in the Warwickshire countryside. It has a job opportunity, a remote shack in its grounds, and Ivy: one part tour guide and three parts loose cannon. Audrey seizes all of these things and secretly makes the shack her home.

Audrey is a wanted woman. The men who murdered her friends want their money – laundered profits from illicit art dealings. The police are anxious she leads them to the truth. Ivy, Olive, and homeless Graham all want to help her. But which of them can she trust?

Paranoia, isolation, and fear are just a few of the obstacles Audrey must overcome in order to fight for survival. And prove her innocence.

Printed in Great Britain
by Amazon

37427985R00185